PRAISE FOR THE SARA STORIES

SARA'S YEAR
AFTER SARA'S YEAR
THE EMMELINE PAPERS

Gerson is a superb storyteller…I could not put it down!
"THE SUBURBAN" – MONTRÉAL, QC

An amazing, captivating story!
KIM MELROSE – SAN DIEGO, CA

When characters become so real they feel like family,
you know you've found a gem of a book and a brilliant writer!
KAREN HELENE WALKER – AUTHOR OF "THE WISHING STEPS"

A masterful journey with a brilliant cast of characters.
CAROLYN FLOWER – AUTHOR OF "GRAVITATE 2 GRATITUDE"

Honest and heartfelt. Brilliant!
JOAN CERIO – HOST OF RADIO'S "EARTH ENERGY FORECAST"

An emotionally charged page-turner!
PAUL Q. GROSSMITH – EDITOR OF "THE GAY JEWISH ANTHOLOGY"

A classic in the making!
D'ARCY MAYO – MITTAGONG, AUSTRALIA

Thrilling…bittersweet…triumphant!
DAN STONE – AUTHOR OF "ICE ON FIRE"

Brilliant story and setting…magical!
DEBRA LOUISE BARRY – MONTRÉAL, QC

I absolutely loved it!
MAHABBA AHMED – ST. CATHARINES, ON

Vivid…fantastic!
PAOLA RIZZATO – GLASGOW, UK

MORE FROM MARK DAVID GERSON

FICTION

The MoonQuest

The StarQuest

The SunQuest

The Bard of Bryn Doon

The Lost Horse of Bryn Doon (coming soon!)

The Sorcerer of Bryn Doon (coming soon!)

MEMOIR

Acts of Surrender: A Writer's Memoir

Dialogues with the Divine: Encounters with my Wisest Self

Pilgrimage: A Fool's Journey

SELF-HELP & PERSONAL GROWTH

The Way of the Fool: How to Stop Worrying About Life and Start Living It

The Way of the Imperfect Fool: How to Bust the Addiction to Perfection That's Stifling Your Success

The Book of Messages: Writings Inspired by Melchizedek

RESOURCES FOR WRITERS

The Voice of the Muse: Answering the Call to Write

The Voice of the Muse Companion: Guided Meditations for Writers

From Memory to Memoir: Writing the Stories of Your Life

Organic Screenwriting: Writing for Film, Naturally

Birthing Your Book...Even If You Don't Know What It's About

The Heartful Art of Revision: An Intuitive Guide to Editing

Writer's Block Unblocked: Seven Surefire Ways to Free Up Your Writing and Creative Flow

Time to Write

Write with Ease

Free Your Characters, Free Your Story

Write to Heal

Journal from the Heart

THE EMMELINE PAPERS

The Sara Stories

MARK DAVID GERSON

THE EMMELINE PAPERS

Copyright © 2017, 2020 Mark David Gerson
All rights reserved

No part of this book may be reproduced, stored in a retrieval system
or transmitted by any means, electronic, mechanical, photocopying,
recording or otherwise, without written permission from the author,
except for the inclusion of brief quotations in critical reviews and certain
other noncommercial uses permitted by copyright law.

This is a work of fiction. Names, characters, businesses, places, events and
incidents are either the products of the author's imagination or used in a
fictitious manner. Any resemblance to actual persons, living or dead, or to
actual events is purely coincidental.

First Edition 2017. Second Edition 2020.

Published by MDG Media International
2370 W. State Route 89a, Suite 11-210
Sedona, AZ 86336

www.mdgmediainternational.com

ISBN: 978-1-950189-22-9

Cover Photograph and Title/Section Pages Sketch: Fitzroy Square, London
(cc) Peter Church
*https://commons.wikimedia.org/wiki/File:Fitzroy_Square,_London_-_geograph.
org.uk_-_1225411.jpg*
*Adapted from the original image and used under Creative Commons License
Attribution-Share Alike 2.0 Generic license*
https://creativecommons.org/licenses/by-sa/2.0/deed.en

More information
www.markdavidgerson.com
www.thesarastories.com

Art is a wound turned into light.
Georges Braque

The power of imagination makes us infinite.
John Muir

I don't get ideas. Ideas get me.
Robertson Davies

*Life is to be lived to its fullest
so that death is just another chapter.
Memories of our lives, of our works and our deeds
will continue in others.*
Rosa Parks

For the Emmeline in all of us

There's a good chance that you will recognize some of the Yiddish words and phrases scattered through "The Emmeline Papers." After all, many Yiddishisms have slipped into everyday usage. Still, you probably won't recognize them all. Flip to "Sara & Sadie's Yiddish Glossary" at the back of the book when you need help deciphering the less common ones!

Just as I am fussy about my first name (it's "Mark David," not "Mark" or "David"), Emmeline is particular about hers. Emmeline pronounces it "Emme-line" not "Emme-lean."

1974
LONDON

1

Jeremy Reese-Thorpe's breath evaporated into the guttering yellow of the Victorian streetlight as he clasped the unmarked brass urn tightly against his pea jacket. With his free hand he gripped the wrought-iron enclosure bordering the front walk and shuffled toward the cab idling at the curb. The last thing he wanted to do was slip on the icy pavement and scatter Emmeline's ashes into the gutter. Emmeline wouldn't care, but he did.

"Trust Emmeline to die at the coldest, dreariest time of the year," Jeremy groused as he let go of the glacial metal for the final few yards to the car door. It would not yet be light by the time his taxi crept through six miles of central London rush hour to Regent's Canal. If it was bitterly damp here, it would be worse once he was on the waterway.

"Serves you right, you sentimental fool," he could almost hear Emmeline proclaim from wherever the pugnacious landed when they died. "You ought to have done what I asked."

"Bollocks," Jeremy muttered.

"Guv?" the cabbie asked.

"Nothing. I loathe this weather is all."

"Then you're living in the wrong town, I'd say." The driver chuckled. "Wrong country, p'raps."

"You'd be right."

"Where are we off to, then?"

"The moorings behind The Palm Tree in Mile End. Do you know it?"

"I know it well, guv. But there'll be no boats running at this time… not there nor anywhere."

"There will be one," Jeremy replied. *A special boat.* He settled into the rear of the cab and tucked the urn next to him on the seat.

"Righty-o." The driver shifted into gear, then turned onto Fitzroy Square and up Conway Street toward the A400.

It was not only a special boat that Jeremy was heading to, it was a special boatman. Andrew McGill, or Cap'n Andy as he fashioned himself, no longer offered the canal hires and tours he had done for decades, but it was on his *Cotton Blossom* that Jeremy had asked Emmeline to marry him and that had she turned him down, monthly for a nearly a year. When she at last agreed, it was with one condition, that they tie the knot immediately, on Andy's boat.

"I'm seventy-nine," she declared. "I could be dead tomorrow. With any luck, I'll make it through the weekend so that we can get on with the bleeding thing."

Emmeline had wanted Cap'n Andy to perform the ceremony, but he'd refused. "This isn't much of a ship and I'm not much of a captain," he'd said. Besides, he explained, it was only in books and pictures that sea captains could marry people. He studied the two of them — the rail-thin spinster with her sharp nose, pointy chin and horsey teeth and the thirty-nine-year-old bachelor, slight, balding and a full head shorter than his fiancée — and scratched his stubbly chin. "Even in the pictures," he said, "no one would credit the two of you's getting hitched."

In the end, Jeremy and Emmeline conscripted a retired vicar who, along with them, frequented The Palm Tree, and on a Tuesday afternoon in June, with the *Cotton Blossom* floating between The Narrowboat Pub in Islington and The Palm Tree, they stood in the bow and were wed — to the cheers of spectators on the towpath. The bride wore a burgundy-and-teal pantsuit in not-yet-trendy paisley and the groom wore sandals and Indian-style kurta pajamas: gold silk top and white trousers. Hippies before there were hippies.

"I cannot believe that I am having a June wedding," Emmeline later grumbled as she slurped down her second pint at the surprise reception their pub mates had arranged. "Could any of this get more clichéd?"

Andy chortled. "You're lovin' every minute of it."

She was, though she would never admit it, not even to Andy. And they went way back, all the way to the Blitz, when she had saved his life on this same street. Only The Palm Tree had survived that 1944 air raid.

Andy was one of the first people Jeremy called after Emmeline died, and although her death was not unexpected, Andy wept at the news. Rumor had it that the two of them had once been lovers. Jeremy didn't doubt that it was true. Most men and women of Emmeline's acquaintance had found their way into her bed at one time or another, it seemed. Whether or not a much younger Andrew McGill had ever been one of them, he had instantly agreed to Jeremy's not altogether legal request, as long as it could be handled before dawn.

"I am a sentimental fool," Jeremy sighed as the taxi pulled into The Palm Tree's drive at the end of Haverfield Road. A scattering of lights flickered inside, unusual at this early hour.

Jeremy stepped out into a light Scotch mist and strode the few dozen steps to the towpath, where Andy and the *Cotton Blossom* were waiting for him. Ten minutes later, with the slightest hint of pink silhouetting the trees in Victoria Park and with tears streaming down his face, Jeremy popped open the urn, whispered a silent prayer and flung Emmeline's ashes in a broad arc out over the bow.

*H*appy Birthday, Emmeline Marguerite Marie Mandeville.

I cannot decide whether having been born minutes before midnight on 31 December is a blessing or a curse. On the blessing side, I have always been guaranteed some form of party, because who does not want to celebrate the ushering in of a new year? For all my parents' stern Victorian demeanor, they managed to set aside a small proportion of their propriety on New Year's Eve and were generally willing to allow their precocious daughter at least some benefit. On the curse side, my birthday generally seemed to have been an afterthought, a sometimes grudging postscript to a more noteworthy occasion.

None of that matters, anymore, of course, other than that as we grow older we tend to spend more time looking backward then forward. I vowed I would never become one of those dotty old spinsters who lived out her senescence in a rearview mirror. Thanks to Jeremy, I am not the former. I fear, however, that I may be aging into something of the latter. This writing regimen that has been prescribed to me could well accelerate the trend.

It is a prescription that I did my utmost to resist. In years past I could easily have fended off the joint forces of Jeremy and Sir Benjamin Barnett, my pertinacious Harley Street physician. My nineties, alas, have dulled my fight, although none of my feistiness, at least according to my husband and my doctor.

That feistiness was in full view yesterday afternoon when Sir Benjamin stopped by the house to see me. Rather, he stopped by to blackmail me, having already enlisted the support of my turncoat spouse.

"Unless you agree to slow down, Emmeline, and considerably, I shall resign as your physician," he announced.

"Slow down?" I huffed. "I am only ninety-one. Grandmama lived to one hundred and three with all her faculties intact. She continued to entertain regularly and extravagantly until a week before her death. I expect to do at least as well."

*Sir Benjamin would not retreat. "I was not your grandmother's doctor,"
he retorted, "and having scrutinized the results of your latest examination, I
doubt that you possess either her heart or her lungs."*

*I drew myself up, intent on storming from the room. "I refuse to slow
down in order to add a day or a week to my life," I fumed. "I plan to live as
I have always lived and bugger the consequences." I glared at Jeremy for his
part in the assault. Sir Benjamin gently laid a hand on my arm.*

*"I am not ordering you to your bed," he said. "Nor am I insisting that
you never leave the house. I am merely asking you to rearrange some of your
obligations so that they can be carried out from here and to give up a few
others. I am merely asking you to stop running around London like you did
when you were twenty-two."*

*"I have a notion," Jeremy offered with an unusual degree of timidity. "A
surprise, really."*

*"Out with it," I spat, more sharply than I had intended. Or perhaps it
was just as sharply as I had intended.*

*"Come," he said, taking my hand and leading me up two flights of
stairs to this room, which he had outfitted as a "writer's studio" without
my knowledge. It was easy enough for him to do as I rarely ventured up to
this part of the house anymore and never into this room, which for more
years than I could remember had been stuffed with overflow from the attic
— mildewed furniture and rusted trunks stuffed with musty papers and
moth-eaten clothing that I could never be bothered to attend to.*

*Now, the room was immaculate, its walls freshly painted a creamy ivory.
A Wilton rug covered most of the wood floor. An easy chair, ottoman and
side table sat next to the fireplace, already ablaze. Above the mantle hung a
Marc-Allan Cameron original, an early birthday present that Jeremy had
intercepted before I could see it. Many of my favorite volumes, collected
from all over the house, filled a pair of beech Arts and Crafts-style bookcases.
And a matching desk and padded chair sat in front of a spotless window,
angled so that were I to glance up from my writing I could gaze out toward
Fitzroy Square Garden.*

*I was at once outraged and moved, nearly to tears, my mind teetering
between the two extremes and my tongue uncertain to which of those
emotions it ought to succumb.*

*That I now sit in the wing chair in what has drifted into the early hours
of my ninety-third year and the early minutes of 1974 reveals which side of
me prevailed in that inner struggle.*

I do not know what I shall write. I do know that what I write will be neither private journal nor public book. I have no desire to diarize my thoughts in some form of ersatz therapy. Nor do I wish to share what emerges from this pen with a public which, unquestionably, has better ways to occupy its time.

Whatever ultimately fills these pages, it will write itself precisely as my life has lived itself — from instant to instant and with minimal regard for all custom and convention but one: the custom and convention that has one inaugurate a new project at the start of a new year; two new years in my case: the calendar's and my own.

Having launched this questionable enterprise within moments of both, I shall now slide this sheet of monogrammed vellum into its folder, extinguish the light in a room I am reluctant to admit an attachment to and climb down the stairs to our bedroom, where Jeremy, should he have managed to remain awake and alert, awaits with a bottle and two glasses. Champagne, of course. One is never too old, or young, for champagne.

2

The radio was playing when Jeremy opened the front door to 33 Fitzroy Street. Since Emmeline's death he had taken to leaving either it or the telly switched on in order that the house not seem so echoingly empty when he returned. The volume was set to low, so that all he heard was a comforting hum from upstairs as he slipped off his dripping coat and soggy shoes in the front hall.

After Cap'n Andy dropped him back behind The Palm Tree, Jeremy had wandered through the rubble still littering the neighborhood thirty years after the last bomb fell. When, eventually, he reached Grove Street, he hailed a taxi to take him to Claridge's for a late breakfast. From there, he walked the mile home through a dewy fog that perfectly matched his mood. It was only as he climbed toward the first floor bedroom to change out of his wet clothes that he was finally able to make out the song playing on the radio. It was Barry White, with the week's hit single.

I know there's only, only one like you
There's no way they could have made two
You're, you're all I'm living for
Your love I'll keep forevermore
You're the first, you're the last, my everything
He crumpled onto the steps and sobbed.

1988

MONTREAL & LONDON

3

Marc-Allan Cameron watched the airport sprawl of Montréal-Mirabel and the hundreds of acres of abandoned farm fields that surrounded it dissolve into golden clouds of dusk as his British Airways jumbo jet banked sharply and pointed its nose toward the Atlantic Ocean and London-Heathrow. When nothing of his adopted Canadian soil remained visible, he shut his eyes and sighed.

Another trip home, another funeral. Last time, it was for his mother. This time, it was for his step-uncle, although calling Jeremy Reese-Thorpe any kind of uncle made about as much sense as calling the UK home. Jeremy was eight years younger than he was, had been nearly forty years younger than his Aunt Emmeline, whose funeral he would have returned for in 1975 had her will not expressly forbidden any kind of memorial. "Burn my remains and have Jeremy empty the urn into a dustbin," her instructions had read, wired to him by an embarrassed solicitor. "No crowds. No service. It's all tripe, and you know how I feel about tripe."

As for home, the instant the wheels of his American Overseas Airlines DC-4 had left the Bournemouth Hurn runway in 1945, just a few months after his demobilization from the RAF, not only his native Glasgow but all of the British Isles seemed to shrink, becoming little more than a place he had lived once upon a time and, through happenstance, been born. By then he already knew that his final stop on this still-rare transatlantic passenger flight would be his real home: in the Canada of artist Anne Savage; more specifically in the Halifax of Anna Leonowens, the real-life Anna of *Anna and the King of Siam*. Anna had set out to civilize the then-rough garrison town when she arrived there soon after retiring from her time in the

Siamese royal court. One of her pet projects was Marc-Allan's destination that postwar autumn: the Nova Scotia College of Art. It was a journey that Marc-Allan would never have undertaken had it not been for his mother's older sister.

Emmeline had been right to trick him into becoming an artist. Mac, as he chose to be called shortly after his arrival in Canada, was never cut out to take over his family's retail emporium. As a boy he invariably sulked when his father demanded that Mac accompany him to the thriving Cameron-MacCready department store on Sauchiehall Street. As a sullen teenager he simply refused.

Mac had also been right, about his early instincts about Canada. Although he would travel extensively as the celebrity artist he never expected to grow into, only Nova Scotia would ever feel like home to him: first, Anna's Halifax and later, the rural orchards and farmland sixty miles away in Kings County.

Now, with Jeremy gone, the last of his links to family and the old country had gone with him. Mac would see to his uncle's final wishes, certain to be as eccentric as those of his aunt, sell the Fitzroy Street terrace house that Emmeline had lived in for more than half her life, pay a final pilgrimage to the Tate, which had helped launch his improbable career choice a half-century earlier and, if he could manage it, never return to England. He would be seventy in a day. It was time to start cutting back on the nonstop overseas travel that came with international renown. Even first-class, a luxury he was grateful to be able to afford, exhausted him these days. He didn't know how many years he had left, but he intended to spend more of them in front of an easel and fewer on airplanes.

That was the plan. However, Mac knew from sometimes bitter experience how easily and often plans could go awry. "The best laid schemes o' mice an' men gang aft agley," Robbie Burns had written. It was Esther Freed's voice he heard whenever he thought of those words, not his countryman's Scottish burr.

One example: Mac had expected to spend his birthday with his son. That was why he was in Montreal when the previous day's call from London found him. Now, he would spend his seventieth birthday in the same place he had spent his twentieth, in the same house where, again, thanks to Emmeline, he had daubed his first tentative splotch of yellow on his first terrifyingly blank canvas.

When he had finished that inaugural painting, Emmeline refused to let him destroy it. Worse, she insisted on hanging it in her front room, where she could boast about it every Sunday to the assemblage of artists, writers and assorted hangers-on who piled into the room for her weekly gatherings.

"This painting," she maintained, "will support me well into my dotage. I shall hang it between my Nina Hamnett and my Aleister Crowley, and when the name Marc-Allan Cameron is considerably more well-regarded than theirs, I shall sell it and live comfortably off the proceeds."

Yet despite numerous offers, Emmeline had never sold it. As far as he knew, it hung where she had left it. Now, thought Mac, marveling again at his aunt's canniness, *Primus* was probably worth more than the combined sales value of her townhouse and all its neighbors. Perhaps he would donate it to the Tate, for old times' sake. Or maybe he would give it to his son, to Bernie. Yes, Bernie ought to have it.

His son. How odd that still sounded, barely four years since discovering that he had one. How odd and how remarkable. If only he could have shared all of Bernie's thirty-one years. If only he could have shared them with Bernie's mother, with Esther.

Mac shook his head to clear it of that doomed love affair from so long ago. He had wasted too many years mourning what might have been, what in the end was never meant to be. Bernie was meant to be. Thank God for Bernie. And thank God for all the strange synchronicities that had brought them together.

He smiled at the memory of that October afternoon when a shy, fearful young man had knocked on his farmhouse door and announced that he was Bernie Freed, Esther's son…and his, Mac's. That moment was the most disruptive and wondrous of his life, more wondrous than his times with Esther had been. It also heralded the most creatively productive period he had experienced in decades. Art critics, no doubt, already had a name for it. He would have to ask Sylvie what it was. She would know.

Mac leaned his head against the shuttered window. No first-class on this flight, at least not for him. It didn't matter to the booking agent that he was *the* Marc-Allan Cameron, the world-famous artist who was a Companion of the Order of Canada, whose *Expressions* hung in former Prime Minister Pierre Elliott Trudeau's Montreal home, whose *Thrice Blessed* hung in the White House and who had turned down a commission to paint a new portrait of Queen Elizabeth. Not that he would have attempted to parlay those achievements into special treatment, but Sylvie Ryan had no such qualms. Sylvie, his new live-in assistant, was really an art historian gathering material for what she was determined would be the definitive Cameron biography. Short of a private-jet hire, this was the only seat to London she could arrange for him at such short notice. If Sylvie couldn't manage anything better, Mac knew that it couldn't be done.

"Sir?" A soft British voice wafted toward him from the drinks trolley in the aisle.

Mac ignored it, pretending to sleep. A few minutes later, he no longer needed to pretend.

4

"So much for surprise parties," muttered Erik Donnekin, glumly scanning the half-empty room. "I guess the surprise is on us."

A few knots of smartly attired guests clustered by the windows, ignoring the gray drizzle of a gloomy late-October afternoon — both the parade of black umbrellas on the pavement eight stories below and the skeletal limbs of the oaks and maples climbing the upper slopes of Mount Royal a few blocks to the northwest. Across the vast, velvet-walled grand salon, another knot of visitors edged closer to the marble fireplace, drawing whatever warmth they could from its tentative flames. In between, the remainder of the assembly was dispersed among the eclectic and not entirely comfortable blend of French and oriental antiques that made up the room's various sitting areas. No one paid any attention to the slightly scruffy McGill music student hunched over the ebony Bechstein softly crooning "Blue Moon."

Blue moon you saw me standing alone
Without a dream in my heart
Without a love of my own

"Maybe we shouldn't have tried to cancel," Bernie said. "It was so last-minute, there was no way we were ever going to be able to reach everyone. We should have let the party happen, without Mac but with *all* the guests, instead of just with those we couldn't get hold of. It could have been the world's first surprise birthday party that was a surprise for the guests instead of for the birthday boy."

"Mac still doesn't know about this?" Erik asked.

"I didn't have the heart. It's bad enough he had to fly to London yesterday. I didn't want to make it worse by telling him that he would miss his own surprise party." He draped his arm around Erik and planted a kiss on his lightly stubbled cheek. "How come you're taking it so hard? I'm the one who usually gets depressed about stuff like this. You're the one who's usually trying to cheer me up."

Erik said nothing.

"You'd think Mac was your father, not mine," Bernie added.

"Well, I have known him longer than you have. Besides, he's kinda my father now, too."

"More like your common-law father-in-law." Bernie grinned.

Erik traced a paint-splattered finger across the carved gilded back of a Louis XVI armchair then kicked it aside. "I used to love this room," he muttered. "Now it just seems over the top. Way over the top."

Bernie pulled Erik closer to him. "You used to love it *because* it was so over the top. It brought out your inner *Cage aux Folles.* At least that's what you keep saying." He hummed a few out-of-tune lines of from the Broadway musical.

I am what I am

And what I am needs no excuses

Erik covered Bernie's mouth. "You're no George Hearn," he objected, picking up the lyric in a voice as sonorous as Bernie's was grating.

I deal my own deck

Sometimes the aces sometimes the deuces

Only the pianist noticed. He executed an awkward segue from "Hello, Young Lovers" to "I Am What I Am" and gestured for Erik to join him at the piano. Erik ignored him.

"You're right, hon," he sighed, gazing around the room. "This place really is a gay interior decorator's wet dream." He wiggled the chair back into its indentations in the Japanese rug. "I guess I'm in a mood." He turned to the window and watching the fat snowflakes that had replaced the rain fuse themselves to the glass then slide down to the sill. "I wish they'd all just leave. Even the piano player looks bored." He scanned the room again. "No one's having any fun here."

"Least of all you." Bernie swept a loose strand of blond hair out of Erik's eyes.

"Yeah." Erik plunged his hands into his jeans pockets.

A young, muscular server in black tuxedo pants, white shirt and black bowtie glided toward them, bearing a platter loaded up with morsels of smoked salmon on pumpernickel, garnished with capers and dill remoulade.

"Lox," Bernie said stuffing a canapé into his mouth. "Ritz-style. For Sarah, if she shows."

"Monsieur?" The server presented his offerings to Erik.

"No." He gently pushed the tray away. "Merci."

"You sure?" Bernie asked. "It's really good." He grabbed another. "It's probably Nova Scotia smoked salmon."

"I'm not hungry."

Bernie frowned. Erik was always hungry, especially for anything that reminded him of home. Smoked salmon, absolutely. But also lobster, Acadian fricot and the pickled herring and onion concoction known down east as Solomon Gundy. If Erik was turning down any kind of Maritime delicacy, something was seriously wrong.

Erik was also an unapologetic flirt, rarely passing up an opportunity to chat up a cute guy, even if chatting was as far as it ever went. Yet he had ignored the waiter, who could easily have stepped off the screen of a porn film.

That was how he and Bernie had connected four years earlier; because of Erik's flirting, that is, not at a dirty movie. Bernie had been on his way to Sarah Swartz's for dinner, hours after walking out on his mother's funeral, when some irresistible force pulled him into Westmount's Galérie Cinq Arts and deposited him on a bench in front of Erik's painting. It was an awkward initial meeting, at least for Bernie, who had not yet acknowledged his homosexuality but found himself disturbingly attracted to this indigo-eyed art student who talked at him nonstop. Erik, uncharacteristically nervous in front of this fidgety bearded man with glasses who, between his dark suit and melancholy demeanor, looked like he had just lost his best friend, was terrified that his chatter was scaring Bernie off. As Bernie left the gallery, Erik thrust his business card at him, never expecting to hear from the attractive stranger again. But twenty-four life-changing hours later — after Bernie had discovered truths about his mother he could never have suspected, had quit his civil service accounting job to pursue a newly discovered artistic passion, had accepted his sexual orientation and had committed to searching out a father who didn't know he had a son — Bernie called Erik. They had been a couple ever since.

One server was swiftly replaced by another, this one a young woman with close-cropped auburn hair who was expertly balancing a silver tray filled with a dozen crystal flutes of bubbling Moët & Chandon. "Messieurs?"

Bernie lifted a glass from the tray. He passed it to Erik.

"I've had enough. You drink it."

Bernie took a sip. "Free food, free booze and the most exclusive hotel's most exclusive suite," he said. "You'd think people would be having a better time."

"I bet they're wondering whether they can take their prezzies back, now that the guest of honor's a no-show." Erik tilted his head toward the brightly wrapped gifts stacked on and around a marble-topped pedestal table by the door.

"It is quite a haul."

"Especially considering we told everyone no presents. Now we'll have to shlep the lot down to the post office to get it back to Nova Scotia."

"Shlep?" Bernie laughed. "Your Yiddish is coming along just fine, mister."

"For a WhiNoLu, you mean." Erik forced a fleeting smile.

"More like a Whiny Lu today. What's up?"

"You know us White Nordic Lutherans," Erik replied. "We never talk about our feelings." He raised Bernie's champagne glass to his own mouth, slurping loudly. "Maybe I will have another." He snatched a flute from a passing waiter.

"Forget about the post office," Bernie said. "This is the Ritz-Carlton, remember? And the royal suite. We'll just call down to the concierge after everyone's gone and have him take care of it."

"And tip him handsomely for his effort."

"As long as it's the hunky one. Short, dark hair, mustache. Green eyes. Nice hands. You know the one I mean?"

Erik shrugged.

"You really are a Gloomy Gladys. First you pay no attention to the cute waiter and now you show no interest in the cuter concierge. What's really going on, love? And don't give me that stoic Norse crap."

"Is Sarah coming?" Erik asked.

"You're ignoring the question."

"What about Sadie?"

Bernie gripped Erik's chin and pivoted it so that they were nose-to-nose.

"Talk to me, Erik."

Erik gestured toward the guests. "What about them?"

"What about them? Fuck them. They don't know we're here." He grabbed Erik's hand, pulling him out of the grand salon and down the hall to the study. He slammed the padded door behind them, shouldered Erik onto the leather settee and leapt on top of him, kissing him hard on the mouth while tickling him mercilessly.

"Mmmfff." Erik struggled to jostle Bernie off. "Nnnng. Mmmfff. Pfff." He wrenched his head from Bernie's, giggling. "Stop!"

Bernie shifted position and forced his face back into Erik's. This time, Erik laced his fingers into Bernie's and relaxed into the kiss. After he pulled free, he lay with his head on Bernie's lap. "I'm sorry," he murmured.

"There's nothing to be sorry about."

"Yeah, there is. I've been acting like a jackass."

"As stubborn as one, for sure." He stroked Erik's forehead. "You're scared."

Erik nodded.

"Italy?"

"And the show. How will I ever produce enough good work by next summer, even with all of Tuscany as inspiration?"

"And me as your muse."

Erik opened his eyes and pulled Bernie toward him. "And you as my muse."

Bernie kissed him softly on the eyes. "I love you, Mr. Whiny Lu."

"I love you, Mr. Whiny Jew."

"Look," Bernie said, "if I could produce enough good art to fill a gallery show, with no training or experience, you sure as hell can do it. You have an art degree. Two art degrees. One." He poked Erik in the stomach. "Two." He poked him again.

Erik grabbed Bernie's finger. "Art degrees don't mean shit. You know that."

"They mean more than my lousy business degree."

"Not hardly. Nuh-uh. Nope. And what about you, mister? You had Canada's primo artist as a full-time, live-in mentor. What's an art degree, or two, next to that?"

Bernie pulled his finger free and tousled Erik's hair. "You were there, too, sunshine. Remember?"

"That was you?" Erik squinted up at Bernie. "No, it can't have been. The guy I was with back then had a beard and mustache." He tapped his chin. "Yup. I'm sure of it." He ran the back of his hand across Bernie's cheek, clean-shaven since August. "It's okay, stranger. You're much hotter than he ever was. I think I'll stick with you."

"You're insane." Bernie pressed his lips to Erik's hand. "You're still a better artist than I am. Way better."

Erik guffawed. "That's bullshit, but thank y—." He jerked up, slamming into Bernie's nose. "Crap!"

"Ouch! Anyone ever tell you you've got a hard head?" Bernie rubbed his nose.

"Anyone ever tell you you've got a big nose?" Erik kissed it.

"You!" they exclaimed in unison and burst into a fit of giggles.

"I—," Erik started. "No, wait a sec." He bolted from the room. "Don't move," he called back over his shoulder. "I'll be right back."

"What? What is it?"

"Don't move!" Eric shouted from the hall. "Not an inch." He raced back almost immediately, carrying two overflowing champagne flutes and leaving a trail of bubbly on the carpet behind him. He shoved one glass at Bernie then grabbed his free hand and pumped it furiously, pulling him to his feet.

"Wha—?"

"Mazel tov times a million. Mazel tov times a billion. Times a gazillion!"

"What are you talking about?"

"I can't believe I forgot to tell you. I'm such an idiot." He clinked glasses with Bernie. "L'chaim. Drink, O Great Artist."

"Will you tell me what this is all about?"

"Oh yeah." Erik nudged Bernie back onto the couch. "You'll want to be sitting down for this."

"For what? What is it, already?"

"Right." Erik plopped down next to Bernie. "Walter called a

couple of hours ago. From the gallery. You were in the bathroom so I couldn't get you to the phone. Then guests started showing up. Then I got into my funk and totally spaced." He clinked glasses with Bernie again, gulped down half his champagne and belched loudly. "You're sold out," he said.

"What?"

"Those last two paintings? The Montreal skyline and your mother's house?"

"What about them?"

"They were bought this morning."

"Huh?"

"You heard me."

Bernie stared blankly at Erik.

"That's a record," Erik continued. "That's what Walter said. Selling out two weeks before a Klinkhoff show closes is a fucking record! So drink your champagne." He directed Bernie's flute-clutching hand toward his mouth.

Bernie took a sip. He tasted nothing.

"You, Bernie Freed, are no longer plain old Bernie Freed," Erik gushed. "You're now Bernard Marc Freed, celebrity artist. The next Marc-Allan Cameron. A star!" He chugged down the rest of his drink. "In fact you're more than an ordinary, everyday star. You're a 'shimmering, glowing star in the artistic firma*mint*,'" Erik proclaimed, adapting the classic line from *Singing in the Rain*, one of their favorite films, and doing his shrill, screechy Lena Lamont impersonation.

"Shit," Bernie said. "For real?"

"For real, buster. So don't tell me I'm as good an artist as you are. Cuz I'm not."

Bernie wrapped his arms around the man he adored more than anything else in the world and croaked in his best Bette Davis-*Whatever Happened to Baby Jane?* voice, "But ya are, Blanche. Ya are!"

My hand still reaches for a cigarette when I sit up in bed first thing of a morning. It was a longtime pleasure that I was reluctant to abandon, but Jeremy insisted that he would marry me only were I to give it up. I came close to suggesting that he stuff his marriage proposal, that I would rather go on smoking than marry him. The words were already in my mouth. For some reason I swallowed them.

Oh, how I loved smoking. Watching that sinuous vapor curl off the end of a glowing cigarette tip and feeling its smooth, smoky warmth wash down my throat: It was a sensual experience like few others I have known outside the bedroom. Not that I had experienced any notable pleasures inside a bedroom when I had my first fag. I was barely eighteen then and a virgin… although not for long! Let me see… That would have been 1899, I believe. At that time a girl or woman of any age seen smoking was immediately branded as little better than a "fille de joie." If I am honest — and why should I not be all these years later? — that was part of the attraction. To be mistaken for a prostitute? What fun!

It was a Saturday evening soirée at the Knocktons', one of those dreary "young people's affairs" that Lady Knockton was so fond of organizing in the hopes that Penelope Knockton would finally meet a suitable young man. Her London season had failed to produced a likely candidate, not surprising given that Penelope was deathly boring and even homelier than I was and that the Knocktons, for all their title, their estate in Sussex and their posh terrace house in Mayfair, had barely tuppence to rub together. It was whispered about that Knockton fancied horses — not winning ones, alas — and that he owed money across three counties…which ought to have rendered him interesting. It did not.

Where was I? Oh yes. Smoking.

When I pulled the Embassy cig from Percival Masterson's mouth that evening, then placed it between my lips and inhaled deeply, conversation *in the room ceased. It was difficult to determine, in the next moments, who was more shocked: the men or the women. I suspect Percy was amused, though he did not dare show it. Only after two more draws did I relinquish the cigarette. Reluctantly. "Bloody hell," I remember thinking as I thrust it back between Percy's lips, succeeding in being more provocative still. "Here we are, standing on the cusp of a new century. There is nothing that a man now does that a woman should not be equally free to do. Smokes today. Votes tomorrow."*

I bought my first packet of Embassies the following day — the vote took considerably longer to acquire — and I smoked for sixty-two more years, until shortly after breakfast on the morning of the 13th of June, 1961.

Oh, I know they are not good for me, even if all those films and early adverts made it seem otherwise. Smoking was sexy. Smoking was sociable. Smoking the right brand was a hallmark of breeding and success. For a time most physicians endorsed it. It was all bollocks, of course. By the time Jeremy forced me to quit, I knew they were bad for me. Possibly, they might have killed me before now, had I not stopped.

As I said, I lit my last one the morning of the wedding, just to be certain. After all, I had successfully avoided marriage for more than half a century, despite the many proposals I had received, most of them dubious, some of them clearly unsuitable (those were the only ones that ever truly tempted me) and only a small number by gigolos after the money they were confident I possessed.

Why Jeremy? I could say that by seventy-nine, it was time for me to settle down. I could say that Jeremy had an irresistible je ne sais quoi... that I had at last fallen in love. It was all those things and none of them. To this day I cannot say why I said yes, only that I did and that I have never harbored an instant's regret, even if it forced me to renounce a favored vice.

In truth, and I have bound myself to absolute truth in these writings, it was not solely the loss of a potential husband that persuaded me to stop smoking. It was the prospect of having to return to Harley Street. I had not been to a doctor since Sir James Allen died, and that was decades earlier. I had continued seeing Sir James more out of habit than conviction and because he always indulged my idiosyncrasies, including my smoking. Although he paid lip service to his duty and regularly urged me to give it up, he did so in the halfhearted manner of someone who ignited a secret pipe or cigar the second his final patient of the day departed his surgery.

Once Sir James was gone, I declined to see another doctor until six months after we were married, when Jeremy threatened to throw me over his shoulder and haul me to Harley Street were I to persist in refusing to go on my own. At one time I might have challenged Jeremy, simply for the pleasure of watching him try…and fail. He has never been a large man, and in earlier years I know that I would have possessed the requisite force to resist him.

That was then. In more recent times, even as I have repelled most of the physical indignities that equate infirmity with aging, I have been unable to stop my body from losing height, mass and strength. Thus, I am forced to concede however peevishly, that I have reached an age where it is wise to have one's health monitored.

"You may look anywhere you feel called to look," I declared to Sir Benjamin on my initial visit to his surgery. "You may poke and prod and draw whichever fluids and other bits of me that you are convinced will assist you in making your diagnoses. But be aware that I have known my own mind about most things since before you were born, and I am not about to alter that practice without irrefutable evidence. I shall not take drugs that require other drugs to mitigate their side effects. Nor shall I alter my diet to satisfy your quackery or submit to any other of your prescriptions and proscriptions. While I am not eager to hasten Death's arrival, I am not prepared to cut short my enjoyment of life in order to delay it." I rose to my full height, somewhat shrunken but a half-head taller than his. "If you agree to my terms, Sir Benjamin, I shall agree to having you as my physician. If not, you can sod off."

He agreed. "Your terms are acceptable, Mrs. Reese-Thorpe."

"Miss Mandeville," I corrected. "I am not my husband's chattel."

"I stand chastened," he murmured. "My job, as I view it, is to keep you as healthy as I am able, for as long as I am able, without interfering with the quality of a life you have been enjoying without my assistance through the reigns of six monarchs." He bowed and kissed my hand. "I am here to serve you, Miss Mandeville."

After a grave silence, during which I could not be certain whether he was being obsequiously serious or was putting me on, Sir Benjamin roared with laughter and I joined him. We have had an unspoken understanding ever since: He will say what he believes he must, and I shall do what I bloody well please. It is an arrangement that suits both of us and one that might have been more difficult to come to had I not already given up smoking. That is one subject on which he will not compromise. I understand that. I have many more than one and am sure to collect at least several more before I am finished here.

Do I act unreasonably? I dearly hope so. Advancing years (what an obnoxious phrase) offers few benefits to those upon whom the years advance with such alacrity. At a minimum, we ought to be granted the privilege — nay, the right — to live them out in as curmudgeonly a fashion as decaying mind and body permit. Granted? Bloody hell, no. We ought to seize it, with both hands!

5

The liveried doorman, his lambswool hat dappled with snow-flakes, leaned into the late model Chevrolet Impala and opened the rear passenger door.

"Mesdames," the doorman said, reaching in to help Sadie Finkel out.

Sadie waved his hand away and gripped her handbag. "I should never have come, Sarah," she said to her companion. "Mr. Cameron—"

"Mac," Sarah Swartz interrupted. "He said you should call him Mac."

"Fine," Sadie muttered. "Mac. Whatever." She huddled into a thin cloth coat that provided little warmth against the chill blowing in through the open taxi door. "He isn't even going to be here. You told me so yourself. We should just leave."

"Mesdames?" The doorman straightened up and stepped back, his gloved hand resting on the roof. "Will you be coming inside the hotel?"

"*I* will be," Sarah declared, "if I can get past this eingeshpahrt machashaifeh. *Alteh* machashaifeh," she snorted.

The doorman suppressed an unseemly smirk. He didn't intend to let on that from his dozen years working at Cavendish Mall in Jewish Côte-Saint-Luc before coming to the Ritz-Carlton, he probably knew as many Yiddish insults as this woman did. She had called her friend, if she was a friend, a stubborn old witch.

The thin one did look a bit like a witch. With her grim, angular face and beaklike nose, he could easily picture her replacing Margaret Hamilton as the Wicked Witch of the West in *The Wizard of*

Oz. The other one was oddly familiar, although with her Brillo Pad hair, crooked lipstick and generous proportions, she didn't resemble the typical Ritz regular. If he had seen her somewhere, it sure as hell wasn't here.

"It looks like someone is making me negotiate my way out of here," Sarah continued, glaring at Sadie then gazing up at the doorman. "So don't wait."

The doorman glanced at the Haitian cabbie, whose eyes remained gratefully fixed on the still-ticking meter. He gently shut the door and retreated to his post by the elegant Edwardian hotel's brightly buffed, brass-handled doors.

"It doesn't matter about Mr. Cam— about Mac. I shouldn't have come," Sadie said, chewing on her right thumbnail. "Bernie doesn't really want me here. He was just being polite, inviting me. Why would he want me here? You stay. I'll go home."

Sarah rolled her eyes and grunted. "Don't be so meek and humble, Sadie. It doesn't suit you."

Sadie dropped her right hand to her lap and covered it with her left. "I don't know what you mean. All I'm saying is that the way I treated Bernie and Esther all those years... I wasn't such a mensch, you know."

"I know, Sadie," Sarah sighed. "Believe me, I know." *You weren't such a mensch to me all those years either, Sadie Finkel. All the way back to Bancroft School where I first met Esther, you weren't much of a mensch. That's more than fifty years, a half a century and then some, of being an old witch and only a couple months as maybe a mensch. Maybe.* She paused. *That's witch with a b. It's my own damn fault. I should never have talked her into coming.*

When Bernie had called Sadie with his invitation to Mac's surprise birthday party, she thanked him for including her then apologized that she wouldn't be able to make it, manufacturing an excuse that she immediately forgot.

"Look at me," she said to Sarah when they met later for tea at Café Bistro Chez Dominique. Sarah had not wanted to have tea or anything else with Sadie. Ever again, if it could be helped. For sure not at her favorite restaurant in all of Montreal. Her and Esther's both. Still, she had promised Bernie. Bernie believed in his aunt's miraculous conversion from shrew to saint two months earlier. But

Bernie had experienced only thirty-one years of being treated like drek by his mother's older sister. Sarah had suffered through nearly twice that. She wasn't a hundred percent convinced. Or it could be that Bernie was a better person than she was. "It's possible," she muttered.

"What's that?" Sadie asked, clutching her cup.

"Nothing," Sarah replied. "So, I'm looking at you. Why am I looking at you?"

"My hair is like something that someone took garden shears to. And my clothes? We won't talk about my clothes. If I set one foot in that Ritz lobby, they'll throw me out. Or they'll send me around back to the alley, to the chambermaids' entrance."

"Don't be an idiot," Sarah retorted. "How many more invitations to the Ritz do you think you're going to get at your age? It isn't like you don't know fashion. You know it better than I do. I'm not the one who sold ladies' dresses at Reitmans and Morgan's and The Bay all those years."

Sadie was not being an idiot. How could she admit to Sarah that she couldn't afford a new dress, despite her store discount?

"Do you still get your ten percent at The Bay now that you're retired?"

Sadie nodded.

I'm crazy. Sarah shut her eyes. *Tell me I'm crazy, Esther, for what I'm about to say to your sister.* But her oldest friend, who still talked to her sometimes, even if she had been dead for four years, said nothing. Sarah opened her eyes and smiled weakly.

"Then you'll take me to The Bay with you," she said to Sadie. "We'll run you through the beauty parlor there to fix your hair and get some makeup on you, then I'll buy you an outfit. Something pretty. Something for an afternoon at the Ritz. Something for a party." She looked at her watch. "We should go now. For the outfit. The beauty parlor you should do the day before, or that morning, so you don't make a mess of it."

Sadie wanted to shriek *no*, that she wasn't worthy of it, not any of it — not the Ritz, not the new clothes, not any kind of hairdo. Instead, she did her best to keep her voice level. "You can't do that," she said. "How can you do that? Why would you do that?"

Sarah lifted her teacup. "Because I can," she said. "Because Jack

left me comfortable and because, miracle of miracles, I got a big —
what do they call it? — yeah, an advance, for that book I wrote, for
Sara's Year. Can you believe it?"

"It's tsufil," Sadie replied. "Too extravagant. When will I wear
something like that again? You'll be wasting your money."

"Whose money is it to waste?" Sarah slammed her cup into the
saucer. "Mine, that's whose."

The old Sadie would have accused Sarah of flaunting her wealth.
The new Sadie caught herself in time and kept her mouth shut.

"When was the last time I bought you a birthday present, Sadie
Finkel? Never, that's when."

Sadie shrugged. "It isn't my birthday."

"It was one day and God willing, it will be again. Happy
birthday." Sarah took one final sip of tea, set her cup down — gently,
this time — dabbed her mouth with a napkin and signaled for the
check. "Now," she said after she had counted out the necessary bills
and added a few, "let's catch ourselves a taxi, and let's shlep ourselves downtown."

Sadie trailed Sarah out to the street. "We could take a bus," she
offered weakly. "The 24 will take us almost right there."

Sarah ignored her and hailed a cab.

By the end of the afternoon, Sadie had a new dress, new shoes
and new stockings. New underwear, too. "You can't wear such nice
new things over such old schmattas," Sarah insisted as she hustled
Sadie into the fitting room for the umpteenth time.

The one item Sadie refused was the one she needed most to accept:
a new fall coat. That's why she was shivering into her old cloth one
outside the Ritz as she continued arguing against going in. "So, like
I said: I don't deserve to be at some fancy affair at the Ritz, especially
since he isn't even going be there, your Mac. Not that I'd have any
kind of right to be there if he was coming, not the way I was all those
years with Esther and Ber—"

"Enough with your narishkeit," Sarah barked. "Just get out of the
damn cab." She gave Sadie a not-so gentle shove. "You know," she
added, "I think I almost liked you better when you were a bitch."

Sadie watched package-laden Saturday afternoon shoppers
scurry past on Sherbrooke Street. "I'm sorry," she said softly.

Sarah placed a gloved hand atop Sadie's. "No, Sadie, I'm sorry.

Now I'm the one being a bitch." She waved at the doorman who was still watching them. "We've already scared one nice man away. Now we're making this one wait for no reason. At our age, we can't afford to let any nice men get away."

"You go in," Sadie insisted. "I'll take the taxi home."

"Not to be rude, but you couldn't afford to take a taxi to the nearest Metro station, let alone all the way home to Côte-Saint-Luc."

"I can walk to the Metro. It isn't so bad out. It's just a few blocks to the Peel station."

"Are you meshugena? In this weather? You'll slip and fall and break a hip and die, and it'll be my fault. I have enough Jewish guilt. I don't need any more from you." She leaned across Sadie and unlatched the car door. The doorman rushed back. "You seem like a good boy," she said to him. He was in his forties. "Can you help this old la— this friend of mine into the lobby? I'll be right in after I pay this Sidney Poitier of a driver." She tapped the cabbie's shoulder and pointed to the meter. "You can turn that thing off now. We're finally getting out of your hair."

"Oui, madame," the doorman said. He reached for Sadie's arm.

"A hiltsener tsung zol zi bakumn," Sadie cursed, barely under her breath, dispatching a poisonous glare back at the taxi.

The doorman stifled a chuckle. *I bet* this *is the one who would be better off with a wooden tongue!*

"Now that's the Sadie I remember," Sarah mumbled as she dug into her oversized handbag for her wallet.

6

Mac lay in his oversized marble tub in Claridge's, watching soap bubbles rise and vanish into the blackness beyond the glow of the five flickering tapers strategically placed around the cavernous bathroom. He had asked the hotel butler assigned to his suite to procure the candles that morning when he had checked in. He had also requested a copy of Loreena McKennit's *Elemental* CD, and McKennit's haunting voice and Celtic harp now filtered in from the stereo in the Brook Penthouse's sitting room.

Come by the hills to the land where legend remains
Where stories of old fill our hearts and may yet come again…

By all rights, Mac should have been soaking in the extra-deep clawfoot tub in his Aunt Emmeline's townhouse. But when his taxi from Heathrow had pulled up in front of 33 Fitzroy Street, Mac asked the cabbie to wait. As he fumbled with a front-door lock that was as temperamental as his aunt had been, he wished he were still at the Ritz-Carlton with Bernie and Erik, helping launch them on their upcoming Italian odyssey. With Bernie's art show at Galérie Klinkhoff now a stunning success, Mac's son was ready for the fresh inspiration that would fuel the next phase of his painterly journey. Erik, too, needed to view the world with renewed vision as he prepared for the gallery show he had just committed to a year hence. Ten months in the Tuscan hills south of Siena would be just the ticket, for both of them.

They had been resistant at first, Bernie in particular. The four years he had spent in rural Nova Scotia with his newly discovered father had been magical, and he had been reluctant to see them end. It had also been hard for Mac. When he told Bernie and Erik, the afternoon of the Klinkhoff opening in August, that they would have to move out, he had been close to tears. The unexpected miracle that was Bernie had been just as magical for him.

"You don't need me as an art teacher anymore," Mac forced himself to say. "You don't need any art teacher anymore. It's time to let the world teach you. It's time to go where the art is." Mac suggested New York, Paris, London, Florence or Venice. Even Toronto, if they wanted to remain in Canada. In the end, Bernie and Erik opted to eschew established art centers in favor of a hilltop villa just outside Montalcino. There, they would house-sit for artist friends of Mac's who would be on an adventure of their own, in Gaugin's Tahiti. And they would paint.

That was the other reason Mac had been in Montreal: to move Bernie and Erik out of Nova Scotia and see them off to Europe. Now, Jeremy's sudden death had compelled Mac to fly out of Canada ahead of the boys. Perhaps he would take an Italian detour before returning home. It would depend on the size of the mess Jeremy had left him; or, rather, the size of the mess Emmeline had left, because Mac was certain that 33 Fitzroy, along with everything else about Emmeline's estate, had changed not at all in the fourteen years since her death. Who knew how long he would have to remain in London sorting it all out. He couldn't remain at Claridge's the whole time. Could he? No, he would have to settle in to the Fitzroy Street house at some point. For now, though, he was grateful that his celebrity status and frequent Claridge's stays had made it possible for him to walk into the hotel unannounced at ten and be installed in his favorite suite by ten-fifteen, with all the necessary adjustments to cater to his eccentricities handled while he was enjoying lunch in the dining room.

Mac's art may have been largely nonfigurative and modern — his portrait of Esther was his most noteworthy exception — but his design taste was more catholic. His home was furnished in an eclectic blend of sixties sleek and country comfortable, and when he traveled Mac generally chose to immerse himself in the past: the delicate, eighteenth-century elegance of the Ritz-Carlton's royal suite, the Georgian style of the Waldorf Astoria's White House-like presidential suite, the Napoleonic opulence of the George V's empire suite and the streamlined, art-deco poise of Claridge's.

Once he had jimmied open Emmeline's front door and stepped

inside, Mac knew it could only be Claridge's, at least for the first few days. He was not yet ready to tread this far back into the past. After all, he had not set foot in this front hall in decades, not since he began to be able to afford five-star hotels. From then on, most visits with Emmeline had been over afternoon tea, if not at Claridge's then nearby at either Brown's Hotel or the upscale Fortnum & Mason department store. Through all that time, nothing here appeared to have changed, not even the faint floral fragrance that greeted him as he advanced across the threshold: Jean Patou's Joy, which Emmeline had been lightly dabbing onto her neck since its release in 1929. How had the house held onto Emmeline's scent so many years after her death? Mac ran his fingers lightly over the mahogany handrail. As a child, he had helped keep its mirror-like finish buffed by frequently sliding down it…after Aunt Emmeline demonstrated how to do it without falling. Knowing Emmeline, she was probably still sliding down it until the day she died.

Mac peered into the front room. Here, too, little was different. The furniture pieces — an eclectic jumble of Victorian, Edwardian, art deco and mid-century modern — stood precisely where they had long stood. Even when shifted for Emmeline's legendary Sunday morning literary salons, they had been religiously returned to their proper places immediately after the penultimate guest's departure. It was the final guest who was inevitably charged by Emmeline with restoring the room to its disordered order.

One of the few additions was the mirror by the door, a 1960s oval monstrosity framed in shiny gold and silver discs that served as further testament to Emmeline's indifference to aesthetics and that reflected back a Mac much changed from the last time he had been in this room. The tall, slender man in leather bomber jacket and jeans was not as slim as he had then been, and his once-auburn hair had long ago lost its pigment and fullness. His hazel eyes, normally bright, were puffy and bloodshot, the result of seven hours of trans-atlantic coach travel. He looked away.

The only other alteration of any significance greeted him from above the fireplace: His *Primus* still stared back at him from over the mantel. However, its Hamnett and Crowley neighbors had been removed, giving his yellow-and-red monstrosity more unfortunate prominence.

Mac backed out of the room, overwhelmed by the sensory assault. Maybe he would stay at Claridge's for the duration after all. He snatched the thick envelope that Jeremy's solicitor had left for him on the hall table and fled back to the safety of the waiting taxi.

Now, a few miles away but galaxies distant, Mac dropped deeper into his hotel tub, a crystal flute of birthday champagne in one hand and the solicitor's envelope in the other, a thick, cream letterhead envelope that was embossed with "Dunedin" in block letters and inscribed with Mac's name in flowery cursive. The envelope, he had been advised in the brief phone conversation informing him of Jeremy's death, contained a cover note, a letter to him from Jeremy outlining his final instructions and a second from Emmeline, which had been withheld to this moment at her request. There would be a formal meeting with Miles Dunedin on Monday, but Jeremy's wishes were, like Emmeline's had been, singular enough that Miles determined that they could not wait.

They could. Mac flung the envelope toward the bathroom door, raised the champagne flute to his lips, lay back with his eyes closed and let Loreena McKennit's voice wash over him.

Where the past has been lost and the future is still to be won
And cares of tomorrow must wait till this day is done.

7

A discreet tone signaled the elevator's arrival on the eighth floor. Gleaming brass doors whooshed open and Sarah and Sadie entered the cab, ushered in by an olive-skinned young woman with coal-black hair and eyes as dark. She was dressed in Ritz-Carlton colors: a taupe blouse, dark-umber skirt and matching jacket. "Mesdames?"

"Lobby, please," Sarah said.

"Oui, madame."

The doors slid silently shut and the elevator began its effortless descent.

Sadie shut her eyes and steadied herself against the back rail. *Only one glass. Not even a full glass. And I'm all farshnickert.* Had she ever drunk champagne before? She must have, at some wedding or other…but decades ago. Could it have been as far back as Esther and Morris's wedding? She tried to do the math through her champagne fog. *Forty-five years ago? It can't have been forty-five years since I've had a glass of champagne. It must be. Where else would I have had something so fancy?* Sadie could come up with no other possible occasion. She received few party invitations and accepted fewer. If she could have avoided this one, she would have.

Sarah was chatting with the elevator girl, something about her hair, but Sadie wasn't listening. She was remembering: a wedding reception forty-five years earlier — in Outremont, of all places. You could say one thing about the Freeds: they had money. When Max Finkel couldn't afford a proper wedding for his daughter, Esther's Freed in-laws-to-be had stepped in. The ceremony had taken place at the Bagg Street shul in the Finkels' inner-city neighborhood. But the Freeds had hosted the reception in their spacious home on

Stuart Avenue. *Treelined* Stuart Avenue. Across from a big park, no less. That was as big a novelty for Sadie as the champagne had been. The Finkels' Clark Street boasted few trees and no park.

Sadie inhaled sharply. *Gott in himmel. That wedding of Esther's was forty-five years ago,* today? *That can't be right.* It was. Her sister had married Morris Freed on the twenty-fifth birthday of the man who would become her lover and would father her son. That was just too modne, too peculiar. Bernie and Sarah would use that five-dollar word of theirs to describe it. What was it? Synchronicity. That was too exotic a word for Sadie. Synchronicity was for the Ritz or for Stuart Avenue. Modne was Clark Street. Modne was perfect.

"So," Sarah asked Sadie as the doorman shepherded them to their Diamond taxi, sheltering them from the snow with a giant coffee-colored umbrella. "Was that so bad? The party, I mean." She ducked into the taxi. Sadie followed.

"Kildare Road by Cavendish Mall," Sarah directed the cabbie then turned back to Sadie. "Is that right?"

Sadie nodded.

"Was it? So bad?"

"No one seemed to be having a very good time."

"No," Sarah agreed. "You're right. Even Bernie and Erik were out of sorts, when they came back into that grand saloon room from wherever they were hiding. Erik, especially, is always so freylekh, always smiling, always making jokes."

"Not today."

"No, not today." Sarah lapsed into silence. She had promised herself that she wouldn't play the Jewish mother to Bernie and Erik, yet something was wrong and she couldn't help but worry. *It doesn't matter how long ago my Morty died. Once a Jewish mother, forever a Jewish mother.*

"You aren't his mother," Sadie said sharply, as if reading Sarah's mind. "Or Bernie's, for that matter." Sadie immediately regretted her tone and turned to the car window. The snow was coming down more heavily, unusual for late October. Their doorman's umbrella looked more like one of those overpriced cappuccino drinks than a regular coffee. Sadie watched as he waited until the sidewalk cleared of pedestrians and shook it out. Minutes later, the umbrella was snow-covered all over again. A minute after that, their taxi pulled out into the Saturday afternoon traffic on Sherbrooke Street.

The two women sat in tense silence as the cab drove east for a block, passing Galérie Klinkhoff with its window poster for Bernie's show, then turned south onto Stanley Street to circle the block back to Sherbrooke. As the car made its way west toward Sadie's dingy basement apartment in Côte-Saint-Luc, Sarah wondered how she could learn what was troubling Bernie and Erik and whether she could manage it before they flew to Italy in a few days. Sadie, meanwhile, angrily reproached herself for not having had the backbone to resist Sarah — first, about the party, and just now, about sharing this cab. She should have insisted on taking the Metro. Only when their taxi had passed Sadie's impossible-dream fantasy home, the castle-like Trafalgar Apartments near the top of the Côte-des-Neiges hill, did either of them speak again.

"Your book," Sadie said softly, still staring out the window.

Sarah opened her eyes. She had slipped into a light doze.

"It was good," Sadie added, turning slowly back to face Sarah.

"What?"

"*Sara's Year*. I read a bunch of it that day back in August, when I crashed Bernie's gallery opening."

"You didn't crash it, Sadie. We were surprised to see you there is all."

Sadie fidgeted with her purse strap. "I was surprised to see me there."

"I bet you were." Sarah wasn't sure what she wanted to say next. There was a lot she could say and lot she probably shouldn't. She and Sadie had met only twice before the afternoon tea that turned itself into a shopping expedition. On each occasion, she had forced herself to be civil, to try to ignore a past that Sadie had repeatedly poisoned, to try to believe that her oldest friend's older sister was truly as contrite as she acted. Sarah liked to think of herself as a generous, forgiving woman. Yet it was hard for her to believe that a single day, as harrowing as Sadie insisted that it had been, could have so transformed her Wicked Witch of the West into Glinda the Good. Maybe it was time she tried?

Sarah took a deep breath. "You know," she said slowly, "when I never liked you all those years? It wasn't because of who you were. It was because of how you were — to me, to Bernie, to Morris. Mostly to Esther."

"I—"

"No, Sadie, let me finish. Please. If you read *Sara's Year* like you said, I'm not telling you anything you don't know. If you read *Sara's Year*, I'm surprised you're talking to me."

"Sarah, I'm sorry. I—"

"Please, Sadie. You'll have your turn. I promise. What I want to tell you is that you have a lot of courage. To show up like that at Bernie's opening— At first, I thought it was chutzpah. Not the good kind. The unmitigated gall kind. I see now — and it isn't easy for me to see it or to say it — that to walk up to people you've treated so bad for so long and apologize…well, it's like walking into enemy territory waving a white flag and praying they won't fire on you. That takes courage. That takes the good kind of chutzpah."

Sarah paused. "It's almost your turn," she said, "but I need five minutes more." Five minutes more was all she had. They would soon be at Sadie's. "After you came to the gallery," she continued, "I think I was mad at you. More mad than I already was, because you were forcing me to be agreeable to you after you had been so mean to me all those years. I know you weren't forcing me to do anything, but that's what it's felt like since that day at the gallery. Like our places were switched, and suddenly you were Billie Burke and I was Margaret Hamilton.

"I was thinking about Bernie and Erik, just now. Not so much about what's bothering them. More about the fact that they're half my age, and here I am acting like I'm half theirs. I don't know your story, Sadie, about why you were so horrible to us. Maybe you'll tell it to me and maybe you won't. It shouldn't matter. And I don't know everything that happened to you that day, before you showed up at the gallery. Maybe you'll tell that to me and maybe you won't. That shouldn't matter either. What matters is that I'm a sixty-six-year-old adult. It's time I started acting like one. Like you."

Sarah gazed out the window. They were crossing over the Décarie Expressway, not far from where her Jack had been driving when a truck jumped the median and slammed into his car. First, God had taken her son, then He had taken her second husband (her first had been a son of a bitch; no loss), then her best friend. God would have a lot to answer for when she finally got to meet Him.

"Life is too short to hold grudges," Sarah said, turning back to

Sadie, who was wiping tears from her cheeks with the back of her hand. "Even if we're not ever going to be best friends, we don't have to be worst enemies." She took Sadie's other hand. "We could be not-best friends?"

Sadie squeezed Sarah's hand weakly.

"Now," Sarah said. "Now it's your turn."

"You've said everything there is to say."

A few minutes later, the taxi pulled up in front of Sadie's apartment building. "I can go home," Sarah said, "or I can come in, you can make me a cup tea and we can talk. Really talk, for once."

"I—" Sadie held her left hand down with her right to stop herself from gnawing on her thumbnail. "My apartment. It's—"

"A hekdish?"

Sadie gripped her left hand more tightly. "Uh-huh. A dump."

"You never saw where I lived in NDG with Sammy, did you?"

Sadie shook her head.

"If I lived in a hekdish with a nishtik mamzer for thirty years, I can spend an hour in one with a—"

"Reformed klafte?"

Sarah chuckled. "Yeah."

8

33 Fitzroy Street
London W1
10th August 1974

My Dear Marc-Allan,

If you are reading this, it is because Jeremy is a sentimental fool...a dead sentimental fool, that is. For the condition I set were he to choose to act on his silly sentimentality was that the ultimate fate of my papers — "The Emmeline Papers," as he has so pompously dubbed them — not be decided until after his death.

Should Jeremy live as long as I have, you will be decidedly old by now, Marc-Allan. With any luck for all concerned, you will be too old to fulfill this request. With somewhat less luck (for you, at least), you are dead as well. In that instance, the three of us could well be sharing a celestial pint-and-snigger over all this rot in whatever otherworldly place we have landed...should there be such a place, which my C of E upbringing insists there is, but which my nature denies as more ludicrous than ludicrous.

In that same instance, some bewildered heir or solicitor is reading these words and is wondering what manner of madwoman wrote them. I assure you, whoever you are, that I am not mad. What is the phrase used in all those American films when a will is read? Ah, yes. I am "of sound mind and body." Well, of sound mind, at any rate. Having labored, as of this day, through nearly ninety-three years on this planet, my body is not as sound as I would prefer it to be.

Regardless, whether it is you, your heirs or your solicitors who read this, I grant you my full permission to do what I continue to urge Jeremy to do; that is, destroy the bleeding lot. "The Emmeline Papers," that is. For that is what we are talking about.

Should you have the misfortune to share my husband's misguided romanticism, you now have my permission to read through the reams and reams of it and determine whether you concur with Jeremy's view that my papers are historically or literarily significant and ought to be dealt with accordingly or with my view that it is all twaddle and ought to be consigned to the nearest dustbin. I wash my hands of all of it, easy to do when one is only ash in the wind.

One final note, nephew, as you will learn when James Dunedin or, more likely, his son Miles, shares the details of Jeremy's will with you. You will know by now, of course, that on my death I left everything to him. What you will not know is that it was bequeathed to him with the proviso that nothing of mine be dramatically altered and that all of it be passed to you at his death. That means that this house, most of its contents, including your despised *Primus* and, you may be surprised to learn, the Cameron-MacCready stores are now yours. When you turned your back on your "destiny and your family obligations," as your father so melodramatically put it, he willed the stores to your mother and me. They, too, will pass to Jeremy when I die, with the aforementioned stipulation. A capable and well-remunerated Mr. Campbell has been running them with inordinate profitability since your father's death. You may remember him as the unruly grandson of your father's general manager. Mr. Campbell is young enough that he is surely still acting in this capacity when you read this; I am certain that he will be prepared to carry on doing so, should that be your wish.

As for Jeremy, he is, of course, free to dispose of his own money and property as he sees fit. Yet, if he continues to be estranged from what remains of his family, I have no doubt that his holdings have now passed on to you and that when the relevant Dunedin reveals to you their scope and breadth, you will be astonished. The bottom line, as they say so vulgarly in America, is that you are now a remarkably wealthy man, wealthier than your art will have rendered you by the time you read this.

My dear Marc-Allan: Jeremy reprimands me repeatedly for being excessively blunt with my criticisms and miserly with my praise. He is right to do so. That is my excuse for never having expressed to you my boundless pride in your extraordinary artistry and astounding achievements, all of which I have followed with the misplaced self-importance of one whose sole talent is to recognize the gifts of others. My tribute may be belated and posthumous. It is no less genuine for that.

In closing, I know that you choose to be called Mac. However, I feel safe in assuming that that cannot extend to anyone old enough to have attended your christening. So, Marc-Allan it is.

Yours,
Aunt Emmeline

9

Mac folded Emmeline's letter back into its envelope and reached for his Royal Doulton cup, deco-styled like much of Claridge's. Frederick, the earnest young butler assigned to his suite, had just departed after setting out the breakfast Mac had ordered the previous night: a basket of croissants, brioches and muffins, a selection of jams, jellies and Dundee marmalade and a salver of mixed berries and sliced melons. The tea, served from an angular sterling silver service, was not Claridge's standard morning Assam but Mac's favorite blend from Fortnum & Mason. As soon as the hotel manager had been alerted to the artist's arrival, a junior porter had been dispatched to Piccadilly to procure a dozen canisters of the store's signature Royal Blend.

This was Mac's second morning in London and he still couldn't face the full English breakfast that Frederick had proposed. The mere thought of black pudding made his stomach turn, however tarted up it might be to appeal to a discriminating Claridge's palate. Even eggs felt impossibly rich. Mac smiled wryly as he recalled a young RAF pilot who would once have eagerly cleaned his plate of a traditional fry-up, especially were it to include kippers or lorne sausage. Both, preferably. A serving or two of rumbledethumps, a dish unlikely ever to find its way to a Claridge's table, would also have been welcome. The potato, cabbage and onion hodgepodge had been a particular favorite of a much younger Marc-Allan, especially as prepared by Morag McTavish, the Cameron's long-ago housekeeper and cook, whose generous proportions suggested that it had been a favorite of hers, too.

This was the fifth time Mac had gone over the letter and he was no less surprised by its contents, now that he could practically recite them by heart. But then Emmeline had always been full of surprises — as much to her nephew's delight as to her brother-in-law's dismay.

Mac's father had rarely bothered to conceal his disdain for his wife's older sister. A stolid Scots businessman whose Tory leanings were so pronounced that he had once been approached by the party to stand for Parliament, James Angus Cameron III had done his best to protect his son and heir from "the corrosive sorcery of that radical suffragette socialist sister-in-law of mine." Unfortunately for him, his best had not been good enough. Outrageously encouraged in his willfulness by Emmeline, Mac had chosen to exchange a solid future at the helm of the family's department store for the uncertain and certainly unsettling life of an artist. James Angus (never simply James) died before he could witness a future for his son that eclipsed anything he could have imagined: an international artistic success staggering in its scope and far more enriching than any Glasgow mercantile establishment could ever have hoped to be, regardless of how profitable it was.

After all my youthful rebellion, I am to be a department-store magnate after all? Mac marveled at the vagaries of fate. Now that he was in charge at Cameron-MacCready, perhaps he ought to prevail upon the capable and well-remunerated Mr. Campbell to establish a fine arts department in what now numbered a half-dozen stores scattered across England, Scotland and Ireland. That would set all three James Anguses spinning wildly in their graves. Mac laughed.

More startling was the revelation about Emmeline's mysterious "papers." Had his aunt been writing a book? A memoir or autobiography? Had she been keeping a journal or some other daily record? Had she maintained a correspondence with one or several of her ultimately better-known literary salon creatives? Former lovers? Could any be alive after all these years?

None of those alternatives seemed plausible. As uncommon as her life had been, the Emmeline Mac remembered would never have sat still long enough to write a book. She was constantly flying from project to project and cause to cause, barely establishing one before turning its leadership over to a subordinate and moving on to the next. Even the longest-lived and most locally renowned of her undertakings, her literary salons, didn't survive the war. And her letters? This near-death letter was the lengthiest and most personable of hers that he had ever read. All her previous letters to him had been as crisp as telegrams, and nearly as brief.

Of course there was a simple way to find out: He could return to Fitzroy Street and search for the damned things. Yet Mac could not shake the unnerving sensation that returning to Emmeline's would be far from simple and that some not-yet-knowable something about those papers would shatter his plans to be gone from the UK within a few days.

Miles Dunedin had revealed little in his brief phone call to him in Montreal, other than to assure him that the firm would take care of cremation arrangements (a relief), that Mac was Jeremy's sole legatee (a shock) and that his presence in London was required, at his earliest convenience (an annoyance).

Now that he was here, Mac's intention was to see to his uncle's final wishes, remove from Emmeline's house any personal mementos, including *Primus*, meet with Dunedin to sign whatever papers were required to sell the house and auction off the remainder of its contents, and then get the hell out of England as quickly as possible.

Yet everything about Emmeline had been disruptively if endearingly Machiavellian while she was alive. Why would he expect her to not go on orchestrating the lives of those around her fourteen years after her death?

Mac stared out the hotel window toward Buckingham Palace, less than a mile away and directly south. If he squinted he could almost make out the Royal Standard fluttering in the wind, indicating that the Queen was in residence. Under other circumstances, that might have proven convenient. Not on this trip. Mac had again been asked to paint the Queen's portrait, a rare honor for someone who had had the effrontery to turn her down once before. This time the request had not arrived through normal channels. Someone at the Palace had taken the time to research the reluctant artist and had discovered that whereas Marc-Allan Cameron found it easy to turn down official invitations, he had a tougher time refusing friends. Thus, the Palace had discreetly reached out to Donald Macdonald, the new Canadian High Commissioner in London, who had discreetly reached out to his former boss, a certain former Canadian prime minister.

Pierre Elliott Trudeau was already a fan when he and Mac bumped into each other in the Ritz-Carlton dining room the morning of Bernie's Klinkhoff Gallery opening in August. When Trudeau followed up with an invitation to join him and his sons for a family dinner, Mac accepted, but only because he wanted to get inside Maison Cormier, the landmark art deco masterpiece that was now Trudeau's home. That, and the fact that Bernie and Erik had been included in the invitation. It didn't seem right to deprive them of an opportunity to meet the retired statesman.

To Mac's astonishment, he and Trudeau hit it off. Mac had expected Trudeau to live up to his arrogant, imperious reputation, a persona already experienced during their brief Ritz encounter. Instead, he was seduced not only by Trudeau's warmth, wit and generosity of spirit but by his genuine and informed interest in art — Bernie's as well as Mac's. The two men had kept in touch ever since.

So it was Pierre Elliott Trudeau who had telephoned Mac at the Ritz and asked — unofficially, of course — what the artist's response might be were he to be reinvited to paint Queen Elizabeth's portrait. Although Jeremy's death gave Mac an excuse to delay his response, he was leaning toward another no. The Queen could not be expected to come to him in Nova Scotia, and he was not eager to spend months traipsing after her from Buckingham Palace to Windsor Castle to Balmoral and back. He was flattered, of course. Yet flattery no longer worked the same magic on him that it once had. He was now old enough, successful enough and decorated enough that the honor and prestige of the request did not tempt him, even if the subject did.

Mac agreed to consider the request but begged Trudeau to reveal nothing of his impending London trip to either the High Commissioner or the Palace.

"They'll find out," Trudeau warned. "They do every time." Once word of Mac's presence reached the Palace, he added, they would undoubtedly enlist another emissary. Unofficially, of course.

Mac tore his eyes away from Buckingham Palace. *With any luck, I'll be gone before that can happen.* He glanced down at the envelope from the solicitor's office. *Or not.*

Sighing, he splashed a touch of milk into his cup, poured in some fresh tea and reached for the envelope, which still contained

Jeremy's letter and Dunedin's note — both as yet unread. Perhaps he was overdramatizing the situation. Perhaps his uncle's words and those of the solicitor would reassure him about Emmeline and Fitzroy Street. He doubted it. Leaving the envelope where it was, he reached instead for the bakery basket. He ripped off the flaky end of a buttery croissant, slathered it with apricot jam and washed it down with a fortifying gulp of tea, all the while peering at the envelope. Finally, he picked it up, pulled out the relevant sheets, unfolded them and laid them on the table, face down. He then tore another hunk off the croissant, spreading this one with marmalade, and stuffed it into his mouth. When he had finished the croissant and consumed most of a blueberry muffin, he drained his cup and picked up the pages: Dunedin's, a half-sheet on heavy legal stock, and Jeremy's, on the same vellum as Emmeline's.

The solicitor's was succinct, repeating the circumstances of Jeremy's death, assuring Mac that his uncle's cremation and related arrangements would already have been attended to, advising him to peruse the attached letters from Jeremy and Emmeline and summoning him to his offices in the City first thing Monday morning to receive both the ashes and further instruction. Dunedin closed by including his home telephone number and inviting Mac to call any time over the weekend should he have pressing needs or questions.

Jeremy's letter, written in a neat public-school hand, was equally straightforward, if nowhere near as concise. Mac poured himself another cup of tea and began to read.

10

33 Fitzroy Street
London W1
1st January 1976

Dear Mac,

I trust that this letter will not reach you for many years, but it strikes me as wise to have it prepared in the event that the capriciousness of fate eclipses my expectations. I am, after all and by most rankings, still a young man. At the same time, the death of your aunt, if not unexpected, has shaken me deeply, and my health has suffered as a consequence. Hence, this note, written to you only twenty-four months after her passing, which contains my "final" requests and instructions.

Although we have met only twice, Mac, I consider you to be more "family" than my remaining blood relations, all of whom are mean-spirited, narrow-minded, grasping gits, which is the most generous way I know to describe them. For that reason, you are my sole heir — not only by rights to the property that Emmeline entrusted to me on your behalf, but to the Reese-Thorpe holdings that I inherited upon my father's death and that are infinitely more vast than I can know. Whichever Dunedin is handling my affairs when you read this will sort all that out for you, if he has not already.

You are aware, of course, that Emmeline insisted that there be no memorial service for her and that her ashes be unceremoniously disposed of. What you cannot know is that even as I obeyed her first request, I flouted her second, most flagrantly. What I am about to ask of you mirrors my decision about her final disposition.

Before I continue, I must apologize for the uncharacteristic sentimentality of my appeal. However, when it comes to your aunt and our improbable union, I have always been more of a romantic than Emmeline ever was or approved of. I like to believe that she did more than indulge my more overt displays of affection, that she secretly delighted in them. Yet for all her outspokenness and public eccentricities, when it came to matters of the heart, Emmeline retained her English reserve until the end.

Like Emmeline, I see no reason for any formal memorial, nor am I concerned with how my corporeal remains are converted to ash. What I would request is that you engage a particular Regent's Canal narrow boat and, from it, scatter my ashes into the canal between The Palm Tree Pub in Mile End and The Narrowboat in Islington, where they can follow Emmeline's ashes, if belatedly, out to the Thames and, thence, to the sea. Should it suit you and the landlord to arrange for it, an intimate gathering afterward at The Palm Tree would complete the sendoff. Dunedin can assist you with all the necessaries.

I spoke earlier of your aunt's aloofness in matters of the heart. That aloofness was not reserved uniquely for me, as I am certain you experienced in your times with her. Emmeline had no use for such phrases as "I love you" or "I am proud of you." Yet she spoke of you often enough with that possessiveness of tone and phrase that she employed only when referring to those about whom she cared deeply that I know and must share that she loved you very much and was profoundly proud of you and of your accomplishments, as am I.

It would be absurd for you ever to consider me your elder, or even your uncle. Perhaps you might consider me a friend. It is a peculiar request, I know, coming from beyond the grave, as I can only assume that it now does. As I am coming to learn in these difficult months that have followed Emmeline's passing, love and friendship know none of the restrictions that we attach to physical form. Love and friendship are eternal. If you would hold that thought in your heart as you scatter my ashes out toward Emmeline's, I would spend all eternity expressing my gratitude.

Your "uncle" and, I hope, your friend,
Jeremy Reese-Thorpe

11

"Thank God that's over," Erik declared as the royal suite's front door clicked shut on the final guest. He cocked his ear and waited until the elevator had chimed its arrival and then a moment more to ensure its departure. "I thought she'd never leave," he added.

"She might not have if you hadn't kept staring at the clock," Bernie said. "That was brave of you. After all, she *is* the art critic for CKO."

Erik grimaced. "I don't know how you can put 'CKO' and 'art critic' in the same sentence and keep a straight face. She's a joke and so is the radio station." He tugged his turtleneck out from his jeans, kicked off his sneakers without untying the laces and dropped onto the Chippendale chair next to the door.

Bernie planted himself on Erik's lap. Erik tried to push him off. "You're heavy! You shouldn't have eaten all those hors d'oeuvres." Erik pronounced it horse doovers.

Bernie solidified his position by wrapping his legs around Erik's. "So why did you invite her?"

"Me?" Erik asked incredulously. "Never. Not in a million years. Not in a billion years. Not ever." He tilted his head. "You mean you didn't?"

Bernie shook his head. "You were in charge of the art world invitations. I just figured you'd had a change of heart."

"Not where Maryse Pelletier's concerned. Not unless she magically sprouts some art savvy *and* gets an instant personality transplant."

"You're saying Maryse crashed Mac's party?" Bernie asked.

Erik guffawed. "I'm sure it wasn't the first."

"She's got chutzpah. You've gotta give her that."

Erik stood, forcing Bernie off his lap. "I don't gotta give her nothing, let alone all the champagne and canapés she tucked away. Did you see her go at them? I don't know where she puts it all. She's thinner than I am." He tugged off his Salvador Dali socks and stuffed them into his back pocket. "You know she's Gérard Pelletier's great-niece fourteen times removed or something like that, right? I'm sure that's how she got the job at CKO. Don't forget that Pelletier was Trudeau's arts minister. That's probably why she showed up."

"What do you mean?"

"Mac knows Trudeau. Ergo, Maryse gets to go to his birthday party. By divine right."

"*Ergo?*"

Erik giggled. "I'm practicing to be an intellectual." He stiffened his posture and made a scowling face in the mirror. "I'm counting on them giving me Mac's old teaching job at NSCAD."

Bernie circled Erik, inspecting him with mock seriousness. "Let's see," he said. He tilted his head and tapped his chin. "Permanently tousled hair." He mussed Erik's hair. "Permanent scruff." He ran the back of his hand across Erik's unshaven cheek. "Permanent paint." He flicked the colorful stains on Erik's fingers and jeans. "You know," he went on, "you look seedy enough to be an academic, but..." He pulled Erik toward him and kissed him. "Disreputable artists are much sexier. Ergo, no professorship for you, mister."

Erik kissed him back then leaned away, mimicking Bernie's inspection. "You're right," he concluded, leering. "Disreputable artists *are* much sexier." He padded toward the grand salon. "That calls for more champagne." Bernie followed after him.

Erik stopped just inside the door to the grand salon and surveyed the disarray. "Oh, shit." He picked up a pair of half-empty champagne flutes from a side table and scanned the room for somewhere to put them. "Maybe we shouldn't have pushed Maryse out so fast. I bet she would have gladly emptied all these plates and glasses for us." He elbowed aside a platter of picked-over hors d'oeuvres on a room-service trolley and deposited the glasses there. "What are we supposed to do with this mess?"

"Absolutely nothing," Bernie replied. "This is the Ritz. I'll call down in a minute and they'll immediately dispatch a disaster crew to clean it all up."

Erik smirked. "I'm so glad I married you for your money."

"Me, too." Bernie pulled Erik toward him. "Even though it's Mac's money."

Erik found a clean glass and poured himself some champagne. "Just don't get that old man of yours mad at you," he said. "If he cuts you off, I'm going to have to divorce you and find myself a new sugar daddy."

Bernie snatched Erik's champagne flute from him. "Just don't go losing your boyish looks, blondie," he warned teasingly, "or I'm going to have shop around for a new boy toy."

Erik slid his hand under Bernie's shirt. "You can barely keep up with me as it is, Grandpa. What would you do with fresh meat?"

Bernie fiddled with Erik's belt. "How's about I show you?"

"How's about it?" Erik steered Bernie out of the grand salon and down the hall toward the bedrooms. If during their first stay at the Ritz in August they had occupied the opulent royal bedroom in honor of Bernie's Klinkhoff Gallery art opening, for this visit they had turned it over to Mac, for his birthday. They had selected instead the suite's second-grandest, the vice-regal bedroom, which was still more spacious than Erik's old one-room apartment had been.

"Wait." Bernie stopped by the hall phone. "I'll call the front desk for that cleaning crew."

Erik slapped Bernie's hand away. "No, you won't."

"What about the mess back there?"

"Later, big boy." Erik slapped Bernie's butt. "Now's the time to make a mess of our own."

"You're on." Bernie ogled Erik and propelled him toward the bedroom.

The phone trilled.

"Or not." Bernie turned back to pick up.

Erik kept pushing him down the hall.

"It might be Mac."

"So?"

"You want Pops to cut me off and force you back out onto the street? You aren't as young as you used to be, you know."

Erik frowned. "Well, if you put it that way, especially now that winter's coming."

Bernie ran back to the phone. "Hello? Oh, hi." He covered the mouthpiece. "It's KC," he whispered. "It went great," he spoke into the phone, "considering that the guest of honor wasn't here… Huh? Sure… How's your mom doing?… Bummer… Erik? Yeah, he's here… Yeah. Later… You, too." He passed the receiver to Erik.

"Hey, sis… Yeah, what Bernie said, except the part where he said it went great. It was the worst party ever, and I've been to some turkeys." He laughed. "Actually, no. I was about to have my way with this hot guy I lured up here. Can I call you back in a bit?… What?… Oh, okay… No, I didn't. What happened?… Shit." His voice quavered. "You're sure? That's a stupid question. Of course you're sure." He paused. "Yeah, I'm here. No, I had no idea. Not a clue. I haven't talked to him in, well— Not since, you know… Go on… Uh-huh… What a slime… And?… Fuck. Fuck, fuck, fuck, fuck, fuck…" He wiped his eyes with the back of his hand. "Yeah, I'm okay… No, you're right. I'm not… Yeah, okay. Call me after, if you go. If you talk to her, tell her I'm sorry…if you think she'll remember me. Unless you think she'll think it's my fault. It isn't, but…well, you know… Yeah, okay…

"Wait. How's Mom doing? She always says she's okay, but… Shit. Really?… You think Bernie and I should cancel?… You're sure?… No, you're right. If I don't go, she'll kill me. But—… As long as you promise. I'll call her in the morning, and every day while we're over there… Okay. And call me back, collect, if you hear anything else about—… Right… Love you, too. Bye."

Erik slid to the floor and let the receiver fall. "Shit," he muttered. "Shit, shit, shit, shit, shit." He swallowed a sob. "Fuck."

"What is it? You're pale as a ghost." Bernie dropped to the floor next to him. "You're shaking." He put an arm around Erik to steady him. "Is it your mother? KC said—"

"It isn't that. It's—" Erik gulped back his tears just long enough to blurt, "It's Calvin. He's dead." Then he collapsed into Bernie's arms, sobbing convulsively. "AIDS," he gasped when he could speak again. "He died from AIDS."

12

The Diamond taxi skidded to a halt in front of a palatial, two-story house across Kildare Road from Cavendish Mall, its wipers thwacking back and forth in a noisy battle to keep the windshield clear. An SUV-shaped snowdrift filled the driveway.

Sarah climbed out of the car after Sadie. "This isn't so bad," she said, eying the broad front staircase that swept up to an expansive terrace and a set of heavy double doors trimmed with wrought-iron fixtures and leaded-glass panes. Buff-brick lower floors made way for mock-Tudor half-timbering on the upper story and gables.

"Ongepatshket," Sadie muttered. She led Sarah along an icy walk at the side of the house, sliding her palm along the wall to steady herself. "Be careful," she said. "Feldman usually clears the way or at least salts it. But they're in Florida, and the boy who's supposed to take care of it while they're gone isn't so reliable. He's their nephew and they haven't raised my rent in five years. So what am I supposed to say?"

She pulled a loose key from her purse and jiggled it in the lock. "It's a little fussy," she said. When it finally caught, Sadie pushed open the door, reached inside to switch on the light, then moved aside to let Sarah go first down the dozen steps. "It's unlocked," she called after her. "Just go in. It'll be cold, so keep your coat on."

Sarah opened the flimsy door at the foot of the stairs and stepped into a tiny one-room apartment. A studio, they probably called it, but it was too fancy a name for something you couldn't swing a cat in. More like a giant walk-in closet with its own bathroom and with a narrow strip of snow-covered windows at eye level.

Filling most of the apartment's shortest wall was a compact

kitchenette. A 1970s fridge and stove in now-unfashionable avocado green bookended a matching Formica counter, itself topped by particle-board cabinets and bisected by a single porcelain sink, chipped but scrubbed shiny. A few feet away, a pink plastic rose poked out of a lead crystal bud vase at the exact center of a cafe table that was covered in the same Formica as the counter. A bentwood chair served as its it sole companion.

The only other seating was a compact sofa bed, also green, that together with the three-fixture pole lamp to its left, served as a makeshift room divider. A wobbly, faux-walnut coffee table and matching end table completed the grouping.

Tucked into a corner on the far wall was a narrow dresser that doubled as a nightstand for the twin bed next to it. The bed was covered in a surprisingly feminine bedspread: tufted, if threadbare pink chenille in a floral medallion design, with a fringe dusting a waxed and buffed wood-plank floor. Had this been Sarah's apartment, clumps of lint and God knows what-all else would have been clinging to the fringe. Whatever else Sadie was, she was a first-rate balabusta. Her apartment may have been shabby, but it was spotless. Not a single smudge marked the walls, doors or light switches. Not one dirty dish could be seen in the sink or anywhere else. Nothing was out of place.

On top of that, the lingering aroma of chicken soup suggested that Sadie's microscopic kitchen got plenty of expert use. This wasn't a Campbell's-can smell; it was the from-scratch bouquet known to generations of Jewish mothers and their offspring. Ironically, Sadie had never been a Jewish mother; Sarah had been but couldn't cook worth a damn.

The apartment's walls were bare except for a framed sepia photograph from the 1930s and two unframed art prints. The photo, Sarah was certain, was of Sadie in her twenties. She was smiling, a rare sight for Sadie, with her arm around a young man, an even rarer sight. Sarah squinted at it. She was sure she had known the boy but she couldn't place him, not fifty-something years later. Did she dare ask Sadie about it? No way. As for the reproductions, Sadie must have returned to the Klinkhoff after Bernie's opening to buy them. One was Bernie's *At Stella's*, which depicted Sarah and his mother as teenagers at the restaurant that had for decades been their favorite hangout; the other was *Queen Esther,* Mac's luminous portrait of his lost love, Sadie's sister.

Sadie followed Sarah inside and crossed to the Honeywell dial-thermostat between the kitchenette and bathroom door. "I'll turn up the heat and put the kettle on," she said. "Soon you'll want to take your coat off. Not yet. The place is either shvitzing or like an icebox. That's in the winter. In the summer there's an air conditioner, so it's fine." She paused. "When they get around to putting it in." She paused again. "If it's working." She filled the stainless steel kettle and plugged it into an outlet.

"Sit, Sarah," Sadie continued. "On the sofa. My other dining room chair broke and I didn't see any reason to replace it. It's more comfortable on the sofa anyhow." She opened a cabinet door and pulled out a pair of Expo '67 mugs and two turf green Fiestaware plates that nearly matched the Formica. "Tea or coffee? Coffee's instant. Taster's Choice. Tea is Red Rose."

"Tea, please," Sarah replied. She lowered herself onto the lumpy sofa and hugged her coat more tightly around her. The heat had yet to kick in. "With lemon if you've got. Plain is fine if you don't."

Sadie opened the fridge, holding the door close to her body so that Sarah couldn't see how empty it was. She hardly ever bought fresh fruit or vegetables in the winter; they were too expensive. But by some miracle her fridge contained not only a lemon, it contained a third of a Sara Lee chocolate cake, both left over from a party at the senior center. "You like chocolate?" she asked, holding up the Sara Lee box.

"What's not to like? I'm not real hungry after that feast at the Ritz," Sarah added, "but who am I to insult Miss Sara Lee?" She shoved her hands into her coat pockets. "Just a small piece, please."

A few minutes later, Sadie arranged two mugs of tea, two plates of cake, a dish of lemon slices, two forks, two spoons and two napkins on an aluminum tray and carried them to the coffee table. She pulled over the bentwood chair and took off her coat. "If you get hot," she said, picking up one of the mugs, "I can open a window. It's narish, I know. But that's how it is."

"Sara Lee is one of my best friends," Sarah said stabbing a piece of cake onto her fork, "next to Dominique with her pies." She closed her eyes as she chewed. "I can't keep this in my house or I'd eat the whole thing in one sitting. I'm big enough as it is." She patted her ample belly. She swallowed another piece. "Dominique," she explained, "is Stella's niece. It's her restaurant now." She pointed to *At Stella's*. "It isn't that different now, is it, even after all these years."

Sadie lifted her mug, letting the heat warm her hands and face before taking a sip. "So what do you think of my hekdish?" she asked. "I bet yours was bigger than this one."

"Bigger, yes," Sarah said, "and it had a small backyard, which helped. And Morty, which also helped. It also had Sammy, which didn't help at all." She squeezed a lemon slice into her tea. "It was also nowhere near as clean as this. My mother, aleha hasholem, would turn her visits into all-day cooking and cleaning marathons. It was embarrassing." She laughed. "Not so embarrassing that I would ever have stopped her."

Sadie said nothing. She didn't know what to say. Any conversation about the past would only make her look bad. And what was there to say about the present? Instead, she focused on her tea and cake and on trying to not chew her nails.

Sarah half-shut her eyes. *What am I supposed to say to her, Esther? If I talk about the old days, it'll sound like I can't let go of what a bitch she was, and I want to try to let go of it. If I talk about now…well, what's there to talk about? She's lonely. I can see that. She has no money. I can see that, too. She's not happy. Who knows if she's ever been happy? Except maybe in that picture.* She stole a peek at the framed photograph. *Who's that boy, Esther? Do you know?* If Esther knew, she wasn't telling. Sarah scraped the last of the chocolate icing onto her fork.

"More cake?" Sadie asked.

Sarah shook her head. Was it time to leave yet?

"Are you sure? Me, I'm going to have one." Sadie carried her plate to the kitchen counter. "There's just two more slices," she said. "You might as well help me finish."

"To help you out," Sarah said. If she had to stay, eating more cake was something to do. Besides, if she kept her mouth full, she had an excuse not to talk.

"Can I ask you a question?" Sadie asked. She slid the final slice from the Sara Lee box onto Sarah's plate. "You can say no, if you want. I'll understand if you say no. It's just that— Wait here."

"Where am I going with a piece of chocolate cake sitting in front of me?" Sarah asked, wishing that she could take her piece of cake and be gone.

Sadie crossed to the closet and retrieved her copy of *Sara's Year* from the top of a low bookcase. She held it out to Sarah tentatively. "Would you sign it?"

"You want me to sign it?" Sarah was astounded.

"Y-yes."

"With all the bad things I said about you in it?"

Sadie nodded. "It wasn't so easy to read, parts of it. It was also hard to put down. It doesn't make so much sense when I say it out loud, but that's what it was like." She sat, still holding the book. "Without *Sara's Year*," she added, "I would never have gone into the gallery that day." She hesitated, riffling through the pages. "Or back to Esther's grave. That's where I went after, to apologize."

Sarah rummaged in her purse for her special fountain pen, the gold Parker 51 Signet she had bought to sign her McClelland & Stewart publishing contract, and her books.

"What do you want me to say?"

"Just your name would be good. Or whatever you want."

Sarah opened the book, tugged the cap off her Parker and let the nib hover over a blank spot on the title page, just above her name.

"To the new Sadie," she wrote, underlining the word *new*, "living proof that it's never too late to be a mensch." Could she write "Love, Sarah"? No. Not yet. Just "Sarah"? She sensed Sadie's eyes on her. *Not that, either. It's cold.* She touched the pen to the page. "Mit fil respekt," she added, "Sara(h)."

Sadie set the book on the coffee table, open to the inscription. "Thank you," she whispered, her voice trembling. "That means a lot."

"It also means a lot to me that my book can make such a difference in someone's life," Sarah said. "In *your* life, especially." She drained the last of the tea from her mug and returned it to the tray. *Now, maybe, it's time?* She smoothed her slacks and pressed down on the sofa cushions to push herself to standing.

"More tea?"

"Oh. Uh…" Sarah sighed and settled back into her seat. Sadie was already adding fresh water to the kettle.

"So, are you going to write another book?" Sadie called from the kitchenette. "An *After Sara's Year*?"

Sarah groaned. "Everyone wants I should write another one. Except my publishers. They're waiting to see if this one sells first." She accepted a fresh mug of tea from Sadie. "Not that I know what I'd write." She set the mug down and squeezed another lemon slice into it. "Not that it matters. I sort of have to, or at least try. I promised Bernie's Erik." She blew on the tea and took a sip. "Not so much a promise," she added. "More like a deal."

"A deal? What sort of deal?"

Sarah leaned into the sofa and let her mind drift back to that day in August where so much happened. How could it be only ten weeks ago? Somehow, it was.

After four years' not knowing what had become of him, she and Bernie had reunited, not exactly according to plan, at Esther's grave. From the cemetery, he and Erik had whisked her downtown to join them first for lunch at the Ritz with Mac, then at Bernie's art opening a few doors away at the Klinkhoff. But it had been over lunch when she and Erik had struck their deal.

She couldn't tell Sadie that it had been Esther, Sadie's dead sister, who kept insisting that she pull Erik aside for a private chat. *She'll think I'm more meshugena than she already does.*

Sarah hadn't known what she would say to Erik when they left Bernie and Mac at the table and went outside to the Ritz Garden. But Esther had been right. There were things to say. As they sat by the duck pond, Erik confessed that he had passed up an opportunity for an art show of his own in order to follow Bernie to Nova Scotia.

"I had to give it up," he said. "I couldn't risk losing Bernie."

"Like Mac lost Esther."

"I never told him about the show," Erik said. "If I had, he never would have let me come. You won't tell him, will you?"

"I think you and I should have a pact," Sarah replied after a moment's thought. "Like Bernie and me did."

"A pact? What do you mean?"

Sarah's arrangement with Bernie had been that if he would agreed to surrender to his newly discovered passion for painting, she would recommit to the writing she had abandoned decades earlier. It had paid off: Within four years *Sara's Year* was finished and published and Bernie had his first show, at one of Montreal's premier galleries.

"I don't know if I have another book in me," she had explained to Erik. "I know you have lots of paintings left in you. So here's my deal: I know the boys at your gallery haven't given up on you. So you call them to arrange for a new show and then you get back to your painting, really get back to it. You do that, and I promise to try to write this *After Sara's Year* book you boys keep nagging me about."

Erik had agreed. That was one of the reasons he and Bernie were leaving for Italy in a few days, to paint.

"A lot happened that day," Sadie said softly, recalling her own experiences. "Too much."

Sarah waited. She knew that *Sara's Year* had been partly responsible for Sadie's transformation. She didn't know the rest of the story.

"Maybe I'll tell you all what happened…another day."

"Maybe you'll write it."

"Narishkeit. You're the writer. Me? I'm the…" Sadie gazed up at the band of windows immediately below the ceiling. A single shaft of light pierced through the sole fissure in the snow that the storm had packed up against the glass.

"The what?"

Sadie turned to Sarah. "That's it. I don't know. Your book did that. Not only your book. Everything that day. It erased that alteh mach-ashaifeh that I was. Well, not all of it. Just enough to leave me all farblondzhet. It's like it ripped up the old Sadie recipe and didn't replace it with any kind of new one. I can be a pretty good cook with the right recipe and the right ingredients, but…"

"You haven't found the right cookbook yet," Sarah offered.

Sadie shrugged. She wasn't convinced that there was a right cookbook.

13

Erik eyed the cherub perched on a ball in the center of the shallow pool. If that angel-baby could speak, what would it say to him? Had it any constructive counsel to offer after its sixty years of watching humanity pass through its glass-enclosed oasis a few hundred feet from the noisy bustle of Sherbrooke Street? Or was the soothing burble of its fountain the best it could do? Erik leaned in toward it, hoping the stone sculpture would come to life just long enough to issue a Yoda-like pronouncement that would make everything okay. As with all great masters, however, the cherub spoke most eloquently through its silence. Erik dropped his head into his hands and shut his eyes, once again reliving his brief time with Calvin Hutcheson.

Erik had been a high school senior when, not yet eighteen and already comfortable with his sexuality, if inexperienced, he began to suspect that the school's star athlete and girl-magnet was cruising him. Trusting neither his crude gaydar nor Calvin's intentions, Erik did his best to ignore the subtle overtures — until one afternoon in the school cafeteria, a stuttering, red-faced Calvin came out to him.

For three weeks after that extraordinary encounter, Erik and Calvin met most days, out of public view at the edge of town. As they walked, Erik reassured Calvin that he wasn't sick or deviant, Calvin appeared to grow increasingly comfortable with his feelings and the two boys fell for each other, agreeing by the end of that third week to explore the physical side of their attraction. They planned to skip school the following morning and meet at Erik's house, after his mother had left for work.

Calvin never showed up. He never again spoke to Erik, nor would he acknowledge him.

\# \# \# \# \#

Bernie touched Erik's shoulder. "Are you ready to talk about it yet?"

Erik rose from the wrought-iron bench and knelt by the water, trailing his fingers in the cool wetness. He was half-tempted to make the sign of the cross on his forehead, as if that sacramental act would somehow unlock the mysteries of the universe. Instead, he dried his hand on his jeans and returned to the bench.

"It isn't that I was in love with him anymore," Erik said, "or that I ever really was. But Calvin was the first guy I cared about, the first guy who ever cared about me. Now he's…he's…" Erik swallowed back his tears. "Dead," he whispered.

Those were the first words Erik had spoken since the previous evening. After the phone call from his sister, he had let Bernie lead him to bed, where he fell asleep, fully dressed and crying. That morning, he refused breakfast with a wave of his hand then retreated to the bathroom for an hour-long soak in the tub. When he emerged, flushed from the heat and in fresh clothes, he still wouldn't speak.

Bernie hadn't pressed him. Instead, he stuffed Erik into a taxi bound for the Victorian-style conservatory two miles west of the Ritz. With its exotic plants and tinkling fountain, the jewel-like greenhouse next to the Westmount Public Library was a favorite refuge for both of them. Bernie's mother had first brought him there when he was seven. He had never stopped coming back and introduced Erik to it soon after they got together.

The cherub may have had no answers for Erik, but its setting helped quiet his agitation.

"I know it was only a high school crush. It didn't feel like that at the time. It felt like he was The One. Then, to be dumped like that. I know he was scared, but— Now this." He turned to Bernie. "He couldn't have been The One. That's you." His eyes teared and he gazed out the window to the naked maples, oaks and crabapples of Westmount Park. "If I feel this way about Calvin," he whispered, "what would I do if anything happened to you? I couldn't bear it."

"I'm not going anywhere," Bernie reassured him, "and neither are you. We're a forever couple, you and me."

Erik rested his head on Bernie's shoulder. "Last I heard, Calvin had graduated from Osgoode Hall and was in Moncton, practicing some kind of law. Corporate, I bet, given his father. And he was engaged. I guess he never dealt with the gay thing. He must have, though, right? Sometime…somewhere…with someone."

"To have something you're running from, running so hard from, kill you," Bernie said. "It's so sad."

"All of it's sad, period. If my father was alive, he'd be screaming that AIDS is God's punishment, that we're all wicked and that we all deserve to die. Me and KC, too, probably. How he and my mom ever hooked up is beyond me."

"How's she doing?" Bernie asked. Britta Donnekin had been diagnosed with leukemia the week before she had been scheduled to travel to Montreal with her current boyfriend, Sven, to see Bernie's show at the Klinkhoff. Her doctor had urged her to stay home and begin immediate chemotherapy. She told him to go to hell, told Bernie, Erik, KC and Sven nothing and made the trip.

"It's hard to know. She won't let the doctor talk to me or KC, and we can never figure out if she's telling us the whole story. Even Sven isn't sure what's going on." He sighed. "That's my mom."

"Does she know about Calvin?"

"I don't know," Erik replied. "Wolfville's a small town. She's gotta have heard something. If she hasn't, she's better off. This whole AIDS thing is freaking her out more than it's freaking me out. And I get pretty freaked out every time I hear about someone else dying. The minute she read about Rock Hudson in *The Chronicle-Herald*, she called me to make sure I was fine. Same thing happened a couple of years ago with Liberace."

He stood up. "I know it's cold, but can we walk in the park for a bit, and then over to Cinq Arts and Dominique's? Maybe if we do that, the day will start to feel normal again. We could ring Sarah's doorbell on the way, if you want."

An overnight downpour had melted much of the previous day's snowstorm and the park smelled damp and loamy, more like the start of spring than of winter. It wasn't always wise, even in 1988, for two men to stroll in public holding hands. But with so many men their age getting sick and dying, and with Calvin's death still so fresh in their minds, Erik needed more than Bernie at his side. He needed to feel Bernie holding him up.

At first it hadn't seemed real to Bernie, this talk of a gay cancer. Before he came out, it was little more than a curious news story with little impact on his life. Then he found himself in a new world, where people his age got sick and died of a disease that screamed itself out in capital letters that denied its deadliness: There was nothing helpful about AIDS.

First it was strangers. Then it was acquaintances. Then it was Ray David Blackman, his best friend in college until Ray David came out to him and awkwardly suggested that he, Bernie, might be gay as well. Bernie never spoke to him after that, but a few years later it was Ray David's book, *A Blessing on My Head: Gay, Jewish and Proud*, that helped him to ultimately come to terms with his sexual orientation. Ray David had died in June.

Now, Calvin.

Bernie wasn't worried for himself. Erik was the only guy he had ever slept with. He wasn't worried for Erik either. For all Erik's bravado, he didn't have much of a sexual history: two short-lived relationships before Bernie and a sparse scattering of other partners in between.

"Poor Calvin," Erik continued. "I wish— I don't know what I wish. I guess I wish that it had all been easier for him. He deserved better." He said nothing as they exited the park and turned west on Sherbrooke. "From what KC found out, Calvin came back to Wolfville after he was diagnosed, without his fiancée. He had KS, Kaposi's sarcoma, and his face was covered with those horrible purple sores. When he got home, his father wouldn't let him in the house. He wouldn't even look at him. In the end his mother took him to Halifax and rented an apartment for them near the VG, the Victoria General. That's where he died, last week." Erik started to cry again. "His father never went to see him. Not once."

Jeremy, who lies snoring at my side, insisted again today that making love to me is as satisfying now as it was that first time fifteen or so years ago, and that I am as desirable at ninety-two as I was at seventy-eight. He is delusional, of course. As delusions go, it is a convenient one…at least for me.

It would be amusing to examine myself in the looking glass and see what it is that Jeremy sees: not a woman eight years shy of a century, not even a woman of seventy-eight; rather, some fairy story princess conjured up by the Brothers Grimm themselves. Not that I would recognize that reflection. My mirror is not as magical as was the one those Grimms created for Snow White's stepmother. Nor are my eyes tuned to the same Robert Burns fantasy as are Jeremy's. "My love is like a red, red rose" is naught next to Jeremy's florid flattery. As for his prose, Barbara Cartland might be forced to step aside were he to set his romantic notions to the page. Perhaps he ought to. She does well. Well enough, I'm told, to lunch every Wednesday at Claridge's.

At a minimum, my husband would do well to set an appointment with an oculist to have his vision checked. Whatever it is that he sees, my mirror prefers to show me scrawny arms, sagging breasts, chicken legs and more wrinkles than a prune.

I am not complaining, mind. Even as a young woman, I possessed neither a film starlet's face nor a beauty queen's body, nor have I ever truly yearned for either. It is not that I wish to be what Jeremy sees; I simply wish to catch the briefest glimpse of it. We so rarely see with any clarity or insight what others see in and of us. It could be instructive. It would be entertaining.

Wasn't I talking about sex? I was. There is one thing I know about growing older. Growing old, I ought to say. Ninety-two is not "older." It's bloody old. And when one is bloody old, one's mind bloody well wanders. It does more than wander. It takes off on extended holidays from which it does not often or easily return.

Sex. That is where this began, with Jeremy snoring and I, pleasingly sated.

I have always enjoyed sex. That may not be a shocking admission in 1974. Even in this age, however, many would find it startling to hear it from a woman of my years. Yet, for a woman born when Victoria reigned to say how much she relishes sex, and to speak it out loud with neither blushes nor shame? That is shocking. Or it would be were any of my more strait-laced relatives or contemporaries still alive to be shocked.

Women of my generation were expected to squeeze our eyes shut, do our duty to Queen and country and produce an heir and a spare. We were expected to tolerate sex as necessary to the perpetuation of our lineage and to the survival of the Empire. We were not expected to savor it. We were absolutely not expected to seek it out — within a marriage or, worse, outside of it.

Sexual mores loosened up after the First War, of course, but I had not waited. I was nearing my forties by then and was already in possession of a past that no amount of smelling salts could have successfully revived Grandmama had she learned about it. I had a body, albeit an unshapely one, and I saw no reason why I should not extract from it as much pleasure as it could offer me. Nor did I see any reason to limit myself to men of my own class...or to men at all, come to think of it.

Although I choose to name no names here, it is not out of any sense of modesty or to protect my reputation or that of anyone else. Why should I do either when I have had no hesitation, in casual conversation, to name certain names in the past? But setting those names in ink on a page is a different matter altogether. When I list past paramours to a current lover, I have made the choice as to what is told to whom. Fortunately, my lovers have been gentlemen or gentlewomen enough to limit their gossip. Yet, despite the fact that these pages are not being written to be read, I cannot control who might ultimately view them. So I shall choose an uncharacter-istic discretion.

And orgasms? If a woman of my era admitted to having had one, if she were shameless enough to utter the word, that woman was viewed as little better than the most common of prostitutes. How ironic that Victoria should today be seen as the primmest, most prudish and most humorless of monarchs...of women. I do not believe it. Not for an instant. Any woman who bore as many children as Victoria did clearly loved snogging, even as she was said to hate pregnancy. Had she so desired, she could have barred Albert from her bed once she had produced a male heir, which she did with her second child. She was Queen, after all. Instead, she chose to keep the royal bed bouncing and went on to produce an unwieldy total of nine off-spring. I am willing to wager that Victoria was not the sort to "shut her eyes and think of England." I am willing to wager that she enjoyed her monarchical romps. I am willing to wager that whether or not she ever spoke the word, she, too, enjoyed her orgasms.

I have manifestly enjoyed mine through seventy years and a good score or more of able partners. Had Jeremy been unable to match if not surpass the prowess of his predecessors, I could not have married him, regardless of his other attributes, however admirable. For a man with so little experience of women before me, Jeremy is surprisingly adept and pleasingly passionate. Frankly, if I didn't fear that it would give him a heart attack, I would choose to die in bed with him, in mid-orgasm. I cannot imagine a more satisfying end. Can you?

14

Mac touched a lit match to the crumpled newspaper in the grate and watched as a whoosh of orange instantly devoured fourteen-year-old pages from *The Guardian* and ignited the split wood beneath them. He knelt and rubbed his hands to expel the raw clamminess that sliced through him. London had been characteristically damp this fall, although not cold enough to justify the expense of heating an empty house.

And it was empty. Emmeline's study was the only room that felt alive, which was strange, given that Jeremy appeared to have left it just as it had been the last time his aunt had used it, down to the fountain pen resting atop a virginal sheet of vellum on the desk and the balled-up Hudson's Bay Company blanket shoved into a corner of the easy chair. Only the date on *The Guardian* pages, January 2, 1975, a few days after Emmeline's death, indicated that Jeremy had been in here after she had. That, and the absence of all but a light layer of dust, in marked contrast to the rest of house, which bore the unkempt and neglected aspect of either a bachelor's lair or the home of someone with little interest in life. From the letter Jeremy had left for him, Mac suspected it to be the latter.

After reviewing the terms of Jeremy's will, collecting his uncle's ashes and tasking Miles Dunedin with arranging an informal gathering at The Palm Tree, Mac had found Annie McGill, Cap'n Andy's daughter and inheritor of his *Cotton Blossom* boat, and arranged for a predawn scattering. The following evening's not-quite wake — there was no body, after all — was a curious affair. There were two distinct categories of attendees: Jeremy's contemporaries, mostly gay men who had known him since long before he married Emmeline, and a tiny collection of men and women in their eighties and nineties, nearly all of them, he suspected, long-ago lovers of his aunt's. He couldn't fathom why this latter group had shown up, unless it was to satisfy themselves that Jeremy was truly dead. The two parties occupied opposite ends of the pub and had little congress with each other, reluctantly coming together only when Mac proposed a toast to Jeremy and Emmeline, which, under the circumstances, was more politic than proposing a toast to Jeremy alone. When Mac left the pub a few hours later, it was with a handful of unsurprisingly bawdy stories about his aunt, having discovered little new about his uncle.

That was yesterday. Now it was Friday. Although Mac had been in London for a week, this was his first time in his aunt's study. It was difficult for him to imagine the Emmeline he remembered settling into the sedentary life that this sanctuary of hers suggested. Yet for all its incongruity, this room, so lovingly — or perhaps obsessively — preserved by Jeremy, brought her back to life in a way that startled him. Had he ever seen her sit still for more than a few minutes at a time? Rarely. Even locked into her theater seat for the duration of a film or stage play, she had resembled a caged tiger. Yet despite her chronic restlessness, this room suited her somehow. If Mac raised his eyes to her desk, he could picture her seated there, leaning into the page as she scribbled furiously. Or if he reached for the armchair, he could almost touch her where she sat, wrapped in her blanket, the one he had sent her one Christmas long ago, gazing up from her jottings and into the fire. What had she been writing? What could have so consumed her that it could keep her sequestered in this room so unexpectedly?

Miles had directed him to the compact oak filing cabinet next to the desk. Mac rose from the fire, finally warm, settled into his aunt's chair and reached across to the cabinet. He slid open the top drawer, surprised to find it stuffed nearly to capacity with file folders that were themselves filled to bursting. The bottom drawer was nearly as full. He pulled out a random folder, laid it on the desk and opened it to a familiar scrawl. Among Emmeline's many rebellions was the one she directed, from an early age, at "proper" right-handed penmanship. It took Mac a few moments to reacquaint himself with his aunt's unruly blend of backhanded cursive and blocky non-cursive. It took him no time at all to recognize her blunt, brusque tone.

When he glanced up from his tenth file folder, the fire had died to a scattering of embers and a damp chill was creeping back into the room. Mac didn't notice. All he knew was that Jeremy had been right. "The Emmeline Papers" were significant and ought to be dealt with accordingly.

He knew just the person for the job.

15

"So this is the barimt biblyotek, the famous Westmount Public Library?" Sadie asked, letting her eyes climb the dozen worn steps to the Victorian building's arched entry then travel higher, to the yellow-sandstone frieze above the door where a massive-winged angel hovered over the shoulder of long-bearded gentleman. *Moses? Not with my luck. It's probably God.* Were they inviting her in or preparing to strike her down? Given her history with the place, the latter was more certain. "So much fuss so long ago for so little purpose," Sadie muttered as she stepped into the revolving door.

This was a pilgrimage for Sadie, visiting for the first time the building that had been one of her sister's favorite sanctuaries: the turreted, red-brick library and its adjoining conservatory. It was Sarah, all those decades earlier, who had introduced Esther to this place when they were still in high school. Now, she would introduce it to the woman who had prohibited the teenaged Esther from coming here.

"This is…" Sadie began, making a slow circle on the travertine floor and stopping in one of the pools of golden light that streamed down from the lobby's clerestory windows. She couldn't go on. She had no words.

Sarah understood. She had been equally awed when she stepped into the library for the first time a half-century earlier. Nothing about the cacophony and chaos of her inner city neighborhood could have prepared her for the gracious tranquility of one of affluent Westmount's major landmarks. Sadie, along with much of Jewish Montreal, had long ago traded the immigration gateway of downtown Clark Street and The Main for suburban Côte-Saint-Luc.

Yet where Côte-Saint-Luc was clean, new and, well, sterile, West-mount had history and class. Upper class, and the gentility that came with old money.

"This way," Sarah said. She led Sadie under a series of heavy Romanesque arches and past rows upon rows of walnut shelves crammed with books. When they reached the fine art section, Sarah stopped under a striking oil painting.

Sadie squinted up at the tiny brass plaque set in the picture frame. "Quebec Farm. Anne Savage. ca.1935," she read aloud. "Our Anne Savage?" she asked doubtfully.

Sarah nodded.

Anne Savage had not only taught art at Baron Byng High School when Sarah and the Finkel girls were students there, she had already achieved national renown as an artist. It was Savage who inspired Esther to want to go to college to study art. It was Sadie who convinced their father that art was not something that good Jewish girls did. Before long, Esther had abandoned her dreams in favor of the one thing that good Jewish girls of her generation did do: get married and have a family.

Sadie studied the painting of a woman bent over a flower patch at the edge of a farm. As her eyes followed the road that wound off into distant, rounded hills beyond the pitched-roof farmhouse typical to Quebec, she tried to picture the long-ago Miss Savage of Room 214, Baron Byng's art room. The art teacher had seemed ancient to Sadie, likely because of her white hair. However, it must have gone white prematurely, because Miss Savage could not have been much older than thirty at the time. She also didn't look like what fifteen-year-old Sadie imagined an artist ought to look like. Where was the wild hair? Where were the strange clothes? Where was the compulsory beret? Nowhere to be seen, at least not inside Room 214, where Miss Savage unfailingly showed up in a starched white blouse and simple skirt, her hair neatly coiffed. Often completing the conservative, conventional look was a simple strand of pearls.

Art was a required subject at Baron Byng in those days, so Sadie had been forced to sit through what to her were dreary lessons in art history, taught from a colorless textbook that felt as ancient as some of the paintings it described. *Art Appreciation for Today*. Wasn't that the title? God, how did she remember that after all these years? More than sixty years. Not that there was much that Miss Savage could have done to animate a teenaged Sadie Finkel, whose only dream for herself had once revolved around the eccentric dance moves of Isadora Duncan. By the time Sadie got to art class, those desires had withered. Her mother's death earlier that year consigned Sadie's dreams to the place where all good Jewish girls' dreams belonged in 1928: the kitchen. As the eldest, she was compelled to take on the role of cook-housekeeper to the family and surrogate mother to Esther and their two brothers. She resented every minute of it and never hesitated to take out her bitterness on her siblings, mostly on Esther. Still, perhaps because limited resources forced her to be creative in the Finkel kitchen, she grew to not only love cooking but to excel at it — on those rare occasions in the years that followed when she could afford the ingredients that allowed her the freedom to experiment.

Nine years after Sadie graduated from Baron Byng and herself weary of the approved curriculum, Anne Savage revolutionized the school's art program, abandoning its emphasis on theory in favor of a hands-on focus on paints, paintbrushes and canvases. She also launched a radical project to transform all the school's institutional-green walls into colorful, student-painted murals. Esther had been in the first of those new classes and one of the first of Savage's students to complete a mural.

Sarah eased herself into a worn leather armchair. She was too old to drop to the floor where Esther had once sat, surrounded by stacks of art books. This had been Esther's preferred spot; Sarah's had been on the other side of the building, among the great works of classic and contemporary literature. If Esther's dream had been to be recognized as the first great Jewish Canadian woman artist, Sarah's, postponed until the day after Esther's funeral, had been to be a writer.

Sarah watched Sadie run her fingers across the spines of the art books her sister had so loved. Chagall. Picasso. Turner. Monet. Sadie opened the Chagall to the floating beggar of *Over Vitebsk*, the Monet to a series of water lilies and the Turner to the fiery sunset of *The Fighting Temeraire*. Then she laid those aside and pulled *MAC: A Cameron Retrospective* from the shelf.

"Those other artists," Sadie said as she flipped through page after glossy page of Mac's bold abstracts, "they're strange, but I know what I'm seeing. These?" She stopped at *Anna L.*, a dazzlingly vibrant mass of gold, emerald and crimson whorls that eddied so spiritedly on its circular canvas that it seemed as though it would spiral right out of the book and into Sadie's face. "I know he's talented and famous. And what he did with that picture of Esther..." She shut her eyes and conjured up Mac's portrait of her sister. Not the postcard-size reproduction tacked to her apartment wall; the original that she had first seen at Bernie's opening and that had called her back to the gallery again and again, its glowing, Rembrandt-like face almost more real than she could bear.

"That picture I understand," she continued. "That picture I know what I feel when I see it, even if I don't always like what I feel. But this?" She turned the page to another image, *Thrice Blessed*, a triptych that consisted of a single brushstroke, thick, black and coarse, that slashed diagonally from the bottom corner of the panel on the far left, through the center panel and petered out near the top of the right-hand panel. "Something like this I don't understand what I'm seeing, or what I'm feeling." She shut the book. "I don't like not understanding."

Sarah pushed herself up from the chair. "You know what Mac would say?" she asked.

Sadie shrugged.

"He'd say that art isn't about this." She touched Sadie's head. "It's about this." She touched Sadie's heart.

Sadie shrugged again.

"Don't feel bad. I don't get a lot of it either." Should she go on? She couldn't keep censoring Esther from every conversation she had with Sadie. "Esther would have understood," she said in an awkward tone that was part-defiant and part-apologetic. She cleared her throat. "I suppose that's part of why they were so good together, her and Mac...or would have been, if she could have let herself."

Sadie stared out through the leaded library window to the bare trees in the park. Stray clumps of snow clung to the fringes of the crisscrossing paths. "What if I hadn't been so hard on her?" she murmured. "What if..."

Sarah touched Sadie's arm. "Yes, you were hard on her, and not always for good reasons. Maybe for mostly not-good reasons. But not everything Esther did or didn't do was your fault. She was a grown woman. She had to take responsibility. We all have to take responsibility." Sarah followed Sadie's gaze out to the park. "I wish she had made other choices," she said, then dried her eyes with a handkerchief from her purse. "She made the ones she made." She took *MAC: A Cameron Retrospective* from Sadie and opened it to a photo of a much younger Marc-Allan Cameron, his crooked grin staring directly into the camera.

"Maybe those weren't wrong choices," she said. "Maybe there's no such thing as wrong choices. Maybe one person's 'wrong' choices make it so that another person can make 'right' choices."

"That's too deep for me," Sadie said. "Like a riddle that has no answer. I made wrong choices. Esther made wrong choices. Are you saying your Sammy who hit you was a right choice?"

Sarah considered Sadie's question. It had not been a happy marriage and Sammy had hit her more than once. "I know it doesn't look that way," she said at last. "But without Sammy, I never would have had my Morty. He may have been different from other boys and he may have died too young…" She sighed. "He was no mistake. For nineteen years he was the greatest gift God could have given me. Without a Sammy, there might also never have been a Jack. He was God's second-best gift to me, even if he died too soon, too. And Esther? It's because of her choices that Bernie is the wonderful boy he is. It's because of her choices that there's a *Sara's Year*. It's because of her choices that you and me could be friends. Her choices weren't wrong. Some of them were sad and made her unhappy. But wrong? I used to think so. Now, I'm not so sure."

Sadie said nothing. All the choices she had made through the years…all the choices that had made her so miserable, that had made everyone around her so miserable… Could they have been right choices after all? If she had made different choices, what might have turned out different?

Could she and Jimmy Harcourt still have been friends? Sixty years ago she had condemned him because he was "that way"; they didn't use the word gay back then. Then, he was a faygele. Of course they could never have gotten married like she had hoped. But they had been so close until then. Could they have stayed friends? Who knew?

The baby? Could she have kept it? Could she have dared? What would life have been for her and her child if she hadn't insisted on an abortion? What would life have been like if she hadn't stayed late at work that night? She wouldn't have been raped and there would have been no need for an abortion. Or what would have happened to her and the child if she had carried it to term and given it up for adoption? Would he or she have found her like Bernie found Mac? Would that have forced her heart open years ago instead of waiting until now, until she was almost dead?

What if she hadn't been such a witch of a sister? If she hadn't told Esther all those years ago that she couldn't come here, to this library? What if she had talked their father into letting Esther go to art college instead of persuading him to say no? Would Esther have ended up as the artist she had dreamed of becoming? Would she have lived the life that that long-ago Sadie had dismissed as unsuitable for a good Jewish girl? Would there have been a Bernie?

Sadie's head spun at this infinity of unrealized possibilities. She reached for the shelf to steady herself.

"Are you okay?" Sarah asked.

"I'm a little fartumelt. I need to sit down, I think."

"Not here," Sarah said before Sadie could drop into the armchair. Instead, she guided Sadie past the reference desk and to the passageway that connected library and conservatory. Sadie had known about the library, though she had never been. She had not been aware of the greenhouse until reading *Sara's Year*. When she stepped into its moist warmth, she immediately felt embraced by a comforting serenity that both startled and calmed her. She dropped onto a bench by the fountain and once she had regained her equilibrium, tried to imagine her sister sitting there. Not the Esther she remembered; the Esther she had never let herself see. Her eyes watered as she reflected regretfully on all the years she had wasted, years when she could have loved her sister instead of resenting her. Despite what Sarah said, she wished other choices had been made. Hers.

16

After an al fresco breakfast on the Brook Penthouse's patio, bundled up against the autumn chill, Mac spent the morning walking — first through posh Mayfair and then into the income-mix of Fitzrovia, past the same shops, pubs and bistros he imagined that Emmeline and Jeremy had frequented. Could he do what he was thinking about doing? Of course he could. Would he?

It was lunchtime by the time Mac returned to Claridge's. His hours of wandering had settled it. There could be only one way to repay Emmeline. He wouldn't sell her house. Not yet. Nor would he leave London, just yet. It was five hours earlier in Montreal and so not quite eight in the morning, but he knew that this call could not wait. His next steps depended on it.

The phone was ringing when Sarah stepped out of the shower. She ignored it. No one should call anyone before nine. Before ten, even. Regardless, no one who expected a civilized conversation should call Sarah before her tea and her butter- and jam-slathered toasted poppyseed bagel — from the Fairmount Bagel Factory in her old neighborhood. Sarah had few fixed routines. Her morning shower and regular breakfast was one of them, and the most inviolable. On the fifth ring, she cursed and put the kettle on. On the eighth, she unplugged the kettle and reached for her canary yellow wall phone. What if it was an emergency?

"Hello?" she barked into the receiver. Even emergencies had no right to happen before breakfast. A moment later her voice softened. Why would Mac be calling her? From London, yet. *Was* it an emergency. Had something happened to Bernie? To Erik? Sarah's breath quickened as she dragged a chair over from the table so she could sit down.

"You're crazy," she said when Mac explained why he was calling. He wanted to fly her to London to look through his aunt's papers. Right away.

"I know," he admitted. "But you have to read this stuff. I know there's a book in it."

"I'm no editor or any kind of researcher," Sarah argued, grateful for her extra-long phone cord. She stood, jamming the receiver between her ear and shoulder, and plugged the kettle back in. Then, she sliced her bagel and dropped it into the toaster. "You want to talk to Doug Gibson at McClelland & Stewart," she said. "I bet he could find the right person for you."

"I don't need an editor or researcher," Mac countered. "Aunt Emmeline wouldn't have wanted a biography or a memoir. That's not what I'm thinking."

Sarah dropped a Red Rose teabag into her cup and pushed down on the toaster's lever. "I'm afraid to ask."

"A novel," he said.

Sarah jerked the receiver from her ear and gaped at it like it was an alien creature.

"Sarah?" a tinny voice squawked at her from the speaker.

"Now I know you're meshugena," she shouted at the receiver. She wedged it back in place. "I know all about growing up Jewish in Montreal," she said, "more, some days, than I want to know. What do I know from England? What do I know from writing novels? There are better writers for this, Mac. Find one. Find someone else. Ask Mr. Gibson."

"Why, when I have you?"

Sarah didn't answer. She squeezed a lemon slice into her cup and smeared some butter on her bagel.

"Sarah?"

"What?"

"What would Esther say?" he asked softly.

Sarah raised her eyes to the ceiling, then immediately dropped them. *I know damn well what you'd say, Esther.*

"I'm not asking for promises or guarantees," Mac continued when she didn't answer. "Just come out. Read what I've read, here in the house, where it was all written. Then if you say no, I'll send you home."

Still, Sarah said nothing.

"What's the worst that could happen? You'll have had a nice holiday. But maybe…" His voice trailed off.

Maybe I'll have that new book I promised Erik I'd write. But London? And an English lady like Emmeline? And a novel? It's narishkeit.

Mac set the phone down. Sarah hadn't said yes. Nor had she said no. He picked up the phone again and dialed the porter's desk. He needed to hire a cleaner. For Emmeline's house. As quickly as the porter could arrange it.

17

"Do you think this is what your mom felt like?" Erik asked as he applied a swathe of yellow to the running figure that, like the rest of the mural, had been sketched out by artist Keith Haring on the south wall of the old St. Anthony's Convent.

"Downtown Pisa's a far cry from Baron Byng," Bernie called back from a few figures away, where he was working in red on another ground-level section of the mural. He stepped back to admire his handiwork then crossed to the other side of Via Riccardo Zandonai so as to take in as much of *Tuttomondo* as could be seen from behind the scaffolding and the dozens of paintbrush-wielding students who were fleshing out Haring's rarely comfortable vision of world peace and harmony. Unlike most of Keith Haring's street art, designed to be ephemeral, *Tuttomondo* was meant to last. It grew from a chance encounter Haring had had the previous year with a University of Pisa student, and Bernie and Erik's participation in its execution that November day was equally serendipitous.

Bernie and Erik had flown into Florence that morning and, bleary-eyed from their ten-hour Air France flight, had made their way to the Santa Maria Novella station for the next leg of their trek: the two-hour train ride to Siena. From Siena, a taxi had been arranged for the final, one-hour drive to the hills outside Montalcino.

That was the plan. Unfortunately, a derailment on the main line south had stopped their train at Empoli. Given the choice between remaining in Empoli, returning to Florence or going on to Pisa to wait out the repair, they opted for Pisa. They would visit the Leaning Tower and the cathedral and if it proved impossible to resume their journey that evening, they would spend the night in town and try again in the morning. They checked their bags at the station, picked up a map and set off on the one-mile hike north toward the Duomo. As they crossed the Piazza Vittorio Emanuele II, they noticed a crowd gathered outside a church-like building that their map identified as Chiesa di San Antonio Abate. They wandered over for a closer look and discovered the mural project. It didn't take much for them to abandon their plans and join in.

"I wish we could have had a chance to talk to him," Bernie said as he and Erik passed behind the government building on Via Silvia Pellico. They were heading back toward the train station, their travel clothes lightly spattered with paint. "Keith Haring, I mean. But he was like an orchestra conductor back there at the church; too busy directing all his painters to chat." He chuckled. "I wonder if Anne Savage was like that with her murals."

They turned right onto Via Pietro Mascagni. "We'll come back, though, right?" Bernie asked. "Even if Haring won't be there, the mural will be finished. Won't it be cool to see it and know that we were a part of it?"

Erik walked on, saying nothing.

"I know you don't want to do any touring until after you've finished your first painting," Bernie continued. "That shouldn't take long. We can make this our first outing. What do you say?"

They crossed the station piazza and stopped at the fountain. Erik leaned against the ledge and watched the jets of water spurt up toward the abstract sculpture at its center.

Bernie touched his arm. "You haven't said a word since we left the church."

Erik covered Bernie's hand with his. "You know he has AIDS, right?" he asked, his voice barely audible over the spray.

"Keith Haring?"

Erik frowned at his distorted reflection in the water. "Everyone's dying," he whispered. He looked up at Bernie, his eyes wet with tears. "Don't die, Bernie," he implored. "Promise me you won't die."

18

Sadie stepped off the blue-and-white No. 104 bus in front of the Westmount Library. This time she was alone. She could have found the books she wanted at the Côte-Saint-Luc Library, a five-minute walk from her apartment. Yet if a bus ride could bring her closer to her sister and help her begin to reshape her past, it was worth the trip. Another treat was planned for when she finished at the library: lunch at Dominique's with Sarah.

Sadie glanced at her watch. Ten minutes to opening. The bus had covered the four and a half miles in record time, as though it knew Sadie was on a critical mission. She waited under the arch at the top of the stairs, stamping her feet against the cold and feeling more confident than she had on her first visit that God (or Moses) and the angel would allow her to pass unharmed.

When the doors opened halfway through the ten-bell tolling of St. Matthias' Church a few blocks away on Côte-St-Antoine, Sadie made her way to the fine art section. There, she thumbed through some of the same coffee table art books she had browsed on her previous visit, hoping that this time she would better understand what she was seeing. The exercise proving itself futile, she wandered over to the cookbooks, pulled an eclectic selection from the shelf — from Jewish, French and Italian cuisine to elaborate desserts and heart-healthy meals — and curled up with them in an easy chair. That's where Sarah found her an hour later.

"Ten more minutes?" Sadie asked when she noticed Sarah hovering over her.

"Sure," Sarah replied. "No longer if we want to beat the lunch rush."

Sadie nodded absentmindedly, but she was already absorbed in Julia Child's newest, *The Way To Cook*, poring over her recipe for lamb stew with wine and rosemary and wondering how she could stretch her pitiful grocery budget to accommodate it. The only ingredient she had on hand was the onion. Possibly, a can of tomatoes. No lamb, no peanut oil, no garlic, no rosemary, and for sure no French vermouth…or any kind of vermouth. Not even any flour.

Until now, Sadie had viewed cookbooks as indulgences and their contents as unrealizable fantasies, at least as they involved her meager pension and her tiny, ill-equipped kitchenette. "Fantasies," she frequently muttered, "are for fools." Was she now a fool? Did it matter?

Twenty minutes later, Sarah pulled Sadie from James Beards's *The Fireside Cookbook* and a world of gastronomy that was growing less and less foreign with each recipe. "It's time," she said.

As the two women strolled west on Sherbrooke toward Dominique's, each lost in her own thoughts, Sarah replayed that morning's phone call from Mac, recalling the last words he had spoken before promising to get back to her in a day or so for her answer.

Emmeline, he had confessed, was the parent he wished he'd had, the parent he wished he'd had the opportunity to be. "This book would be my way of thanking her for everything she gave me, including my art and, indirectly, my son. It would be like giving her her life back."

They were a few blocks from Dominique's when Sarah tugged on Sadie's sleeve. "You see this?" she asked, pointing up at the renovated Victorian row houses in front of them. It was the first thing she had said since leaving the library. Sadie had been equally uncommunicative. Part of her was back at the library with Julia Childs and her lamb stew.

"This is the gallery where Bernie met Erik," Sarah said. "This is where Erik's show is going to be in October."

"That's art in there?" Sadie asked, tapping a bony finger on the expansive display window that had replaced the building's original staircase and much of its limestone facade. "How is that art? It's rusty bits of scrap."

"Erik says it's art," Sarah said, "so it must be art."

Sadie wasn't so sure. Cookbooks she could make sense of. Not this. This was more like an indoor junkyard than an art gallery. She walked on.

Sarah trailed behind, still thinking about Mac and London. Should she go or shouldn't she go? Going made no sense. Mac wanted her to turn Emmeline's writings into a novel. How could she write a novel? She hadn't written any kind of fiction since high school, since her "Good Jewish Girls Don't" short story. Not going also made no sense. She hadn't been to Europe since all that traveling she had done with Jack. Without Jack, would she ever make it back to England on her own? Not likely, not unless she were to marry a third time — to another Jack, not another Sammy. Besides, she had loved London, with its history and its art and its architecture and its theater. Montreal had all that, but it wasn't the same. Montreal was Montreal. But London? London was *London*!

By the time Sarah caught up with Sadie at the next corner, she had made up her mind. Of course she would go. She would be an idiot not to, book or no book. She decided something else as well: Sadie would come. She knew Mac would agree. Would Sadie?

19

Mac inserted a shiny brass key into the lock and spun it a half-turn to the right. With a sharp snick, the door to 33 Fitzroy Street clicked open. After four days of fussing with a temperamental latch that had to have predated Emmeline's occupancy, Mac had again enlisted the aid of the porter at Claridge's. The extravagantly mutton-chopped locksmith that the porter had sent to meet him on the doorstep that morning could have been engaged by Robert Adam himself. Adam had designed the elegant Georgian terrace in 1790, dying before he had a chance to see it completed. Its fortunes, like the Fitzrovia neighborhood that surrounded it, had fluctuated through the years — from fashionable to bohemian and back again. The area, sand-wiched between Mayfair, Soho and Bloomsbury, had at one time or another been home to such varied luminaries as Thomas Paine, Virginia Woolf, George Bernard Shaw, Charles Laughton, John Constable, Arthur Rimbaud, Nancy Cunard and Wyndham Lewis. Other writers and artists, like Dylan Thomas, Julian MacLaren-Ross and George Orwell, might as well have lived in Fitzrovia for all the time they spent drinking in its pubs. In fact it was the convenient presence of such a motley collection of the famous and infamous that had prompted Emmeline to launch her prewar weekly salons, themselves as periodically notorious as were her neighbors. At one, for example, Betty May stripped off all her clothes and insisted that Augustus John paint her portrait right then and there. At another, Aleister Crowley conducted an arcane ritual that he claimed had transformed poet Victor Neuberg into a camel and deposited him into an Algiers zoo.

Mac had heard countless stories (mostly from his disapproving father) about Emmeline's salons, held Sunday mornings when respectable Londoners were settling into their church pews, but he had never been given an opportunity to attend one. Emmeline had resolved that she alone would influence her young nephew and she canceled her salons on those rare instances when Mac's parents could be persuaded to permit him to visit. One of those occasions, the one his father would most come to regret, was for his twentieth birthday.

On that trip, Emmeline had determined that she would save Mac from a lifetime of retail servitude. She dragged a reluctant Marc-Allan, as he then still was, to a landmark exhibition of Canadian art at the Tate Gallery, an outing designed to kindle hidden gifts that she was convinced he possessed. It achieved much more than that. By the time he and Emmeline were chased out by museum staff at closing, Mac was hooked. The bold strokes, vivid colors and simple, yet dynamic expressions of Emily Carr, Tom Thomson, Arthur Lismer, A.Y. Jackson and a forty-two-year-old artist-teacher from Montreal named Anne Savage swept the fusty claustrophobia of his native Britain into the dustheap and seduced him into an audacious new world of creative possibility. Hoping for such an outcome, even if not expecting to achieve it so expeditiously, Emmeline had filled a spare room with paints, pallet, brushes, canvas and easel. Ironically, it would be that room that, decades later, Jeremy would convert into Emmeline's writing studio.

Mac stepped into the hallway and closed the door behind him. The house was silent but not lifeless. Yes, that hint of Emmeline's scent lingered on, as if it had steeped into the floor, walls and upholstery and refused to be expelled. Yet it was more than that. Mac shut his eyes. He could almost feel his aunt's presence, larger than life long after death. He shivered and opened them again. He had returned to 33 Fitzroy Street most days since arriving back in London, and although he had remained in the house longer and longer with each visit, he had aways gone back to Claridge's still intent on selling the townhouse and flying back to Nova Scotia as swiftly as he could arrange it.

Until Friday. Until he had read those damned Emmeline papers.

He climbed the two flights of stairs to his aunt's aerie, lit a fire and stood by the window, staring out to Fitzroy Square Garden, its trees naked in the chill of approaching winter. How often had Emmeline stood here during that concluding year of her life? What had been in her thoughts as she watched that final progression of the seasons, not knowing that it would be her last, yet knowing that it could be?

If Mac had inherited his aunt's longevity genes instead of his mother's, he could be around for another twenty years or more. If he had inherited Emmeline's constitution, he could be painting for many of them. Was that what he wanted? Painting had been so much a part of him for so long that he could not imagine doing anything else. That was why he had expected to attend to Jeremy's affairs as quickly as possible and be gone from London just as quickly, back to the paints, canvases and mystical light of his farmhouse studio that waited for him three thousand miles away.

And now? He turned back to the fire and watched the flames dance for him as they had for Emmeline in those closing months of 1974. He owed his artist's life to her. He owed his success to her. He owed his son to her, for without that artist's life he would never have emigrated to Canada, would never have met Esther.

The top log in the Fitzroy Street fireplace crashed down, shooting a stream of sparks up the chimney. He would need a chimney sweep in addition to a house cleaner. Who knew when Jeremy had last seen to the chimney? And the phone would need to be reconnected. He would ask the porter to make those arrangements, too, when he returned to the hotel. He would be foolish not to take advantage of the porter's availability and expertise for as long he could. He would not be spending many more nights at Claridge's.

20

"How do you say, 'Oh my God?' in Italian?" Erik asked as their cherry red Fiat taxi climbed the curving, vineyard-bordered road, and the creamy limestone walls of a two-story villa poked through sentinel stands of cypress.

"Dio mio, signore" replied the swarthy taxi driver.

"Dio mio, signore!" Erik exclaimed.

"No, no!" Bernie chuckled. "Signore is 'sir.' You said 'Oh my God, sir.'" He leaned forward toward the front seat. "Isn't that right?"

"Si, si," the taxi driver replied. "Sir." He pronounced it seer.

The car passed through the trees and onto a dirt driveway. It eased to a stop in front of a pair of umber shutters in aged wood that angled open to reveal a welcoming courtyard. Lush plants in colorful ceramic urns edged the uneven paving stones. A vibrant medley of oleander, bougainvillea, jasmine, alpine pasqueflower and periwinkle overflowed pots that crammed every window ledge. In the center of the courtyard, the Tuscan sun picked out the crystalline water burbling into a pitted stone fountain from four ancient spigots. A nearby cafe table was set with two wine glasses, an opened bottle of Brunello Sangiovese and a platter of antipasti.

The three men stepped from the car and the driver popped the trunk to retrieve Bernie and Erik's luggage. "You like?" he asked, depositing the cases by the courtyard entryway.

Erik nodded, speechless. He reached for Bernie's hand and squeezed it. *Like it? Dio mio, signore! I may never want to leave.*

The driver pulled a card from his wallet and handed it to Bernie. "Call me for anything," he said. "Tours or trip into town. Or out-of-town. I take you where you want to go."

Bernie read the card. "Taxi Montalcino. Francesco Dalmazio.

+39 368 983 899." He shook the driver's hand. "Thank you, Francesco."

"Call me Frank. Like Sinatra," he said. "You American?"

Bernie laughed. "Canadian. I'm Bernie, this is Erik."

Frank pumped Erik's hand, leapt back into the Fiat and skidded off in a cloud of ocher dust.

"I can't wait to see what you're going to paint here," Bernie said as they hauled their bags into the courtyard.

"What we're going to paint, you mean," Erik said. "When does the art stuff get here? I can't wait to get started."

"Sylvie arranged for everything. It's being delivered from Florence tomorrow or the day after. All new. Mac said it was cheaper than shipping our old stuff from Canada." He stopped at the cafe table. "Do we explore the house or do we start with the welcome snack?"

Erik dropped onto one of the chairs and poured out two generous glasses of wine. "I say we start here, then explore the house." He giggled. "Starting with the bedroom."

What is it to grow old? If anyone can answer that question, a woman about to complete her ninety-second year ought to be able to, even if only for herself. Here is what I know...

First in barely noticeable increments, then with increasing velocity, your life starts to fall away. The names you grew up with, for instance. Film stars, actors, singers, musicians, writers, artists: One after the other, they fade into the ghostly shadow that is their movies and recordings, their books and art, and then, should they be sufficiently celebrated, into insipid biographies and flavorless BBC documentaries. In a few cases, you are aware that they have died. In most others, it takes time until you notice that your life has shrunk through their absence.

It is easy, relatively speaking, to watch an older generation get sick and die. Your grandparents, your parents, your aunts, your uncles: We expect them to pass out of our lives, eventually. We expect it less of our contemporaries. However large that circle has been, it, too, begins to shrink — slowly, then more rapidly — as your friends and lovers, siblings and cousins, also disappear.

It is not merely the people around you who vanish from your life. Things you have grown accustomed to, places you have grown to love: They change, they are torn down, they are replaced. It matters not a whit that the replacement is better, cleaner, faster, bigger, smaller, more convenient or more efficient. What matters is that little of what you have come to know, to recognize, to rely upon, remains. A world that was once so familiar has become alien.

Or perhaps it is you who has become alien, you who no longer belongs, who is now more of a misfit than she has long been. A misfit in the greater world, of course, but within your own body as well, a body that increasingly fails to support your will, your desires and, before you realize it, your most basic needs and requirements. Should we be among the more fortunate, it is only our bodies which decay, not our minds. Should we be among the less fortunate, our minds tune in and out of "reality" much as our hands jiggle a radio dial to avoid the static between stations. Whichever is true for us, the physical and mental container that has served most of us reasonably well through the decades starts to do so with less and less ease and effectiveness.

We are born to die. That is the overarching truth of human existence. At the same time we are born to keep our gaze averted from that inevitable moment of extinction or, should your faith or beliefs support it, of transformation. Our appointment with the Angel of Death is always tomorrow, and there is always another tomorrow and another tomorrow after that. That is the illusion not only of the young but of the not-so-young. Yet as we age beyond our middle years and our world grows increasingly unrecognizable, as our bodies themselves grow increasingly unrecognizable, that Angel of Death becomes less an enemy to be kept at bay, less an intruder to be avoided, or should we be among the more philosophically inclined, less a far-distant acquaintance. The Angel of Death becomes a friend.

I have never feared death, but nor have I been eager for it. Frankly, my life has been too filled with, well, life to spend much time thinking about death. Until now.

I am among the fortunate ones. Even at this age, my body is largely cooperative and I believe my mind to be sharp. Yet the world, as wondrous as it has always been and remains, is no longer my world. Be it a thing, a place or a person, the old must ultimately make way for the new. That is the way of the world. The only way. So it must also be my way.

I do not expect to die today or tomorrow or the day after that. But I shall die, soon. That, too, is the way it ought to be. Once that day arrives, I shall no longer be here to miss the people and things I now love. The things I love will manage admirably without me, will not notice my absence. As for the people, they will adapt and adjust to my absence and, in time, move on. We all do, even when we are convinced that we cannot.

Jeremy, who reads everything I write, whether I wish him to or not, insists that these ramblings of mine must move beyond the walls of 33 Fitzroy Street. He claims that they have value beyond the hours in my ever more inactive days that they help to fill, that they contain wisdom that will assist others. I say bollocks. I say that each of us must find his own way and that these words of mine have little intrinsic value, even for me. Whether he is right or wrong does not matter to me. I shall be dead and, in his own time and whether or not he honors my wishes, so will he.

21

A yellow Urgences-Santé ambulance peeled onto the street from the curb in front of Dominique's, its siren shrieking and red lights flashing. Sarah grabbed Sadie's elbow and propelled her across Claremont Avenue, against the traffic light. "Something's happened!" she exclaimed.

Sarah hoped it wasn't Dominique. The cafe's owner wasn't due back from Toronto for another few days. She had gone, against her better judgment, for a rare mini-vacation. Could it be one of the customers? "That won't be good for business," Sarah muttered.

The cafe's lights were off when Sarah pushed open the door, ignoring the "fermé/closed" sign. "What is it?" she called out when she saw Sylvie Ryan by the kitchen door. "What happened? Is it your mother? Is Dominique okay?" Sarah paused, confused. "What are you doing here? Shouldn't you be in Nova Scotia at Mac's?"

Sylvie locked the door behind them and hugged Sarah. "Mom's fine," she said and motioned for them to sit. She touched Sadie's arm. "Ms. Finkel. Sadie, I mean."

"You know each other?" Sarah asked.

"We do," Sadie replied. The day of Bernie's Klinkhoff art opening, the day when so much happened that changed Sadie's life so radically, many of those changes took place while she was sitting a few doors away from the gallery in Café des Artistes. Sylvie, just finishing up her MFA in art history and not yet Mac's biographer and assistant, had been her waitress.

"Wait," Sarah said, slipping off her coat. "First things first. What happened? Is someone dead?"

"I hope not," Sylvie replied. "It's the temp Mom hired to cook while she's away. He suddenly collapsed in the kitchen, so I called 9-1-1. He was still alive when they took him away. The paramedics said he'd be all right, but I'm sure he won't be back." She glanced at her watch. "And the lunch rush is coming up. Or was. Mom's back day after tomorrow, so we'll just have to close until then." She shook her head at the couple peering in past the closed sign.

"You're right," Sylvie continued. "I'm not supposed to be here. But when Mac's uncle died and he had to take off for London so unexpectedly, he asked me to come out to make sure that Bernie and Erik got off to Italy." She shook her head again, this time at the two women knocking on the door. "I just happened to be here this morning. Thank God I was. First Mom's waitress didn't show up for work. Now this." She sighed. "Now I know why Mom never wants to take a holiday. I know I'll have to call her, but I can't bring myself to do it. Not yet. She'd hop on the next train back. Or plane, even though she hates flying."

Sadie scanned the dimly lit cafe, its dozen linen-topped tables set for lunch, her eyes resting on the two circles of light pushing into the dining from the swinging kitchen doors. She then watched as two more groups read the closed sign and walked away. She looked back toward the kitchen and tried to imagine what lay on the other side of those doors. This wasn't some cookbook from the library. This was real life. A real-life restaurant. It wasn't some prost deli on The Main. It was Westmount. Could she do it? Did she dare? She pushed herself up from the table. "You aren't closing," she declared.

"Huh? What do you mean?" Sylvie asked.

Sadie scanned the cafe again and tried to picture it filled with customers. Satisfied customers. "Your lunch menu," she snapped. "Show me."

"Uh, sure." Sylvie retrieved one from a serving station.

Sadie ran her finger down the page from item to item, nodding her head at each one. "You," she said to Sylvie a minute later, "switch on the lights, unlock the door and turn that sign over. You're open."

"You." Sadie pulled Sarah up. "You're coming with me. I need an assistant." Then she marched Sarah through the swinging doors.

"You'll think I'm crazy," Sadie said three hours later, "but I can't remember the last time I had this much fun." With the lunch rush over and the restaurant empty, at least until mid-afternoon shoppers started to trickle in, Sadie, Sarah and Sylvie had collapsed at a table by the window. Sadie and Sylvie were drinking coffee. Sarah had her usual tea with lemon. All three were greedily devouring slices of Dominique's legendary apple pie.

"Fun?" Sarah exclaimed. "You call that fun? You really are meshugena."

Sadie laughed. It felt good to laugh. Who knew when she had last laughed? Not a wistful or an ironic kind of laugh; a happy laugh, a laugh from the kishke, a belly laugh. Probably never.

"You have a twisted sense of humor, Sadie Finkel. But boy can you cook. Who knew you were such a gourmet in the kitchen? You were wasted selling ladies' coats and dresses at Reitman's and Morgan's. You should have been cooking all those years. At The Beaver Club or the Ritz."

Sadie laughed again. "That's too fancy for me. I couldn't pronounce most of what's on their menu, let alone cook it."

"Okay. Then Rabiner's or Hotel Vermont in the Laurentians."

"The Laurentians..." Sadie gazed out the window, past the afternoon shoppers on Sherbrooke Street, and let her mind float back through the decades. *No.* She pushed away the flood of memories, mostly unhappy. Sarah had been right the other day. Second-guessing old choices made no sense. "I was never in the Laurentians," she said softly.

"Never?" Sarah was incredulous. Could any Montreal Jew not have spent at least one Sunday afternoon on the beach at Lac des Sables in Ste. Agathe? Not now, but back in the day, when the Laurentian Mountains were Montreal's Catskills.

"The farthest out of Montreal I ever got," Sadie said, still staring out the window, "was when I went to Expo '67. Morgan's gave us all one-day passes." Her voice took on a hint of the old bitterness. "Taking the Metro to St. Helen's Island hardly counts as an out-of-town trip."

"The Brown Derby, then," Sarah offered in an attempt to restore Sadie's good humor. "Or Miss Montreal."

Sadie took a deep breath, held it for a beat, then exhaled. It took an effort some days to dispel a lifetime of ill temper. She returned her attention to her two companions. "The Brown Derby?" She managed a smile. "That's more like it, maybe. Maybe." A longtime Montreal institution, the Brown Derby specialized in traditional Jewish cooking. "Simple, heymishe food, like my mother cooked when she was alive? That I like to do. That I can do."

"I saw today what you can do, and it's more than that." Sarah turned to Sylvie. "You saw. Am I right or am I right?"

Sylvie chuckled. "You're right."

"Of course I am," Sarah said. She rose and stretched her arms out to the cafe's empty tables, all cluttered with dirty dishes waiting to be cleared. "Today, Dominique's," she proclaimed. "Tomorrow, the Ritz." She dropped back to her seat. "Remember," she said to Syvie. "You heard it here first."

Sadie snorted. "You're the one who's meshugena, Sarah-with-an-h-and-without-an-h Schumacher-Kaplan-Swartz-Schumacher-with-more-names-and-spellings-than-anyone-should-have."

"Don't change the subject," Sarah countered. "I saw those piles of cookbooks at the library this morning." She nudged Sylvie with her elbow. "You should have seen it. Up to the ceiling they were. That Julia Child better watch out. Sadie Finkel's in town."

Sadie rolled her eyes. "Believe me, Julia Child has nothing to worry about. Not the Ritz. Not the Brown Derby. But you're right about the library. I've never been so excited by books before. Then, to come here and actually cook. For people, yet. I'm not used to cooking for people, you see. Who would I cook for? So this was different. A whole restaurant full of different." Her voice dropped to a whisper. "The last time I cooked for anyone… The last time was for my sister, when she was sick."

Sarah said nothing. Esther remained a touchy subject, even if Sadie now regretted the way she had treated her. When Sadie talked about her sister, it was sometimes simpler for Sarah not to respond. Sadie was unlikely to explode with fury like in the old days. Now, she was more inclined to implode with guilt. Although Sarah had come to terms with being Sadie's friend, she was not eager to become Sadie's therapist. "It's a pity there weren't cooking jobs for Jewish girls when you and me were young," she said at last. "It didn't matter if you'd wanted to cook at Rabiner's. They wouldn't hire you. Good Jewish girls didn't work in restaurants, not even Jewish restaurants, except as waitresses, unless their family owned the place. The cooking jobs? Those were for the men. It's different now. Now, girls can do anything. Even good Jewish girls."

"Girls, yes," Sadie said, raising her mug to her lips. "Not old ladies." She drained the last of her coffee and reached for the Bunn carafe on the next table. Before picking it up, she touched the glass. Still hot. She refilled her mug and topped up Sylvie's.

"For an old lady, you did pretty good today," Sarah said, squeezing a fresh lemon wedge into her tea.

Sadie beamed, her peevishness forgotten. "I did, didn't I." She speared the final forkful of apple pie from her plate, stuffed it into her mouth and held the dish up for more. "That was my lunch," she reminded Sylvie. "It's time for dessert."

Sylvie pushed her chair back and stood, although at barely five feet, the pixie-like redhead wasn't much taller than a seated Sadie. "Keep your plate," she said and disappeared into the kitchen. She returned a few minutes later, a tub of vanilla ice cream in one hand and in the other, an oversized Pyrex dish that held most of an apple pie. "Dig in, ladies," she said. "You more than earned it."

"Like I said," Sarah said to Sadie, once the Pyrex had been nearly scraped clean, "you did good for an old lady. I've never seen you like that."

"You mean busy and happy, all at the same time?" Sadie asked.

"You did good for any age," Sylvie said, still amazed that the cafe had survived the lunch rush without a single mistake or customer complaint. "If you ever want a job, let me know. Mom would hire you in a flash."

"You're a sweet girl," Sadie said, "but I couldn't keep this up day after day. Twenty years ago I could. Ten, possibly. Now? Now, it's too much for an alteh machashaifeh like me. Of course I'll help tonight and tomorrow, until your mother gets back." She squeezed Sylvie's hand. "Thank you for making me feel like I could be useful. Thank you especially for everything you did for me, back in August at the other cafe. It meant everything to me."

Sarah raised an eyebrow.

"Someday," Sadie said to Sarah, "I'll tell you the whole story, and not just from that day. Someday. Not today." She stood up. "Today, I have dinner customers to get ready for." She poked Sarah's shoulder. "You, too."

Sarah pulled Sadie back down to her seat. "I can have more pie first? I need my strength." She scooped up the last of the crumbs with her teaspoon. "One more thing," she said when the pie plate was empty. "You had fun, you said."

"Uh-huh"

"You like cooking, you said."

"Yes."

"So you'll come to London with me next month."

"London? What are you talking about?"

"I'm going, and you're coming with me." She related Mac's offer.

"What does that have to do with me?" Sadie asked.

"Mac and me are going to need a cook. If I do the cooking," Sarah said, "we'll be eating bagels and tea for all our meals. That, or we'll be dead from food poisoning. Why do you think I eat all my meals here?" She rapped her knuckles on the table. "But with you as our chef, it will be like Buckingham Palace. Better. We'll have the Queen wanting to come over for dinner every night."

Sadie paled. "I can't."

"You sure can." She turned to Sylvie. "Tell her. It's the chance of a lifetime. To go to London, England? All expenses paid? And all she has to do is some cooking? What kind of fool would say no to the chance of a lifetime?" She turned back to Sadie. "Especially when God only knows how much lifetime either of us has left. You're coming and that's settled." She touched Sylvie's arm. "You'll help her? With passports and organizing and things like that? For Mac, you'll do it?"

Sylvie grinned. "For Mac and for me, I'll do it. Mac called me this morning after he talked to you. I'm coming out to London, too."

Sadie pressed her right hand onto the table with her left to stop herself from gnawing on her thumbnail. "I don't know…"

"You're scared. Of course you're scared. You've never traveled."

Sadie nodded her head so slightly that it was barely perceptible.

"I'm also scared. I don't know if I have it in me to write another book. I know I promised Erik, but can I do it? Not just any book, not just an *After Sara's Year* like we joked about. No. A novel. Not just any novel. A story from Emmeline's life and my imagination. That scares me so bad, has me so convinced I could never in a million years do it, that I have to say yes. That, and London. Such a city!" She covered

Sadie's hand with hers. "So I'm going, even though I'm terrified. You come and we can be terrified together."

Sadie shut her eyes and tried to imagine herself in London, tried to imagine herself anywhere outside Montreal. Her mind wouldn't cooperate. She had no frame of reference. She tried to conjure up pictures of London that she had seen in newspapers and magazines and on TV. Big Ben. Tower Bridge. Buckingham Palace. The Tower of London. The River Thames. The Tube. That made it feel more alien, more impossible. *Damn it! I won't let it be impossible. I'm seventy-six. If I don't go somewhere now, I'll never go. If I don't get out of this farkakte city now, I never will. I'll die in that keyver of an apartment, and I'll never have seen anything of anything.* She opened her eyes. "You'll help me?" she asked Sylvie.

"I'll do more than that," Sylvie replied. "I'll fly out with you." The front door opened with the first of the afternoon-shopping crowd. "For now, I need you here."

22

Bernie woke to the golden light of a Tuscan dawn streaming in through the faint etching of frost on the bedroom windows. He pulled the quilted duvet up to his chin. He would soon have to venture from the toasty comfort of his bed to light a fire. For now, though, it was easier to snuggle under the covers and up against Erik, whose Norse ancestry managed to keep his skin warm even in the coldest weather. Erik murmured a few unintelligible words, breathed out a soft snore and pressed himself against Bernie, who stroked Erik's hair and surveyed the room. A heavy, rustic wardrobe in carved chestnut dominated the wall opposite the iron-framed double bed. It rose from the tiled floor to graze the beamed ceiling and matched both the twin nightstands and a one-drawer writing desk that filled the narrow space between the two open-shuttered windows. A circular mirror set in a sculpted copper-patina frame sat above the desk and reflected Erik's face, caught in a fleeting halo of sunlight.

"You look so calm, so untroubled," Bernie whispered to the sleeping face in the mirror. "I wish… I wish…"

What do I wish? That I had never helped talk you into taking on the gallery show? That we had never come to Italy? It seemed like such a good idea. You were eager to do something different with your art, and Tuscany seemed the perfect place to make that happen. Then, everything fell into place so magically, especially getting this house. Can you imagine a more inspiring spot? Views to die for from every window. Light that any artist would kill for. Less than an hour from Siena, less than two from Florence. Even Venice is closer to us than Toronto is from Montreal.

Erik stirred. His eyelids fluttered and his breathing quickened.

Then they both stilled. If a mouse in the next room could waken Bernie, Erik, Bernie was convinced, would sleep through the apocalypse. Bernie stroked Erik's cheek, its usual light stubble beginning to fill out into a soft beard.

We'd planned to visit all of them. Rome, too. But you wanted to get a start on your show first. Outings like that, you said, would be your reward. Your incentive. Every painting you finished would earn you another trip. We flew into Florence, so we saw a bit of that. And there was Pisa, the little we could see between the mural and the train station. You let me talk you into a one-day trip to Buonconvento. But that terrified you more than it inspired you, so I never mentioned it again.

Bernie kissed the top of Erik's head and buried his now tear-streaked face in Erik's hair. "I don't know what to do to help you," he murmured, "and I want to help you so much. So damn much."

The previous morning had been the worst so far. Erik had slumped onto the terrace that faced south past the rolling hills of Siena Province to the snow-dusted peaks of Mount Amiata. Bundled up against the Christmas Eve chill, Bernie was sitting at the table, whipping out a series of quick pencil sketches. He quickly turned over his pad when Erik flopped onto the bench next to him.

"What's up?" Bernie asked. He no longer dared inquire about how things were going for Erik in the room across from the bedroom that they had outfitted as a shared studio. Spacious, with extra large north-facing windows that looked out onto acres of vineyards and hill country, it had seemed the ideal setting in which to make art. Seemed.

Erik said nothing. He opened the sketchbook and leafed through the newest drawings, stopping at the one Bernie had just been working on, an abstract rendering of the view from the terrace that evocatively captured the essence of the Italian countryside, without any hint that what you were seeing was a landscape.

"Hard to believe I'm the same angst-ridden accountant you picked up in Galérie Cinq Arts that day four years ago, when I didn't know I was an artist and I didn't know I was gay and I didn't know I was in love with you." Bernie waited for Erik's usual smart aleck retort. It didn't come.

"Now I'm the angst-ridden one," Erik said. He slid the pad back toward Bernie.

"Should I ask?"

Erik shrugged. "I feel like Mac must have when he was trying to paint your mother. I keep staring at that blank canvas until I'm seeing crosseyed, but nothing comes." He stared out toward the mountain. "Maybe this was a bad idea."

"Italy?"

"Italy. That fucking show. Maybe even being an artist."

Bernie reached for Erik's hand then pulled away when Erik clenched his fist and pounded it on the table — again and again and again, until he started to cry. Only then did he open his hand to Bernie's. "Everything here is so beautiful, Bernie. I love it. I really do. I love our villa. I love our village. I even love Evil Evelina." Evelina Maria was the irritable cook-housekeeper who came with the villa and acted as though she despised not only cooking and house-keeping but people. Short, stocky and clad head-to-toe in black, she spent her mornings at the villa wandering from room to room, muttering in some incomprehensible dialect and glaring at anyone who crossed her path.

"The only time I don't love it is when I'm in the studio…or outside the studio if I have a paintbrush in my hand and a canvas on an easel in front of me. I've tried every trick that Mac taught me at NSCAD, but nothing comes out." He stood and spread his arms out to the view. "How can I not be inspired? This is Italy, for fuck's sake! Michelangelo. Leonardo da Vinci. Canaletto. Botticelli. Titian. Raphael. Tiepolo. Modigliani. I could go on and on." He dropped onto the opposite bench, his back to the countryside, his elbows on the table, his chin in his hands.

"We could take a few days off, or more, and go back to Florence. Or spend some time in Rome. You've always wanted to see the Vatican. Seeing some of those paintings and frescoes could get you going."

"Or intimidate me more." Erik tapped his chest. "It's in here. All of it. I know it is. Every damn painting for that damn show. I can feel it inside, pushing to live on canvas, pushing to be free. I just don't know how to get in there to let it out. I've tried everything I know…"

"I know you have."

"We should cancel the show while Jeffrey and Pierre can still slot someone else in."

Bernie reached across the table and twined his fingers with Erik's. "Is that really what you want?"

Erik stroked Bernie's hand with his thumb. "No."

"Good. No more talk about canceling. Let's send Evil Evelina home early and get out of here. We can have lunch at Castello Banfi and check out their museum. From what I've read, it's all old bottles and glass. Not one painting." He scanned Erik's face. No reaction. "After, we can head into town. We haven't checked out the Christmas Market yet. What do you say?"

"I don't know…" Erik freed his hands from Bernie's and laid them on the table, palms down.

"Come on. It's Christmas Eve. You deserve a day off."

Erik inspected the backs of his hands, then turned them over. They were clean. No paint stains. Italy was the first time in more years than he could remember that his hands had been free of multicolored acrylic splotches. "You're right," he said after a moment. "I need to get out of here. The winery, the museum, the Christmas market: They're all fine." He looked up at Bernie. "I know you're Jewish," he began, "and you know I don't care much about religion, but…"

Bernie waited.

"Can we stay in town and…and go to midnight Mass? At Madonna del Soccorso? If you don't want to, that's okay," he added quickly.

Our Lady of Succor? Of course I said yes. I figured we could use all the help we could get. Bernie draped his arm over Erik. He felt the steady rise and fall of Erik's chest and let his breath align with it. He felt the easy beat of Erik's heart and felt his own open more fully than he could ever have imagined possible. *I watched you pray, Erik. On your knees, on that unpadded kneeling rail. I don't think you were following the Mass. I think you were making up your own prayers.* Bernie gazed back up at the mirror, at the reflection of Erik's sleeping face. *You looked so peaceful there. Beatific. Like you do now.* He snuggled closer and kissed Erik's neck. *I prayed, too, Erik. I prayed for you.*

23

"Happy Christmas, Mac. Isn't that how they say it here?" Sarah passed a slender, gift-wrapped package across the table as Cliff Richard crooned the season's holiday hit on the radio, a vintage Ecko AD65 housed in garish lime green Bakelite.

It's Christmas time
Mistletoe and wine
With logs on the fire and gifts on the tree
A time to rejoice in the good that we see.

"What's this?" Mac asked. "Didn't I say no gifts?"

"You're the boss of me since when?" Sarah asked with mock sternness. Sylvie stifled a grin.

"Since never, apparently."

Sadie smirked.

"And you," Mac said to Sadie. "You don't even celebrate Christmas."

"It's a long time since I celebrated any holiday," she said. "It's time I started. What better way than with a good Jewish boy's birthday?"

Mac raised his half-empty wineglass to the miniature tinsel Christmas tree that served as the holiday table's centerpiece. "Gut yontif," he toasted. He then turned his attention back to Sarah's gift, studying its shiny, red-foil wrap and tugging lightly on its lacy, gold bow. "It's too thin to be a box of Laura Secord chocolates," he said, "or a box of anything, for that matter." He turned it sideways then flipped it upside down. "It's not very big, is it?" It was about the size of a large greeting card. "I'm not worth something bigger?" He poked it, sniffed it and raised it to his ear, rubbing it between his fingers.

"You could just open it," Sadie suggested with a hint of her old acerbity.

"What fun is that?" Mac asked. He held it up to one of the silver tapers on the dining room table and squinted at it. "Hmm." He edged it closer to the flame. "I know," he said. "It's my walking papers. You want this house all to yourself and you're evicting me. I knew I should never have introduced you to that shyster Dunedin."

"You'll see," Sarah said, her face expressionless. "Just don't hold it so close to that candle, or you'll never find out."

"Whatever it is," Mac said, slipping off the bow and clawing at the wrapping paper, "you shouldn't have."

"You won't say that when you see what it is." Sarah winked again. "Right, girls?"

"You haven't been here a week and you're already conspiring against me?" Mac asked.

The three women had flown into Heathrow from Montreal a few days earlier. After spending their first night being pampered through their jet lag at Claridge's, Sarah and Sadie had joined Mac at 33 Fitzroy Street, which he had spent the previous weeks preparing for the possibility of longterm guests. Sarah, he installed in the second-floor bedroom next to his aunt's writing studio. He and Sylvie occupied two of the attic rooms originally designed for servants, with a third — the brightest — set up as a basic art studio and office. Sadie was given Emmeline's bedroom, the largest and most comfortable in the house. "You're going to have to put up with a bunch of temperamental artists," Mac joked when Sadie objected to her room assignment. "The least I can do is put you in the best bedroom."

To show her gratitude, Sadie insisted on cooking Christmas dinner — "As long as you don't mind me experimenting with something untraditional." Julia Childs' lamb stew was an audacious goal for someone with big dreams but little experience. It had paid off.

"You couldn't be a bad cook?" Sarah asked Sadie after her third helping. "Not as shreklekh as me, for sure, but bad enough that I wouldn't double in size with you in the kitchen?"

"With all the stairs in this house," Sadie retorted, "you'll have no trouble keeping that girlish figure of yours."

Everybody laughed. Sarah's figure had never been girlish, not even when she was a girl.

Now, dinner was over and despite Mac's ban on Christmas presents, Sarah had gifts for all. She gave Sadie her pristine copy of *A Treasure for My Daughter,* the classic Jewish Montreal cookbook her mother had given her thirty years earlier. "To Sadie," she wrote inside the book. "You'll get better use from this than I ever did." For Sylvie, she had a signed copy of Sara's Year.

Mac's gift was another matter. It was a sort of promissory note, and Sarah still wasn't sure that it was a promise she would be able to keep. She had spent nearly every moment since arriving in London reading Emmeline's papers and had finished the last of them that morning while Sylvie was helping Sadie in the kitchen and Mac was making Christmas calls back to Canada.

"You really think I can do this?" she had asked into what would soon become her writing studio, convinced that both Emmeline and Esther were watching her. "A book I know I can write. But a novel?" She peered at Emmeline's armchair. "A Montreal Jew who knows nothing from nothing should turn your life into a some kind of story? Don't answer. And you." She glared into the fireplace. "I'm not asking you anything, Esther." She shut her eyes.

Twenty minutes before dinner, Sarah opened her eyes, uncapped Emmeline's black-and-gold Montblanc Meisterstuck, now cleaned and refilled, and touched its nib to a sheet of blank writing paper. She would fold the page into an old Christmas card she had found in one of the desk drawers and wrap them in the same holiday wrap she had used for Sadie's and Sylvie's gifts.

"To Mac," she wrote. "You've got a deal. Merry Christmas, from me and Emmeline. Love (I think), Sara(h)."

1988
TUSCANY & LONDON

24

The orange-striped white ambulance screamed through ancient villages and past age-old vineyards, its blue and white lights strobing through the Tuscan dusk. Erik wheezed into the oxygen mask and held Bernie's hand limply. His eyes were closed.

"How much longer to the hospital?" Bernie asked the paramedic.

"Soon," the young woman replied, not looking up from the stethoscope pressed to Erik's chest. "We be in Siena soon. The university hospital. Best hospital."

"Hear that?" Bernie said to Erik. "Siena. You're finally going to get to go." He forced a smile. "You didn't have to be such a drama queen about it, you know. Frank would have taken us in his toy Fiat." His voice caught, and he tried to mask his alarm. "You're going to be all right," he whispered, praying that it was true. *You have to be.*

When a week earlier, Erik had begun waking in the middle of the night short of breath and soaked in sweat, he had convinced Bernie that he was having panic attacks, that he would be fine once he got a painting going. It was just that the show was coming up and he seemed no closer to having even one painting ready, let alone the dozen that Jeffrey and Pierre were expecting. There had also been bad dreams, each more terrifying than the last and too many involving violent torture and death with Erik as either victim or tormentor. Sometimes the terror would strike multiple times in a single night. Erik would thrash restlessly, moaning loudly. Then he would wake with a start and shiver uncontrollably while Bernie dried him off, helped him into a chair, covered him with a blanket, changed the sheets and got him back into bed, only for the hell to recur more viciously a few hours later.

"It's artistic angst," Erik would insist next morning. "It'll pass."

Bernie wasn't convinced. He doubted whether Erik was. It didn't matter. Erik refused to let Bernie call a doctor.

Then this.

Erik had woken that morning with a cough and a fever. By mid-afternoon the fever had shot up and the cough was a dry, hacking bark that left Erik clutching his chest with each eruption. By dinnertime, with his respiration shallow and forced, Erik had to concede that this was no ordinary flu. Panic-stricken, Bernie wrapped Erik in another comforter and raced downstairs to call 1-1-8, grateful that the medical-emergency operator spoke fluent English. She dispatched the ambulance before Bernie had finished describing Erik's symptoms.

Now, they were headed to the Azienda Ospedaliera Universitaria Senese. The paramedic's preliminary diagnosis? Pneumonia.

25

Sarah glared at the blank screen of her Macintosh II. Instead of glaring back at her, a little black arrow — a cursor, Mac said it was called — blinked mockingly.

"It's like a typewriter without paper," Mac had assured her as Kevin, the black-haired, black-clad, black-booted young man from the computer store, set it up on a special table in the writing studio. Emmeline's desk was not deep enough to accommodate all the computer's bits and pieces.

"What's wrong with paper?" Sarah asked.

"The paper comes out of here." Mac pointed to the LaserWriter near her feet.

"You want me to write on a television? A Smith-Corona isn't good enough for your Emmeline?"

"A fountain pen was good enough for Aunt Emmeline." Mac plugged the computer into the wall outlet and switched it on. "Nothing is too good for the author of *Sara's Year*. I read the reviews, you know. You're on your way to becoming a literary superstar, and superstars deserve the best."

"You," Sarah retorted, grinning in spite of herself, "you're on your way to becoming a *narish ligner*." She placed her fingers on the keyboard and pretended to type out the two Yiddish words. "A foolish liar, in case Esther never called you that."

Mac laughed. "Not to my face."

Sarah pulled her hands from the keyboard and rested them on her lap. "Seriously, Mac. This is wonderful. At least, I think it is. But I don't know what to do with it."

"Kevin here's going to give you lessons. Right, Kevin?"

"As many as you need, Mrs. Swartz."

"I should have that many years left," she muttered.

To her amazement, Sarah picked up the computer's basics after only two lessons. Today's blinking cursor wasn't mocking her lack of technical know-how. It was sneering at her creative incompetence. "I thought each book was supposed to get easier," she complained to the cursor. "Even with this fancy contraption, I don't know what I'm supposed to write."

"Start anywhere, Sarah, with any word." It was Mr. Littleton's voice, from all those years ago in English class at Baron Byng. "Isn't that how you started *Sara's Year*?"

It was. She had sat at her dining room table on Kensington Avenue and pounded an E, a T and an A into her Smith-Corona, for no reason other than that they were the most commonly used letters in the English language. When typing them once hadn't worked, she had done it again and again and then again until, suddenly, she found herself writing a book. Could it work a second time?

"It doesn't matter what the word is or where it takes you," Mr. Littleton had said to her all those lifetimes ago. "If you believe in the story and trust it, it will take you where you need to go...where it needs you to go."

Do I believe in this story? Do I? Sarah covered the cursor with her hand. "I'm not asking you," she said. She rose from the computer desk, installed herself in Emmeline's armchair and draped herself in the Hudson's Bay blanket. "It's just like home, this blanket," she said. "My Jack had one like it. It's in the apartment somewhere. I'll have to look for it when I get home." She hugged the blanket to her. "I need help, Jack. Also from you, Emmeline. I don't think typing ETA over and over will write another book for me."

She shut her eyes and listened to the faint hum of traffic from a few blocks away on Euston Road. *What did it sound like here fifty years ago? Not as many cars and trucks as today. But cars and trucks were noisier then. Clunkier. And the roads, they weren't as smooth.*

Sarah let her mind travel back through the decades. Not to the London of the 1930s but to the Montreal of the same era, the Montreal she grew up in. Had the sounds coming in from Euston Road been that different from the steady thrum from St. Lawrence Boulevard that had lulled her to sleep at night and awakened her each morning?

Of course Clark Street in the multilingual maelstrom of an immigrant neighborhood had not been the same as fancy Fitzroy Square. Still wasn't. Of course Sarah Schumacher had not lived the life of an Emmeline Marguerite Marie Mandeville. Not by a long shot. But people were people, weren't they? Whatever Emmeline had felt and done, hadn't Sarah felt and done some version of it? Hadn't Sarah encountered versions of Emmeline back home in Westmount? The wealthy suburb was not as unwaveringly British as it had once been. Yet enough of a residue remained, right in Sarah's Whitehall apartments, for her to have some knowledge of that world. Besides, she wasn't writing Emmeline's biography. She was writing fiction...or would be once she got a first word into that lekherlekh contraption.

She crossed back to the computer, the blanket still around her shoulders, and rested her fingers on the keyboard. "Emmeline Mandeville woke to the shrill of a siren," she typed. *No. "To the piercing wail of an air raid siren."* Sarah continued, reading aloud as the words took shape on the screen: "Seconds later, the pulsing whir of low-flying planes sparked a too-familiar terror. Emmeline grabbed for the greatcoat that she kept at the foot of her bed, threw it over her shoulders as she thrust the notebook from her nightstand into one of its pockets, slipped into the flats that she made certain were also by her bed each night, then raced down the stairs and out the door to the nearest shelter."

"Not so smug anymore, are you?" she growled at the cursor as she pushed it up to the top of the page and typed *"The Emmeline Papers* by Sara Schumacher." She stared at the three words with her fingers poised over the keys. Finally she added, "Chapter One...maybe."

I have savored every instant of my ninety-two years. Every one. Even the tragic and painful ones have reminded me that I am alive. And what do we live for if not for the constant reminder that we do live.

A life as lengthy as mine has experienced much and witnessed more: exhilarating joys and triumphs, excruciating grief and sorrow — all of them, in a smattering of instances, within breaths of each other. Even as I might choose not to relive some, there are many I would happily revisit. Even as I might prefer specific world events not to have occurred, each has brought into my life treasured gifts that I might otherwise never have known. Even had I not been endowed with such longevity, I would have embraced my years with no less passion and seized each moment with no less gusto.

However drawn-out our interval on this earth, it will come to a finite end for all of us. Let others preach of afterlives and squander limited heartbeats on the futile expectation of a better world beyond this one. I say there is no world beyond this one. I say there is but this moment and the accumulation of connected moments that, in the end, adds up to a lifetime. One lifetime. A single opportunity. We can either choose to live that opportunity to its fullest or we can choose to squint at it from the fringes while all its richness, potency and, yes, ferocity pass us by.

Should my view of the hereafter prove erroneous, I shall unhesitatingly step into whatever nirvana awaits me and dive into its delights with no less zeal than I have into those offered me through this span of existence. Regardless, near as I am to its inevitable conclusion, I will not trade the certainty of this life for the chimera of a next one.

Whatever fixed time remains to me is as precious as all the years that have preceded it, and I am determined to live it out as uncompromisingly as this decaying body will allow.

Tonight, it favors me with a full moon gleaming through the window, a fire sinuating in the grate, a snifter of Armagnac in my hand and, of course, these words.

26

Erik switched off the light by his hospital bed and stared into the darkening Tuscan hills. For a moment he was aware of nothing else, only the gathering pall that was devouring everything around him, everything within him. He saw nothing, heard nothing, felt nothing. Not the mask over his mouth. Not the pinprick connecting his arm to the tubes keeping him alive. Not the blip of the bedside monitor. Not the susurrus of sounds from the corridor.

Not the fear.

Was this what it would be like to die? The steady dissolution of his senses until all that was left was nothingness?

Erik turned his head from the window and reached for the light switch. Maybe he wouldn't die. Not yet, anyway. The doctor had said there were drugs, drugs that might keep him going. He wanted to believe it, but… Drugs hadn't helped Calvin Hutcheson or Ray David Blackman or so many others. Too many others. Not in the end.

He let his hand drop from the light switch, felt the darkness press in on him, felt the weight on his chest return, felt his eyes flood with tears. He clawed at the oxygen mask that was interfering with the sobs that wracked through him, then clenched his fists until his fingernails cut into his palms.

When Bernie returned twenty minutes later, he found Erik asleep, his face still damp, his pillow soaked and his arms folded tightly across his chest.

27

Mac set down the hall phone, his hand trembling. *This can't be happening.* He felt for the wall to steady himself, willing his feet to hold him up. He glared at the telephone as if it were responsible for the message it had relayed and considered jerking its cord from the wall and heaving the bloody thing out the front door. Better yet, he could march it the two blocks to BT Tower, home of British Telecom, and heave it into the lobby. After all, it was their phone and their phone service. Not that that would accomplish anything, other than to eliminate the possibility that good news might follow the bad. Instead, he stumbled the few yards to the front room.

Sadie didn't notice Mac right away. She was too engrossed in eighteenth-century Surrey to be fully aware of what was happening around her in twentieth-century London. Until now, she had never been much of a reader, had paid little attention to books. London changed all that. Between the floor-to-ceiling shelving in Emmeline's bedroom, the bookcases in the writing studio and the scattering of books stacked on floors and tables throughout the house, it was like living in the Westmount Library. The only thing missing were cookbooks. Until she married Jeremy, Emmeline had engaged a succession of cook-housekeepers, each more frustrated than the last by her mistress's demands and eccentricities. Those who didn't quit after a month were generally fired after two. Not one left any cookery books behind, and Jeremy had required none.

Fortunately for Sadie, the Marylebone Library was only a twenty-minute walk away; a Waterstones bookstore was a few minutes nearer. She could find all the cookbooks she wanted in one place or the other. What she found at Emmeline's was something altogether different: an eclectic collection of literature, poetry, biography, memoir, history and coffee table art, along with essays on equality in all its guises — from feminism and gay liberation to US civil rights and the plight of migrant workers.

The books had intimidated her at first. What did she know from writers, artists and thinkers? She had gone to work straight from high school, into the retail side of the same schmatta trade that then employed so many Jewish immigrants and their offspring, the same trade that had killed her mother. For fifty years she had labored at it. Who had time for books? Who had time for culture? For fifty years that world had been closed to her. No, if she were honest with herself, she had closed herself to it. There were libraries she could have borrowed from, bookstores she could have browsed. If she were honest with herself, some part of her had feared that books would open her mind to worlds she believed she could never touch.

Now, Sadie was in London. Not London, Ontario. London, England. Those inaccessible worlds had reached out to her, were forcing her to open her mind to them. Her heart, too.

Sadie had successfully ignored Emmeline's books for two weeks; a fortnight, Mac said it was called here. When she dusted them, she let her eyes glaze over so she couldn't decipher the titles. On day fifteen, however, she came across a title that refused to stay unfocused, a title that could easily have described her life until six months earlier. She pulled *Pride and Prejudice* from the shelf, opened it and began reading where she stood: "It is a truth universally acknowledged, that a single man in possession of a good fortune, must be in want of a wife." Twenty minutes later, she was still standing by the bookcase, still reading.

Two weeks after that, she had not only finished one Jane Austen and begun another — *Sense and Sensibility* — she had her own stacks of books scattered around the house. Novels by her bed, art books in the kitchen, biographies and memoirs in the front room and old issues of *Punch* in the bathroom. As a teenager she could never understand how her sister could read three books at one time. Now, she couldn't understand how people could limit themselves to three.

Just before Mac staggered into the front room, Sadie had been scowling over Dylan Thomas's "And Death Shall Have No Dominion." If she could now navigate the old-fashioned elegance of Jane Austen's prose, poetry continued to confound her.

Though they be mad and dead as nails,
Heads of the characters hammer through daisies;
Break in the sun till the sun breaks down,
And death shall have no dominion.

"Why can't he just say what he means," Sadie muttered, "instead of all that farkakte metaphor!" She slammed the poetry collection down and opened up her newest friend, the less perplexing *Emma*: "The hair was curled, and the maid sent away, and Emma sat down to think and be miserable. — It was a wretched business indeed! — Such an overthrow of every thing she had been wishing for! — Such a development of every thing most unwelcome!"

It was then that Sadie became aware of Mac. His face was ashen, his breathing shallow. "What is it?" she cried. "What's wrong?"

"Sarah...Sylvie," he stammered. "Can you get them down here? Please."

"Let me get you something first. A glass of water? No, not water," she continued when he didn't respond. "Something stronger. Whisky? A brandy?"

"After. Please call them."

Five minutes later, with Sarah, Sadie and Sylvie clustered around him, Mac looked up. "That was Bernie on the phone just now," he said. "From Siena. From the hospital."

"Something's happened," Sarah exclaimed. "What's happened? Is it Bernie? Is he all right?"

"It's Erik." Mac waited a moment. "He has pneumonia."

"He's going to be good, right?" Sadie asked, handing Mac a Scotch and water.

"It's not ordinary pneumonia," Mac said. He downed the Scotch in a single gulp.

"What do you mean, not ordinary pneumonia?" Sylvie asked, fearing she knew the answer.

Mac tried to inhale deeply. Instead, his shoulders slumped. "It's AIDS," he whispered. "Erik has AIDS."

Sarah gasped. She couldn't ask. She didn't dare. No one did.

"They've taken Bernie's blood," Mac replied to the unvoiced question. "He'll call again when he knows."

"Erik?" Sadie whispered. "Is he...?"

Mac sighed. "I don't know yet. No one does."

28

Bernie held the receiver to his ear, deaf to its jarring dial tone and oblivious to the flurry of hospital activity behind him. The past hours had hurtled by in a blur of sirens, paramedics, doctors and nurses. Mostly of dread. Standing here by the bank of pay phones, removed for a few moments from the chaotic urgency that swirled around him, he ought finally to be able to breathe. Yet he couldn't. His heart pounded into his head and drilled into his eyes, where a dammed up flood of tears fought to explode out of him.

He should go to the cafeteria and get some food inside him. Or at least some coffee. When was the last time he had eaten? Breakfast? Lunch? Yesterday? No, if he ate anything, he would throw up. He wasn't sure he could keep coffee down either.

He should get back to Erik. He had to see if he was all right…or at least as all right as was possible under the circumstances. Circumstances. He couldn't bear to think about the circumstances. Maybe if he didn't think about the circumstances, they would go away. Maybe if he clapped his hands, Tinkerbell would materialize. *I didn't used to believe in fairies. Now, I have to. Now, I am one.* He paused. *Forget Tinkerbell.* Fairies couldn't make the circumstances go away because it was to fairies that the circumstances were happening. Were they happening to him?

Should he return to the lab for his test results? He knew he needed to know; he wasn't sure he wanted to know. Would he and Erik end up in twin hospital beds? In twin hospice beds? Under twin gravestones? No, he couldn't go back to the lab. Besides, it was too early for results. Or was it already too late?

He opened his wallet to one of the pictures he always carried, of Billie Burke as Glinda the Good Witch in *The Wizard of Oz*. The *Oz* books had been childhood favorites, until his stepfather declared them to be "too sissy for boys." Bernie still loved the film and watched it at least once a year, if only to remind himself that belief was the key to possibility. But was it? Could he believe Erik's AIDS away? Could he believe a negative test result for himself? What if it wasn't about belief at all? What if it was about courage? He flipped to the next photo, of Lena Horne as Glinda in *The Wiz*. What had she said? He tried to conjure up one of the closing scenes: "Home is knowing," she'd said. "Knowing your mind, knowing your heart, knowing your courage." If he clicked his heels three times, could he get back home? Could he find his courage?

Bernie turned to the final photo, of Erik bathed in the pink light of dawn. Bernie had taken it with his then-new Pentax a few weeks after Erik joined him at Mac's in Nova Scotia. Was it only four years ago? Erik had wakened him while it was dark, shoved warm clothes at him and pushed him into the car for the ten-minute drive to the red-sand tidal flats at Blomidon Provincial Park. It was one of Erik's favorite places, and he had wanted Bernie to experience it at one of his favorite times of day. Would Erik ever look that happy again? Would Bernie ever feel that much joy again? He stroked Erik's face in the photo then shut his wallet.

How long had he been standing here? He should move. But he couldn't. He couldn't even put the phone down. Why was he clutching it? Oh, right. He was going to call KC.

He stared at his wrist and couldn't understand why he was unable to read the time, until he remembered that he had left the villa in such a rush that he hadn't put on his watch. What time was it in Siena? He didn't dare turn around to search for a clock. It was safer to keep his back to the corridor. That way he could pretend he wasn't in a hospital. That way he could forget that Erik wasn't one floor up, attached to tubes and wires and God knows what-all else. No, he couldn't forget.

What was it he was going to do? Oh yeah. Call KC to tell her about Erik. Was it too late to call Canada? Too early? His mind refused to calculate the time difference, just as it refused to tell him whether KC was in Wolfville or whether Britta had been admitted to the VG in Halifax. He knew Erik had told him — was it only yesterday? But yesterday was more than a lifetime ago. As for tomorrow, it didn't bear thinking about. Erik would still have AIDS tomorrow. Would he? Was Erik going to die? Was he?

He leaned into the pay phone, gripping the receiver. The tears, held back for so long, would be held back no longer.

29

Erik opened his right eye a slit. Bernie had fallen asleep in the bedside chair, his head tilted back at an uncomfortable angle and his glasses reflecting the room's only light, the green flicker from the monitor. Bernie shifted in his seat and for an instant Erik feared that he would slip onto the floor, but he righted himself at the last minute, wrapping his arms around his chest in an awkward hug.

"I love you, Bernie Freed," Erik mouthed, then let his eye fall shut. It took too much effort to keep it open, even minimally.

On one of her recent rounds, the nurse had tried to persuade Bernie to return to Montalcino or find a room in Siena. Bernie had refused to leave Erik's side. The nurse hadn't argued, for which Erik was grateful, though he had only been half-aware of the conversation. Just knowing Bernie was in the room made him less panicky. And he was plenty panicked.

"Dear God," Erik prayed silently. "It's been a long time…not since the last time Anders tried to make me talk to you. He called it praying. It sure didn't feel like what I thought praying ought to be. So I stopped. I stopped believing, too.

"I don't know that I ever started again, which means that there's a real good chance I'm just talking to myself. But if you're the kind of God I'd like to think exists, you won't mind. I'm pretty sure you also won't mind if I don't get on my knees by the side of the bed, like Anders used to make me. Even without all these tubes and shit, I don't think I'd have the strength. And Bernie would kill me if I tried. Bad choice of words.

"One thing I'm thinking that you might mind is that I don't call my father Daddy or Dad or Father. Isn't there a Commandment about that? But honor is a two-way street, and if you're as all-knowing as you're cracked up to be, you'll know that Anders was never much of a father and didn't earn a whole lot of honor.

"Can you wait a sec? The nurse has something for me. It's to help me sleep, she says, so if I doze off in the middle of this, please don't take it personally…

"She's gone. This time she made Bernie go. Not for good. Just to get something to eat and some real sleep. He's been in here with me practically the whole time, holding my hand and talking to me, even when he hasn't been sure I've been awake enough to hear. It's stressful to be in any hospital. It's worse in a foreign country where not everyone speaks your language.

"Thank God (oh, that's you), there's been no drama about us being a couple, about Bernie staying here in the room long past normal visiting hours. So that's not why they sent him away. If he's going to be able to take care of me, the nurse said, he needs his strength. I don't know where they sent him, but he promised that he wouldn't be far and that he'd be back really soon. Then he kissed me and left.

"I'm alone. The sleeping stuff hasn't kicked in yet. I'm alone and I'm scared. I'm so scared, God. I've never been this scared in my life. Not ever. I'm not even thirty and I may be dying. That's just too goddamn young to die, pardon my language. I know there are guys younger than me dying…guys who never really had a chance to live. Like Calvin. Poor Calvin. I could have loved him, if he'd let me. If he'd let himself be loved. If he'd let himself love himself.

"I know I'm luckier than the Calvins of the world. I'm only twenty-seven, but I've lived. I've loved too. I do love. I love Bernie so much, God. I don't know that I've ever loved anyone or anything as much as I love Bernie. My family, sure. That's a different kind of love.

"So I'm scared, God. I'm scared that all that's about to end. I'm scared for me. I'm more scared for Bernie.

"I don't know how I got this. There's been no one else since Bernie. I know I didn't get it from him because I know he would die before he would betray me. Bad choice of words again. But I feel the same way. If my dying would save Bernie, I'd tell you to take me right now. But you probably aren't there and if you are, I'm pretty sure you aren't some kind of heavenly Monty Hall. I'm pretty sure you don't make deals.

"The doctor said I could have been carrying this for a while, which means I could have been infected the first time I had sex. Which means I could have been some sort of Typhoid Mary all these years. Which means I could have infected everyone I ever slept with. Including Bernie.

"Oh God. Don't let me have given Bernie AIDS. I could stand anything except that. Because if he's got it, it's me that gave it to him. I don't know that I could live with that. I don't know that I'd want to live with that.

"The doctor tried to tell me that AIDS doesn't have to kill me. They've given me drugs for the pneumonia and he said that there are drugs they can give me to help me stay alive, if I can tolerate them. But you and me both know, God, that there's no cure for this, that whatever they give me will keep me going...but only for a while. I want longer than that. I want what I have with Bernie to keep going and going and going and going some more, until we're a pair of half-deaf, half-blind, curmudgeonly old queens cackling about the good old days from our rocking chairs in the old queers home. I want that more than I want anything else, even more than my art...and you know how much my art means to me. I want those years, those decades, that lifetime.

"If I can't have that, I'll take 'for a while,' if you'll give it to me.

"I know this isn't much of a prayer, but I'm not convinced that you're much of a God. So we're square. If you are there and if you are listening and if you do have it in your power to answer prayers, please answer mine. Please keep Bernie safe and please let me have as much time with him as possible.

"They say God is love. If that's true, then my love for Bernie — our love for each other — is God. If that's true, I do believe in you, God. With all my heart.

"I'm fading. The sleeping drugs must be kicking in. If you are God, please stick around. I could use the help. If you aren't, well...I..."

After weeks of relentless fog and drizzle, the sun could hide its face no longer. When I awoke this morning, it was streaming through the bedroom window as if to proclaim, "I have returned. Did you miss me?"

Indeed I had. I have spent close to a century in this city, yet I have never grown accustomed to the pall of gloom that shrouds it for much of the year. How often through the decades was I tempted to abandon this pit of meteorological melancholy for the eternal glow of Tuscany or the golden sands of the Riviera? How often did I have an estate agent around to discuss selling up? How often did I travel to the Continent to explore the possibility of crossing the Channel for good? Each time, I would awake the next morning, as I did this one, gaze out my window toward Fitzroy Square Garden in the height of its emerald iridescence and know that I could never leave.

But in spite of all temptations
To belong to other nations
He remains an Englishman

H.M.S. Pinafore *may be meaningless piffle, but that lyric of Gilbert's incontestably captures my character. Like it or not, I remain an English-woman, and a diehard Londoner at that. If the noxious fogs before the war, the Blitz during the war and a lifetime of bone-chilling damp and dreary skies have not forced me into exile, nothing will.*

After breakfast, Jeremy and I filled a thermos flask with tea, collected the coveted key from the top drawer of the front hall table, stepped out of the house into the uncommon sunshine and crossed the road into Fitzroy Square Garden.

By rights, I should not possess a copy of that key, nor should I be permitted unrestricted access to the garden, which is the exclusive domain of those who live on the square. My terrace house is as near to the square as it is possible to be without bearing a Fitzroy Square address. Yet it might as well be in Dorking for all the difference that would customarily make. If you lack a Fitzroy Square address, you are not part owner of the garden. And if you are not part owner of the garden, all you are permitted to do is peer enviously through the wrought iron rail at the forbidden lands on the other side.

All that changed last month, at least for Jeremy and me, when I was named an honorary Fitzroy Square addressee and presented with this key.

I have steadfastly maintained that my unwavering support of the arts has conferred upon me innumerable benefits. Little could I know that privileged access to Fitzroy Square Garden would ever be among them, thanks, in this instance, to Naomi Blake.

Naomi and I met not long after she arrived in London, while she was studying at the Hornsey School of Art, and I was immediately struck by her courage, her spirit, her optimism and, of course, her talent. After I purchased one of her early sculptural pieces, we became friends, and she and Asher would often come by the house for dinner.

I had them over at New Year's this year, when I introduced her to Major Bellamy Musgrave, a Fitzroy Square neighbor who had just been tasked with commissioning a sculpture for the garden in honor of the Queen's Silver Jubilee. The Major and his committee wanted Naomi. Naomi, however, insisted that she was too busy to be able to give such an important commission the attention it deserved and turned them down. I talked her into changing her mind, and the garden key was my reward.

With any luck, I shall be both alive and sufficiently compos mentis to enjoy the fruits of my lobbying when Naomi's sculpture is unveiled in three years' time. For now, I am grateful to be able enjoy pleasures so long denied me, especially on a day like this one, with its all-too-rare color and light.

The weather was so ideal that Jeremy and I sat on a bench overlooking the future site of Naomi's sculpture for hours. When the thermos flask was empty, I sent him home for a refill. He returned fifteen minutes later with more than tea: he carried a brown paper bag filled with buttered teacakes, which we shared with the squirrels, pigeons and, eventually, Major Musgrave. Next time, we shall bring a chilled bottle of Sancerre!

1989
LONDON

30

At the beginning, after the pneumonia, after Sylvie had been dispatched to Italy to bring Erik and Bernie back to London, after it became clear that the drugs that might keep him alive only made him sicker, Erik plunged into a listless despair. He spent long hours in bed, took solitary walks and said little, even to Bernie. He was already depressed that he hadn't been able to paint for months. If he wasn't going to live anyhow, why put any more energy into it, or into anything else? The only bright light — more an absence of dark, really — was that Bernie's blood test had revealed no HIV. Yet Erik still had AIDS and, now, little possibility of treatment. What was the point of…of anything?

One thing was clear: If he couldn't paint, if he had no reason to paint, there could be no art show come October. Erik had wanted to call Jeffrey and Pierre immediately to cancel, but Bernie made him promise to wait until they were in London. Maybe getting out of Italy would help. Maybe Mac could help. Maybe there were drugs in London that the doctors in Siena didn't know about. Maybe there would be a miracle.

Erik no longer believed in miracles. He kept his promise…barely. While Sylvie paid the cabbie and Bernie unloaded their bags — their art supplies had been shipped to London and would arrive in a few days — Erik marched into the house and straight to the telephone, indifferent to the five-hour time difference. It was close to midnight in Montreal.

"Cancel the show," he ordered when a groggy Pierre answered, not bothering to say hello.

"Nothing doing," Pierre replied.

While still in Italy, Bernie had warned Jeffrey and Pierre that this call might come. "If you guys want me to let him back out, I will," Bernie offered. "It's your gallery and it's your decision."

Jeffrey and Pierre had refused. Erik wasn't the first of their artists to be paralyzed with fear over an upcoming show. He also wasn't the first to give up in despair over an AIDS diagnosis. "If you can get Erik to paint and if you can get whatever he paints to us," Jeffrey said, "we'll hang it, no matter what it is."

Now that Erik's call had come, the gallery owners were as determined as ever to go on with the show.

"I haven't painted anything," Erik argued. "And now…" He left the sentence unfinished.

"Now you will," Pierre insisted.

Yet he couldn't see how he would.

In those final days in Montalcino, nothing Bernie could say would persuade him to pick up a brush or sketch pencil. Now that he was in London, Mac would have no better luck. It would take Sadie to get Erik painting again and Sarah to get him to recommit to the show.

31

For three weeks, Sadie watched Erik brood. He spent most of his time in the bedroom she had surrendered to him and Bernie and spoke in little more than monosyllabic grunts when he came downstairs for meals. Gone were his trademark playfulness and breezy optimism. Not that she expected a dying young man to be cracking jokes all the time. Yet Sadie had spent too much of her life steeped in gloomy cynicism not to recognize its corrosive effects in someone else. Instead of trying to make some sort of peace with his situation, Erik seemed trapped in a morass of self-pity. Instead of making the most of whatever time he had left, he was squandering it in apathy and inertia.

What could she do? How could she succeed where Bernie and Mac had failed? Who was she to try?

"You're Sadie Finkel, that's who," she declared one sunny morning as she watched Erik leave the house on his own, his arms tightly crossed and his chin tucked into his chest. He had again rejected Bernie's offer to join him.

Erik stood on the pavement for a moment, looking neither left nor right, then shuffled diagonally across the road to the iron gate, unlocked it and disappeared inside Fitzroy Square Garden. A few minutes later, Sadie threw on a coat and followed him.

Once inside the garden, Erik shoved his hands into the pockets of his windbreaker and gazed up into a plane tree where two sparrows were chasing each other from one skeletal branch to the next. The birds didn't know that it wasn't spring yet, just like the buds on the trees and shrubs had been fooled into revealing themselves by the unseasonably warm weather. It was March. It would get cold again. Then all those buds would die. *Like me.* He walked on.

It was easy for Sadie to catch up with Erik. When she did, she walked alongside him in silence, gathering her thoughts and her courage. After their third circuit, Erik stopped in front of *View*, the Henry Moore-like sculpture that stood at the center of the park.

"Do you know this Naomi Blake's work?" Sadie asked.

Erik nodded. Taking advantage of Emmeline's friendship with Blake, Mac had invited her to speak at NSCAD when Erik was a student there. The sculptor had described her open, flowing shapes as expressions of hope in the face of the horrors she had experienced in the Holocaust: She had survived Auschwitz; most of her family had not. Blake even included an image of *View* among the slides she had shown. How odd that Erik should find himself living across the road from it. Dying across the road from it.

"I don't like this kind of art," Sadie said. "Not normally. It's because I like to know what I'm seeing. The angel across from Fletcher's Field: That I understand. Or the statue in Philips Square. I look at it and I see Edward VII keeping an eye on The Bay where I used to work. Or the ones in Dominion Square. You've got horses. You've got men. You've got a lion. What could be clearer than that? Then I look into your friends' gallery in Westmount..." She shrugged. "It's because I'm afraid I'll get it wrong, I think. Oh, I know Bernie and Mac say there's no wrong. Miss Savage told us that all those years ago. I didn't believe her then. I'm not sure I believe Mac and Bernie now.

"But this." She pointed to *View*. "This I think understand." She winked. "Even if I cheated."

Erik smiled in spite of himself. "Cheated?"

"I researched her last time I went to the library." Sadie paused. "She saw so much, this Naomi Blake. She lost so much. As hard as my life has been, I can't imagine how she could keep going, how she didn't get all hard and bitter like I got. And my life wasn't anything as bad as hers."

Erik kept his eyes trained on the sculpture. "You aren't very subtle," he said softly.

"I'm too old to be subtle," Sadie began, hesitated, then plunged ahead while she still dared. "I know I got no right to talk to you like this..." She waited for Erik to give her permission to go on, though she knew it wouldn't come. "I've lived a lot of years, Erik, and I've wasted most of them. So many things I could have done and been if I wasn't so busy being so angry, if I wasn't so busy being poor Sadie. It's different now. You read Sarah's book, right?"

"As soon it came out."

"That wasn't the only thing that changed my life for me. But it was a big part of it. A— What do you call it?" She struggled for the word. "A catalyst. That's it. It was when Sarah said that it's never too late to follow your dreams. It was when I saw how Sarah followed hers. Bernie, also, because Bernie didn't even know he had dreams."

"But—" Erik's eyes were wet. He dried them with the back of his hand.

"I know what you're going to say, boychik," Sadie interrupted. "You're going to say that you had dreams you knew about and now that you're going to die, those dreams don't matter anymore."

"They don't. How can they?" Erik was crying.

Sadie put her arm around him. "We're all going to die, Erik. The only difference between you and me is that you know it. Really know it." She touched his heart. "In here, you know it."

"I don't understand."

"I don't know what it's like to be young and to see time running out in front of your nose. I know it can't feel like any kind of gift. But it is a gift. It's the gift of today. It's a gift that tells you that if there's something you want to do or be, you'd better do it today, because one day there won't be a tomorrow." She stepped back. "Look at me," she said. Even an alteh machashaifeh like me who knows she's got more years behind her than ahead of her keeps putting things off, important things." *Like this conversation, for instance.*

"I'm not sure anything's important anymore," Erik murmured.

"A boy who worships you. That's not important?"

"All I'm doing is hurting him."

"Not as bad as you're hurting yourself."

Erik said nothing.

"Forget Bernie for a minute," Sadie said. "Let's talk about Naomi Blake over here." She tilted her head at the sculpture. "This Naomi Blake went through a lot of bad things. Really bad things. Hellish things. So what did she do? Not like what Sadie Finkel did. She made art that helps people keep living…that helped *her* to keep living. Isn't that what you artists do?"

"We already we agreed that I'm not living," Erik argued. "I'm dying."

"That's not what I said and you know it," Sadie retorted.

Erik turned away.

Damn. Sadie took a deep breath and touched Erik's shoulder. "Sometimes, the old Sadie gets out before I can stop her," she said.

"It's okay." Yet it wasn't. This was not a conversation Erik wanted to be having. He just wanted to be left alone.

Don't ever give up on your art, and your art will never give up on you. It was Naomi Blake's voice, whispered across the Atlantic and across the years in response to a question Erik forgot that he had asked her at the end of her NSCAD presentation. "With my past," Blake had said, "it would have been easy to be pessimistic, to give up on life. I chose to use my art to find my optimism, to find my hope, to find life."

"I have one more thing to tell you," Sadie was saying, "then I'll shut up. I promise. Everyone tells me you're a good artist. Maybe a great one. Not in twenty years or thirty or forty years. Right now. Your dream is already happening. Not the way you hoped or expected. But it's still happening."

Erik moved toward *View* and stroked its bronze-resin surface. He thought about Naomi Blake, about the life that she hadn't expected to have, about the art that that life had produced. What had been young Naomi's dreams? How had they changed? How had they changed her? He wished he would have thought to ask her that.

Sadie joined him at the sculpture. "That dream of yours," she said. "What if you used it to stop dying and start living? Not as who you used to be before this AIDS happened to you. Not as you maybe wish you could be living. As who you are, today. Like this Naomi Blake does. What if?"

What if? Could he do it? He hadn't painted in nearly four months, not since before he and Bernie left Montreal for Italy. He didn't count Pisa. That wasn't his art. That was painting from another artist's sketches. Had it been only four months? It felt like a lifetime. Too many lifetimes. He touched his face. Furrows etched his once-smooth forehead and frown lines framed his mouth. His eyes, if he could see them, would be bloodshot, from a combination of sleepless nights and tear-filled days. He tried to recall the Erik he had been in the weeks leading up to their arrival in Tuscany. That Erik was joyful, exuberant, carefree. That Erik was buoyant, excited, enthusiastic. That Erik was painting. That Erik wasn't dying.

Four months without setting paint to canvas, without touching charcoal to sketchpad: It had to be the longest he had ever gone without making some sort of art. Even as a kid he was constantly creating. When he wasn't pressing a crayon into a coloring book — always *outside* the lines to his father's dismay — his pudgy fingers were either soaked with finger paints or fashioning brightly colored Plasticine into intricate, abstract shapes.

What had changed? It wasn't the fact that he had AIDS. His artist's block kicked in as soon he and Bernie got to Europe. He hadn't tried to paint again since Siena…since the hospital. Could Sadie be right? Could it be time to try again? He stared through the opening at the center of *View* toward 33 Fitzroy Street. He would try.

32

The jangling phone jerked Sarah out of the hypnotic trance induced by her flashing cursor. She forced herself out of 1929 Bognor Regis and back into 1989 London. Pity. She had been enjoying the idea of having Emmeline heap scorn on the seaside resort because of the royal recuperation that was ruining her holiday. "Bugger Bognor," she was considering having Emmeline blurt out in exasperation. Apparently, that had been George V's response to his time in the area.

The phone rang again. Some days, she wished that Alexander Graham Bell had never left Edinburgh. Then he might not have invented the telephone. *Why is no one answering?* Then she remembered. Sadie was a twenty-minute walk away on Marylebone Lane, at Le Cordon Bleu no less. Who could have imagined Sadie Finkel from Clark Street taking classes at a fancy French cooking school in London, England? *Not me.* Sylvie and Bernie had gone to the Tate's Clore Gallery to explore its Turner collection. Mac was bundled up against the April damp in Fitzroy Square Garden. As for Erik, he was painting again, thank God. He never answered the phone when he was painting, though. "I don't hear it," he had told her. *I should be so lucky.*

Another ring. *Maybe they'll hang up?* They didn't.

"An answering machine: That's what this house needs," Sarah grumbled as she hurried into the next room, the location of the only phone on that floor. Ironically, it was her bedroom. It was still ringing when she got there. *Don't these people ever give up?*

"This is Canada House calling for Marc-Allan Cameron," an officious secretarial voice announced. "Is Mr. Cameron at home?"

"Canada House?" Sarah asked. "What's this Canada House? Where in Canada are you calling from?"

"This is the Canadian High Commission calling, madam," the voice explained with forced patience. "From London."

"Oh. I see." Sarah sat on the edge of her bed. "Why didn't you say so? Like the embassy?"

"Yes, madam," the voice sighed. "Like the embassy. Is Mr. Cameron available? High Commissioner Macdonald would like to speak to him."

"High Commissioner? Like the ambassador?"

"Yes, madam." The voice grew condescending. "Like the ambassador."

Sarah pinched her nose and raised the pitch of her voice. "I shall see if Mr. Cameron is taking calls at present, meddam. Will you hold the, ah, wire?"

She dropped the receiver onto the table and threw on a sweater. "Snotty bitch," she muttered as she ran down the stairs, out the door and across the road to fetch Mac.

*S*ir Benjamin knocked on our door this evening. He claimed to have been in the neighborhood. However, I am convinced that Jeremy organized this suspicious "happenstance," as he has on previous occasions.

Although Jeremy and Sir Benjamin are aware that I see through their charade, I pretend not to. I invite him into the front room, offer him a glass of fifteen-year-old Glenfiddich, inquire after the health of Lady Alice and invite him to recount the latest escapades of the "Barnetticles," as I have dubbed his surfeit of offspring. After a polite interval, Sir Benjamin casually asks "how I'm getting on," an Americanism he picked up during his medical studies at Harvard. I reply, as I always do, that I am thriving. He nods with ersatz enthusiasm and mentions, almost too casually, that he has his medical kit with him. Would I care for him to have a quick look-see? I have learned that it is pointless to say no. So I mutter, with a grimace, "How kind."

This evening proceeded according to the established ritual. After poking and prodding and taking the usual "vitals," Sir Benjamin declared me to be surprisingly fit, "for an older person." I told him that were he ever again to utter the phrase "for an older person" in my presence, I would knock him down. "You know I could," I cautioned, "and you know I would."

"Indeed," he replied with the faintest suggestion of a grin. Sir Benjamin stands a head and a half shorter than I, and if not for his generous girth — he must weigh at least twenty stone — I could easily have acted as I had threatened.

I did not threaten Jeremy with GBH when he proposed installing a stair lift, even if I was tempted. He made the suggestion after Sir Benjamin left, when I stumbled on my way up to this "writing studio." I know that I am an "older person." I know that my bones are brittle enough that a single misstep could easily be my last. I know, too, that a stair lift might ease my trips up and down, trips that feel more like treks with each passing day. I know as *well that to submit to these so-called realities will serve only to accelerate them. What is that line from* Lost Horizon? *Oh, yes: "Age is a limit we impose upon ourselves."*

Let Sir Benjamin speak my age, if my health and agility must be expressed in relative terms. I have no reticence when it comes to acknowledging the ninety-two years and some months I have occupied one version or another of this body. Having outlived most of my contemporaries, my age is an accomplishment to be celebrated, not an embarrassment to be hidden away. If he is as fortunate as I have been, he will come to know that fact sooner than he realizes.

I was kinder in my rebuke to Jeremy. I know he is right, and he knows that I know. I shall wait until after my next birthday, if I can, to wave that particular white flag. Until then, the banister will be the friend I need to get me to this room and to these pages, whose escalating value in my life continues to astonish me.

33

Erik stepped back from the completed canvas and scowled. "You have got to be the worst piece of shit I've ever painted," he muttered. "I should cut you into ribbons and dump you into the garbage with the kitchen scraps." He surveyed the attic studio for something sharp enough to pierce the canvas. "Lucky for you my palette knife's blunt, and it's four flights down to one of Sadie's carving knives. Otherwise…"

He frowned at the jumbled mass of black and umber tentacles glaring back at him, each grasping for something it could not reach. "What's the word Sarah uses all the time? Shreklekh." He pronounced it shrek-lick. "You," he charged, "are more shreklekh than shreklekh." Wiping the paint from his hands, he turned away from the easel.

I'm more shreklekh than shreklekh. I'm not an artist anymore. Maybe it's a good thing I'm dying. His eyes welled with tears. *I thought I'd found my art again. If I haven't, if I've really lost it now, what am I?*

Out the window, Naomi Blake's *View* was barely visible through the still-naked latticework of tree limbs in Fitzroy Square Garden. "Have you ever hated your work so much that you wanted to give up?" he whispered across to the sculpture. "Have you ever hated your life so much that you wanted to give up?" He gazed back at his painting. "Have you ever been so scared that you wanted to give up?"

She must have been. How could she have experienced Auschwitz and not have been?

"I hate this," Erik wanted to shout. He didn't dare. He didn't want Bernie to hear. Instead, he wiped his eyes on his sleeve and slunk out of the studio. He would clean up later. One last time.

34

"Aren't you going to ask why I invited you to lunch?" Mac inquired as he and Sarah turned south on Tottenham Court Road from Warren Street.

"I don't get so many invitations from handsome bachelors that I can afford to be so inquisitive," Sarah quipped, then turned serious. "You've been acting strange since that call from your Highfalutin' Commissioner the other day. It's that, isn't it. Not about Erik or Bernie?"

Mac pulled open the door to Caffè Nero and followed Sarah inside. The Italian-style restaurant with its exposed-brick walls and plank floors was a favorite getaway for the residents of 33 Fitzroy Street. A three-minute walk from the house, it served up a delectable array of salads, sandwiches, pastries and desserts. And better espresso than Sadie could prepare, although she was approaching Caffè Nero's standard, thanks to the Gaggia that Mac had purchased for the house.

"Let's order first," Mac said as they stepped up to the counter. "The usual?"

Sarah studied the menu as she always did, then chose the Il Milanese panini and a raspberry Italian soda, as she always did. "What could be better than salami and cream cheese?" she asked. In addition to thinly sliced Milano salami, grilled peppers, arugula and Regato cheese, the ciabatta roll was stuffed with creamy mascarpone. Mac had little appetite and settled for a cup of carrot soup.

The early morning's dreary dribble of a rain shower, which had acted as if it might continue for days, had melted away, replaced by cotton-puff clouds, a cerulean sky and a noonday sun that cast enough warmth to allow Mac and Sarah to sit outside at one of the cafe's sidewalk tables. They watched the street's lunchtime parade of pedestrians in silence until their food arrived. Once it did, Mac stirred his soup distractedly but said nothing. Sarah eyed him through her first few bites then set her sandwich down on the plate, wiped her mouth and rapped the table with her fist.

"Knock, knock, Mr. Mac," she said. "Anyone home?"

Mac looked up. "I'm sorry, Sarah. I have a lot on my mind."

"Which is why I'm here, no?"

"Yes."

"Are you going to play with your soup?" Sarah asked. "Or are you going to talk?"

"You eat," Mac said. "I'll talk." He pushed his soup bowl aside. "Did Bernie ever tell you that I turned down a commission to paint a new portrait of the Queen?"

Sarah gaped at him and shook her head.

"That was a couple of years ago, and everyone was as shocked as you are."

"Such an honor you would turn down? Why?"

"I'll come back to that. When I was in Montreal in October for my surprise birthday party—"

"You knew about that?" Sarah interjected. "How could you know about that? It was supposed to be a state secret."

"State secrets sometimes get leaked," he replied dryly, "but that's another story." He went on to tell her about the call he had received at the Ritz-Carlton from Pierre Elliott Trudeau asking if he might be open to reconsidering his refusal of the earlier commission. "Jeremy's death saved me from having to answer, at least right away." Mac slurped a spoonful of now-cold soup. "No one was supposed to know that I was staying on in London. That was also a poorly kept state secret. Buckingham Palace tracked me down and asked Donald Macdonald, your Highfalutin' Commissioner, to call me."

"You'd better say yes this time," Sarah joked, "or she'll have your head chopped off. The Queen, I mean."

Mac laughed. "I don't think they do that anymore."

"Not after one rejection. Not after one rejection and one vanishing act." Sarah's eyes twinkled. "But after a second rejection? Are you sure you want to risk it? What did you say?"

"I told Macdonald about Erik and that I needed some time." He dipped his spoon into the soup and left it there.

"That kind of time, I'm sure they'll give you." Sarah thought for a moment. "There's more to this, isn't there."

Mac sighed. "It's simple," he said. "I don't think I'm good enough," he added so softly that Sarah wasn't sure she had heard him right over the traffic noise. "That's the real reason I turned it down the first time."

"Not good enough?" she repeated dubiously. "This is Marc-Allan Cameron I'm sitting with, right? Not some phony baloney? You can't be serious."

Mac didn't answer.

"You're serious."

"I'm serious," he said. "I'm not a portraitist. I paint abstracts." Sarah opened her mouth but Mac cut her off. "I know what you're thinking: Esther's portrait. I could paint Esther because I loved her. It still took me decades. It still took Bernie showing up for me to be able to do it." He pulled a shiny one-pound coin from his pocket and flipped it over to the bust of the Queen. "I'm no Raphael Maklouf," he said of the sculptor responsible for Elizabeth's likeness.

"If they wanted a Raphael Maklouf, they would have asked for one," Sarah said. "They wanted a Marc-Allan Cameron. They *want* a Marc-Allan Cameron. They want you."

"I'm terrified."

Sarah hadn't heard him over the sound of a passing No. 24 bus, but she knew what he had whispered. "Now you know how I felt when you asked me to write this Emmeline novel," she said when the double-decker had lumbered by. "But I'm doing it. I'm doing it *because* I'm dershrokn, because I'm terrified like you, because I spent too many years not doing because I was afraid. I figure if I'm going to be scared either way, I might as well have something to show for it."

"I—" Mac began.

"Now it's my turn to do an 'I know what you're thinking,'" Sarah interrupted. "You're thinking it isn't a good comparison. That this is the Queen we're talking about. That this is Marc-Allan Cameron, the celebrity artist who's on a first-name basis with Pierre Elliott Trudeau we're talking about. That we aren't talking about some two-bit unknown author from Kensington Avenue in Westmount who's not on a first-name basis with anyone important, except for you."

"I wasn't going to say that," Mac argued.

"Only because you're polite. It doesn't matter. My fear is as big for me as yours is for you. Here's something else you won't like, but you threw it at me, so I'm going to throw it right back at you: What would Esther say? You don't have to answer because I know what Esther would say and so do you. I'm not playing fair anyhow, so here's one more: You don't only owe it to Esther, to yourself and to England and the entire Commonwealth that's going to get to enjoy your picture. You owe it to Emmeline and to your son. You owe it to Erik, too. He needs every role model for courage that he can find right now, and I can't think of a better one than you."

A speechless Mac stared at Sarah as she bit into her sandwich, chewed slowly then swallowed.

"The Queen, she's okay to wait a bit, because of Erik?"

Mac nodded.

"Then you're going to say yes. Yes?"

Mac threw his hands into the air in surrender. "Yes."

35

A week after he had been ready to give up, Erik was still painting. Whatever else it was — and art, he insisted, it was not — it was a form of therapy. All his bitterness, rage and terror had finally found an outlet.

Erik would climb to the attic studio first thing after breakfast each morning and stand in front of the easel for hours, breaking only for lunch. He paid little attention to what he was hurling at the canvas, less to what was taking shape on it. If he had not been concerned about slopping paint all over the walls and floor, he would have been just as happy lobbing gobs of acrylics at it with his eyes closed.

Once upon a time Erik had been self-conscious about painting while others were in the room with him. It didn't matter whether or not they were watching. That had been his biggest struggle in art school. Meeting Bernie changed that. Through their four years together in Nova Scotia, they had often painted together. Things were different now. Bernie was not painting at all and Erik was afraid to ask why, in case Bernie wanted to join him in the studio. He wasn't keen on Mac's presence either, or Sylvie's. He didn't care if Sarah or Sadie watched; they didn't know enough about art to judge what he was doing. Not that they ever came up to the studio. Although curious, both women were reluctant to do anything that might stunt Erik's renewed creative interest.

"Creative? I could be slinging pea soup at the wall or pitching Emmeline's best china out the window," Erik told them. "It's all the same thing, and it's cheaper than a shrink."

When Bernie mustered the nerve to ask to see what he was

painting, Erik wasn't keen. "I'd rather you didn't discover what a god-awful artist I've become, but you'll find out sooner or later. Might as well be sooner. Go ahead. Just don't expect me to go up with you. I already know how bad it is."

36

Bernie's hand hovered over the doorknob. *Am I doing the right thing? What if it really is as bad as Erik says?* He nudged the door open to the darkened room. *It can't be.* He reached for the light switch. *Can it?*

An hour later, Bernie tiptoed down the stairs. He didn't want Erik to hear him passing their bedroom instead of coming right in. He didn't want Erik to hear where he was going. When Bernie reached the front room, where Mac and Sarah were comparing the exploits of the real-life Emmeline with those of her fictional counterpart, he insisted that Mac accompany him back up to the attic. Stealthily.

"Is it just me?" Bernie whispered when they were standing together in front of Erik's paintings. "Or is this the absolute best work Erik has ever done?" Erik may have been two flights below, but Bernie didn't want to risk being overheard.

Mac's eyes traveled from canvas to canvas. There were three completed pictures and a fourth in-progress. Next to the twisted tentacles of Erik's first was a demonic abstract: a frame of rough, black brushstrokes encasing a fiery stew of boiling orange and red. The adjacent easel held what appeared to be a bird's nest composed of ragged, corkscrew twists and filled with mucus-colored eyes, nearly fluorescent in hue and each a different geometric shape. Leaning against the wall on the other side of the room was the most disturbing of the grouping: a massive single blob of dripping blood-red into which Erik had chipped out a jagged, irregularly shaped opening. The unfinished piece consisted of a giant, off-kilter X that was constructed from dozens of tiny dotted lines, each a different color. Not one of the paintings resembled anything of Erik's that Mac had ever seen.

"He hates them all," Bernie said.

Mac's gaze was locked on the nest of eyes. "He must."

"Oh," Bernie sighed, his voice tinged with disappointment. "You mean he's right?"

"Not remotely." Mac reluctantly pulled his focus from the painting. "Here's one of the things I always told my students at NSCAD. Erik would have heard me say something like this a dozen times. I must have said it to you at some point, too. It's that when we create from the deepest parts of ourselves, from those places we have never created from, from those places we barely know exist within us, from those places we dare not acknowledge exist within us, the result can be so terrifyingly unfamiliar that it's easy to assume that it's horrible. Shameful, even. We're almost compelled to assume that it is because if we don't, then we have to admit that what we painted, that what we created *is* a real part of us. It's easier to dismiss it. It's easier to judge it. It's easier and it's safer."

Mac moved from one painting to the next, remaining in front of each for a full five minutes. "These are brilliant," he said. "They're not only Erik's best ever. They're among the most gut-wrenchingly genuine I have ever seen from someone his age."

"He won't believe it," Bernie said sadly.

"Not right away. Perhaps in time." Mac followed Bernie out to the landing.

"If he has that much time," Bernie murmured. "Will you talk to him?" he asked.

Mac crossed the attic hall to his bedroom. "I'll find an excuse to drop in tomorrow while he's painting."

"Thank you." He started down the stairs, then turned back. "I'm scared for him, Mac." His voice trembled. "For me, too."

37

The ebony Daimler DS420 glided soundlessly to a halt in front of 33 Fitzroy Street. In the front passenger seat, Mac shook hands with the uniformed chauffeur and let himself out. He stood on the sidewalk, his normally wispy white hair combed neatly into place and his signature black t-shirt, jeans and sneakers replaced by a gray bespoke suit from Savile Row and a pair of tan Church's brogue Oxfords from Selfridge's. As the limousine continued to the end of the street and turned west on Euston Road for its short trip back to the Royal Mews, Mac turned in the opposite direction and continued along Fitzroy toward Soho and Chinatown. At Shaftesbury Avenue he made a slight jog to cross through Leicester Square and soon found himself near the end of Charing Cross Road, around the corner from The National Gallery and in front of the imposing Greek Classical facade that was the entrance to the National Portrait Gallery.

It seemed a fitting coda to his just-completed visit to Buckingham Palace. Fifty years earlier, the National Portrait Gallery had been his and Emmeline's first museum stop after the Tate exhibition that recast his life path to artist from retail-heir-to-be. Ironically, it was that same visit that persuaded him to avoid portraiture. It hadn't mattered to him at the time that the gallery's collection was more about the historical significance of its subjects than about the artistic merit of its paintings. The idea of having people sit in front of him for hours while he transferred their essence onto a canvas struck him as tedious. It was a cocky judgment, but he was twenty when he made it and in the years that followed, he never saw any reason to amend it. Even Esther's portrait, once he was finally able to begin it in earnest, was painted from memory.

Now that Mac had agreed to paint the world's most famous woman — and possibly its most fascinating — that long-ago pronouncement of his felt insolent and immature. And now that he had met Queen Elizabeth, if briefly, he no longer dreaded the commission. To his surprise, he found that he was looking forward to it, despite the fact that the magnitude of the undertaking now intimidated him even more.

After Sarah's pep talk with him at Caffè Nero and his with Erik a few days later, he had telephoned Donald Macdonald to let him know that he was ready to commit to the royal portrait. The next step had been that morning's meeting at the Palace with Sir William Heseltine, the Queen's principal private secretary, and then, unusually, a brief audience with Queen Elizabeth herself.

"She comes across as so formal when you see her on TV," Mac later told Sarah, "but she was surprisingly engaging, not at all formidable." He replayed the fifteen-minute encounter during which the Queen posed insightful questions about his art and even referred to his portrait of Esther. "It was after someone showed her a reproduction of *Queen Esther*," he explained, "that she asked for me again."

"Maybe you only do portraits of queens?" Sarah asked.

Mac laughed. "Maybe, or at least queens I like."

"You like her?" Sarah asked. "She's a mensch?"

"Definitely a mensch. I think she knew about the Erik situation. She didn't say anything directly but when he was seeing me out, Sir Michael gave me his card and told me to call when it would be convenient for me to start so that he could coordinate times for her sittings."

"She didn't threaten to have your head chopped off to get you to say yes?"

"She didn't have to. I knew that you'd have my head if I tried to get out of it a second time."

"Damn right," Sarah said.

Mac stepped past the National Portrait Gallery's ornate wrought-iron gates, across the elaborate mosaic on the pavement in front of the building and into the entrance hall. Ignoring the banners for "The Man Who Shot Garbo," the tribute to MGM photo-portraitist Clarence Sinclair Bull that had just opened, he made his way upstairs to the Royal Landing and Pietro Annigoni's monumental, nearly life-size 1969 portrait of the Queen.

The painting was as stark as he remembered it, with Elizabeth robed in scarlet against a spare, almost gloomy background: a potent symbol of remote majesty. That wasn't a criticism. Mac respected Annigoni and admired the portrait. However, Annigoni's Elizabeth was not the one he had met that morning. He had spent time with a woman, not with a symbol, and it was Elizabeth the woman who intrigued him, not Elizabeth the Queen.

No, that wasn't right. Not exactly. In his brief time with Elizabeth, Mac had sensed a tension between the woman and the Queen, between her humanity and her position. That was what he hoped to capture in his portrait. Somehow.

Sir Michael Heseltine had cautioned him that he might not be granted more than two or three sittings with Her Majesty. Mac would lobby for more, for the same eighteen that Annigoni had had. The portrait deserved it. So did the Queen.

38

Bernie let his head drop back against the azure-blue leather of his chair and stared up at a gold-ribbed dome that seemed as infinite as the heavens. If you wanted to be alone with your thoughts, the Reading Room at the British Museum was an ideal place to be. Sitting in this vast circular space, he thought, must be what it would feel like to be a single star in the night sky: surrounded by others, yet completely alone in an immense, soundless emptiness. "In the great circle of the library," Thomas Hardy had noted a few decades after the Reading Room opened, "Time is looking into Space." Bernie could understand why Hardy had viewed it that way: The Reading Room was like a universe of its own in a time zone of its own. He could also understand why so many writers had been drawn here, and not simply because of the twenty-five miles of book-stuffed shelving that comprised one of the most comprehensive research resources in the world, but for the awe that the library's interior inevitably inspired. "It seems to me one cannot sit down in that place without a heart full of grateful reverence," William Makepiece Thackeray wrote.

Obscure accounts of British Museum Reading Room experiences would not normally interest Bernie. However, he'd had too much time to fill in the weeks since he and Erik left Italy and he had spent most of it with Emmeline's books, the more esoteric the better. Of course he would prefer to be painting. Yet it had seemed cruel to flaunt his creative flow when Erik's was so blocked.

He felt freer now that Erik was painting again. The only problem was that Erik didn't want Bernie in the studio and there was nowhere else in the house suitable for easel, canvas and paints. Nor was he eager to shlep his art kit around town and set up in the street or in a park. Instead, he had taken to roaming the avenues of Bloomsbury with a sketchpad. When the weather refused to cooperate, he would spend the afternoon wandering through the British Museum.

Today's persistent drizzle had sent him inside to the mummies, funerary masks and other tomb artifacts of the Egyptian collection. When he'd had his fill of ghoulish voyeurism, he had sprinted across the central courtyard to avoid the rain and settled into the Reading Room.

Bernie returned his gaze to the pad on the library table in front of him. It didn't matter what he set out to draw on each of his outings, he ended up sketching Erik. Not today's Erik, his eyes hooded and his emotions veiled behind a perpetual frown, but the Erik he had first met at Galérie Cinq Arts: funny, flirty and with a grin that rarely left his face. Bernie was terrified that that Erik was gone forever, so he drew him again and again and again. He flipped open his pad, touched his pencil to a fresh page and began to draw him…again.

39

"We made a bargain," Sarah said. She held her cup of tea up to her face and observed Erik through the swirls of steam. She had bullied Mac into painting the Queen. Now it was time to work on Erik and his gallery show.

Erik shoveled bits of scrambled egg around his plate, saying nothing.

"I'm writing my book, like I promised you I would," she said. "What happened to your exhibition?" Sarah sipped the lemony brew and set the china cup back onto its saucer.

"I'm painting."

"So?"

He stabbed a morsel of cold egg, added a sliver of sausage to it and jammed the fork into his mouth. "Catharsis isn't art," he mumbled between chews, avoiding Sarah's gaze. Yes, he was painting. And yes, it made him feel better, some days. But it was drek. Drek was another one of Sarah's words and it fit perfectly. It meant shit.

Erik hadn't wanted anyone to see what he was painting up in the attic, but Bernie had asked. He should have said no. Now Mac had seen it, too. That was another mistake.

"Mac says it's good," Sarah said slowly. "Good enough to show." She didn't mention that Bernie had FedExed copies of Erik's finished pieces to Jeffrey and Pierre at Galérie Cinq Arts a few weeks earlier and that they were eager for more.

She didn't have to. Erik had spied the unsealed envelope on the hall table under some outgoing mail and peeked inside. He had said nothing to Bernie and, instead, telephoned the gallery. "I don't care if you want to show my stuff in October," he declared. "I don't want you to. It isn't for general consumption. It's just for me." What he really meant was that it would be embarrassing to have his self-indulgent dabblings made public. Every few days after that he called again, urging whichever partner answered the gallery phone to cancel the show. He was always turned down. "Fine," he muttered after hanging up on their most recent argument. "They can damn well exhibit their empty walls."

Erik slammed his fork down and glared at Sarah. "Mac's wrong."

Sarah sized him up with that look she had, the look he hated, the look that said "you're full of crap." He turned away.

"So, you're a bigger expert than Mr. Marc-Allan Cameron, world-renowned painter and Companion of the Order of Canada? You're a bigger expert than the only artist ever to say no to the Queen without getting his head chopped off?"

Erik piled the remaining bits of egg into a mound of yellow. He used to build mountains of food on his plate as a kid, until Anders smacked him on the side of the head for playing with what he ought to have been eating. He hadn't done it since.

"My Morty liked to make roads through his mashed potatoes with his fork," Sarah said softly. "It made Sammy crazy." She laughed. "Not that it took much. He was already that meshugena." Sarah watched him for a few minutes. "Can I be blunt?" she asked.

"You've never asked before," Erik snapped. "Why start now?"

Sarah ignored the outburst. Erik's personality had not undergone the dramatic shift that the doctor warned might result from the latest manifestation of his HIV, a condition she couldn't pronounce, something called progressive multifocal leukoencephalopathy or PML. But even if the fatal degenerative condition had yet to express itself that way, Erik was increasingly moody and volatile, not an unexpected reaction from someone in his situation. Still, the last thing Erik needed was to be coddled. Let Bernie do that. That wasn't Sarah's style.

"Let's say for the sake of argument that you're right and Mac's wrong," she said. "So what? So what if it isn't as good as you want it to be?"

"It matters," Erik whispered. "If it isn't good, it matters."

"Why? Why do you care?" *Do I dare?* She dared. "You'll be dead."

Erik's lip quivered.

Sarah reached across the table for his hand. "It's true, isn't it?"

Erik pulled his hand away and stared into his plate.

"You think I'm a klafte?" Sarah left her hand where it was. "That I'm turning into another Sadie?" She paused. "Hear me out before you decide."

Erik looked up.

"You won't be here in October for that show, will you?" she asked gently.

Erik started to shrug, then said, "Probably not."

"Does Bernie know?"

"Bernie acts like there's always going to be a tomorrow."

"That's normal," Sarah said, "especially at his age, even with you being sick. Even with losing other young friends like he has. Like you both have." She topped up her tea from the Brown Betty teapot and cradled the cup in her hands. "At my age," she said, "I've seen enough death to know that that's not how it works." Her eyes followed the steam as it spiraled up from the brew and dissipated into the dining room's frosted-glass light fixture before she continued. "I won't tell you how sorry I am. I think you know how sorry I am. Anyhow, talking like that changes nothing. I'm going to put my klafte hat back on for a minute. What do you say?" She set her cup down and again reached for Erik's hand. This time he took it.

"So you paint your paintings, you have your show and you watch from upstairs." She tilted her head heavenward. "I'm pretty sure it'll be upstairs. If it's good, you can kvell. 'Vos a talant,' you can say. 'What a great artist!' And if it's bad? If it's bad, you can make fun of all us shmegeggies for the suckers we are.

"I'm making a joke and maybe I shouldn't. Maybe it's nothing to be kibbitzing about. What I really mean is that you won't just be mucking around in the attic feeling sorry for yourself. You'll be doing something. *Something.* Something important, because you'll be doing it not just for you. You'll be doing it for all of us."

Erik opened his mouth to argue.

"Let me finish," she said. "You're going to tell me that what you're painting is worthless chazerai. You know it isn't. Not in your heart. What you're doing up there is what that Naomi Blake does. What you're doing is feeling for us what we're afraid to feel for ourselves. Then you're throwing it into our faces to force us to feel it. That's a good thing. I'm not saying it's an easy thing. Or a pretty thing. Or a comfortable thing. For you or for the rest of us. You once told me that art isn't about being comfortable. That art's about telling the truth. You're telling the truth up there in that attic. No, I haven't seen what's on your canvas. I don't need to see it to know that. I know you, and that's enough." She squeezed Erik's hand. "You know I'm right, don't you."

Erik burst into tears.

"I knew you did. You're just scared." With her free hand, Sarah pushed her tea across the table. "Drink this. Isn't that what the English do when they're upset?"

"I'm not English. I'm Norwegian." He tried to smile but couldn't. Instead, he picked up Sarah's cup and held it without drinking.

"So you'll do your show?"

Would he? Could he? Was he brave enough? He set the cup down and pulled a bright-red handkerchief from his pocket. "I don't know." He dried his eyes.

"You'll think about it?"

Erik stood and moved toward the door. He nodded once without turning around.

"Good," Sarah called after him. "Because you made a deal with me and it's binding. You don't want I should call Mac's Mr. Dunedin and sue, do you?"

Erik stopped. The glimmer of a grin played on his lips. He shook his head and left.

Jeremy would prefer that I never speak of my impending demise. "How do you know it is impending?" he asks some days. "Why must you assume it is impending?" he asks on others. "You ought not tempt the Fates," he implores on yet others.

This morning I told him that when he is ninety-two, he will also wake each morning grateful for the day, yet aware of Death's shadow hovering in the corner. I told him that at my age, the Fates need no tempting; they are too busy planning for unequivocal outcomes. I told him that I make no assumptions. Whether it is today, next week, next month or next year, the imminence of my demise is as assured as is tomorrow's sunrise. "It will come, and I shall go," I said. "That is the way of the world. There is no escaping it."

"When I am ninety-two," he retorted, "you shall be one hundred and forty-seven and even tetchier than you are today, although that hardly bears imagining." Then he kissed me.

Have I mentioned what a sentimental fool he is? Whether I have or not, I am certain to mention it again.

Jeremy may wish for me to go on indefinitely. I cannot imagine a more hellish prospect. "If I make it to one hundred," I replied, only half in jest, "you must take me out to the back garden and shoot me. I refuse to linger on into decrepitude." I tried to push myself up out of the bed, but my arms lacked the strength and I collapsed back onto the mattress. "Ninety-two is already bordering on excess," I muttered.

Over breakfast a while later, Jeremy dropped hints again about getting a stair lift installed. It is true that every day those blasted stairs feel more like a barrier, but I shall hold out as long as I can manage on my own, however haltingly. I know that Jeremy is terrified that I shall take a fall that will be as fatal as was Humpty Dumpty's. At my age, it is a distinct possibility. Yet as imminent as my death may be, I remain determined to live out my remaining time on my terms, not Death's. To my continuing astonishment, these writings are helping. I did not expect to look forward to setting pen to paper each day, sometimes multiple times each day. Strangely, I do. It is almost as though as long as I can write, I can continue to live. Who would have thought that I would ever have subscribed to anything as ridiculously metaphysical as that. Perhaps Jeremy is right. Perhaps if I continue with these "Emmeline Papers," I shall live to one hundred and forty-seven.

Note to Self: Not one word shall I write beyond the eve of my ninety-ninth birthday. No one hundred and forty-seven for me!

40

Sarah saluted the cursor on her Macintosh II. This time she wasn't intimidated by its insistent flashing. This time her screen wasn't blank. This time Kevin wasn't hovering over her shoulder, explaining that a mouse wasn't something you set traps for. To her amazement, she had grown to love the strange contraption. No more noisy, clunky keys. No more eraser smears or Liquid Paper smudges. No more scissors and tape. As long as she remembered to hit S and that key near the spacebar, the one with the apple and peculiar symbol on it, she was good.

"I loved that Smith-Corona," she had told Kevin at their final training session together, "but I'm never going back to it. Not ever. This is like magic!" Sure, she'd had to call him a few times since, when something popped up on the screen that she didn't understand. At the same time, no one was more surprised than she was at how quickly she had picked up not only the necessary basics of writing on a computer but some of MacWrite's more advanced features.

"You'll be giving courses yourself soon," Kevin joked as he handed her the mock business card he had created for her. "Sara Schumacher. Macintosh Maven," it read. "No H," he said, "just like on your book."

Sarah chuckled at the memory. She had given Kevin a signed copy of *Sara's Year* as a thank you present and he had called her a week later to tell her how much he had loved it and how much he was looking forward to *The Emmeline Papers*. "You'll for sure get a mention in the acknowledgments," she assured him.

Today, the flashing cursor was urging her to get back to the book.

That she wasn't had nothing to do with writer's block. *Emmeline* was progressing far more quickly than she could have imagined. No, she couldn't get her mind off the previous morning's conversation with Erik.

"Was I too hard on him?" she asked into the empty room. Only, it wasn't empty to her. Up in the corner, like the witch-ladies on that silly *Bewitched* television show she used to like to watch, sat Bernie's mother. Esther might have died four and half years earlier, yet she still talked to Sarah. If not for Esther, there would have been no *Sara's Year.* She wouldn't have had the chutzpah. And in the armchair by the fireplace, wrapped in her Hudson's Bay blanket, sat Emmeline. This would always be her room, whatever Mac decided to do about the house after Erik—

Sarah gazed up into the corner. "I feel bad, Esther. He's just a boy and he's dying. What right did I have to be such a chaleria? I was worse than Sadie at her worst, and you can't get much worse than that."

She refused to consult Emmeline on this. Emmeline was too, well, Emmeline. Not hard-hearted, but hard-headed. Not mean-spirited, but unsentimental. She talked to Emmeline regularly about her book…their book. Not about this. Not about Erik. Emmeline had never been a mother. Emmeline had never lost a child. Esther had. A miscarriage. She had, too. Her Morty.

"Would I have talked to my own child like that?" she asked Esther. "Not Morty. Morty wouldn't understand…couldn't understand. But if Erik was mine, would I? Would you, Esther? If Erik was yours?"

Esther didn't answer.

41

Joseph English pecked Sadie on the cheek, his bushy mustache and full white beard tickling her face. "Will you at least introduce me to your nephew?" he asked. "What are you afraid of?"

"Soon," Sadie replied. "Soon, I'll introduce you to Bernie and all of them. But you have to understand: I haven't dated a man in half a century. I'm still getting used to there being a you and me." She brushed up against him. *A sheyner man like this wants to spend time with me? To get to know me? To date me?* "This is dating we're doing, right, Joey? It's been so long for me, maybe it's something else altogether?"

Joseph laughed. He had never let anyone else call him Joey. Even as a boy, it was Joseph. But Sadie? Sadie was different. From Sadie, it felt right. It felt perfect. He pulled her toward him and kissed her again, this time on the lips until she was breathless. "Does that answer your question, Sadie Finkel?" he asked, his mouth inches from hers.

Sadie blushed and clenched her fists to stop herself from chewing her nails. "I'm not sure I'm ready to share you yet," she said softly as Joseph wrapped his arms around her. It had also been fifty years since she had spoken to a man so affectionately, since she had let herself be so vulnerable with a man. The last time, with Jimmy, had not turned out well.

"You're not ashamed of me, are you, Sadie?"

"Me ashamed of you?" Sadie asked incredulously. She stepped back, shaking her head. "It should be the other way around. You're the one who should be ashamed to be seen with me. I'm not smart like you. You've written books; I'm just starting to read books. You taught at a fancy college; I never got past high school." She looked away, out the open door to the shops on Marylebone Lane. "I'm not a good person," she whispered. "I've told you how not a good person I am."

Joseph gently eased Sadie onto the bench by the door. He waited until the rest of their fellow students had passed, then sat down to join her. This is where they had met, in a pâtisserie workshop. The only septuagenarians in the group, Joseph and Sadie had naturally joined forces when the instructor asked the students to pair off. They did more than pair off, the Jewish spinster from Clark Street, Montreal and the retired political philosophy lecturer from Jesus College, Cambridge. They hit it off.

A coffee after that initial Cordon Bleu workshop turned into dinner after their second workshop together and again after their third and fourth. They had been going out after most cooking classes since — sometimes for a meal, sometimes simply for a stroll. Yet regardless of how they spent their time, Sadie would not let Joseph walk her home.

Joseph may not yet have met her family and friends at 33 Fitzroy Street, but he knew all about them. He also knew more about Sadie than she had shared with anyone, ever. He not only knew what Sarah had written about her in *Sara's Year* — Sadie had insisted that he read it — he knew about how her mother's death had thwarted her long-ago dream of becoming a dancer, about her hopeless crush on Jimmy Harcourt, about her brother Nate who had died at Dieppe, about her life on the retail side of the schmatta trade, about her rape, pregnancy and abortion, and about all the ways she had mistreated Esther and undermined her ambitions.

Joseph's story was simpler: "I was an appalling husband and father. I devoted so much of my time to my work that my wife left me. I didn't notice for several days because I had been staying in my rooms at the college that week. Should I happen to be in Cambridge and see Joyce around town or in the shops, she still won't talk to me." He sighed. "Nor will my son and daughter, although they're more likely to change their minds in the end than is Joyce." He kissed the top of Sadie's head. "If you won't judge me for who I was, I won't judge you for who you were. Who you are now is all that matters to me."

"The same for me, Joey," Sadie murmured. "The same for me."

42

"About our deal." Erik leaned against the door frame. He reached above his head and knocked on the lintel.

"One minute," Sarah called, her eyes fixed on the computer screen. "My Emmeline is about to order lunch at Claridge's." She typed a few sentences. "What did they serve for lunch at Claridge's in 1922?" she muttered. "Were unescorted women allowed in a hotel dining room back then? Would my Emmeline have cared if they weren't?"

"If your Emmeline is anything like Mac's," Erik replied, "she wouldn't have given a flying f—." He caught himself, not that Sarah would have minded. "I bet she would have been thrilled to be turned away, just so she could force her way in."

"Hmm." Sarah tilted her head toward the armchair as though she was engaging with someone sitting in it. "I wonder…"

Erik drummed his fingers on the door. "Anybody home? Can I come in, Sarah Shakespeare?"

Sarah hooted. "Sure, Erik Van Gogh. Come on in."

"Erik Picasso, if it's all the same to you." He headed for the armchair.

"Before you sit down," Sarah cautioned, "you better ask Emmeline. It's still her room and she's particular."

"I hear she has a thing for artists." Erik shoved the Hudson's Bay blanket aside and dropped into the armchair.

"Give me another minute," Sarah said distractedly and started to type: "It was not so long ago that a respectable woman alone would never have been seated in a public dining room, let alone one as fashionable as Claridge's. But the Great War had not only taken more than a million of the country's young men, leaving single young women in an uneasy majority, it had broken down many of the prejudices that would previously have prevented Emmeline from being shown to a table. Not that Emmeline wouldn't have created a fuss had they tried to stop her. Today, however, she was grateful that she could direct her fussing elsewhere."

Sarah swiveled her typing chair around to face Erik. "I'm all yours, boychik."

"Don't forget to save," he said.

"Oy." She reached behind her and hit Apple-S. "Mostly, I remember."

"Mostly isn't good enough." He grinned.

"How'd you get to be so smart, Mister Smarty Pants?"

His grin faded. "It turns out that some people in this house are a helluva lot smarter than me." He twisted the top button on his shirt. "Thank you," he said awkwardly, "for the other day. You were right. About the show, I mean."

"I'm glad." Sarah wheeled her chair over to Erik. "You'll do it, then?"

He dropped his hands into his lap. His eyes followed. "Maybe."

"Only maybe?"

"Only maybe. It has to do with that deal we made. There's one clause I think I need to renegotiate."

"Okay, Mr. Clarence Darrow. Name your terms."

Erik gazed past Sarah to the monitor. "What's Emmeline doing right now? Why is she having lunch at Claridge's? What's she up to?"

"You're changing the subject, mister. What are *you* up to?"

Erik stared out the window. "The deal was that I would do the show and you would write your book, right?"

Sarah nodded.

"I don't know what you'll think about this…" His voice trailed off.

"What? How bad can it be?"

He turned back to Sarah. "I want you to share *Emmeline* with me. What you're writing. Every day as you're writing it."

"Not the finished book?" Sarah asked. "*As I'm writing it? As I'm writing, it's rough. As I'm writing, it's a mess. As I'm writing, it's chaloshes. Why wouldn't you want to wait—"

"Until the book is finished?" Erik asked softly.

"For someone who's supposed to be so smart..." Sarah mumbled. "I didn't think. I'm sorry. Of course I'll share *Emmeline* with you, if that's what you really want."

"I do."

"I can print out pages for you. Would that work?"

Erik shook his head. "It's getting hard for me to read. Even it wasn't, where would I find the time? All I do anymore is paint, eat, paint, sleep and paint some more. Maybe the best thing's if you read to me while I'm working. Could you do that?"

Sarah didn't know what to say. She admired visual artists like Bernie, Mac and Erik. It took courage to stand around and listen to people talking in front of you about what you had created. At least with writing, you never had to be in the same room with people as they were reading your book. Sarah had done a few public readings. She had even been invited to read from *Sara's Year* at Toronto's prestigious International Festival of Authors. Still, that wasn't the same as reading a rough draft aloud to just one person. At least in public, the book was finished, was as good as it would ever be. But this?

What do I do, Esther?

She studied Erik, this boy who knew he was going to die yet had found a way to keep living. He had more chutzpah than she ever would. Yes, she had watched her son die. No one should have to do that. That also took a kind of chutzpah. But living had never been easy for Morty. Not ever. Especially not with a father like Sammy, who treated his son like garbage, who never stopped questioning whether Morty was really his. Besides, as painful as it was, she had known all along that Morty would not live long. Children like him never did. He was lucky to have made it to nineteen.

But Erik? Here was a boy who was smart and talented. One minute, he's healthy with a full life ahead of him. The next... She would never be as brave as Erik. Could she be brave enough to do what he asked? She would have to be.

*I*s thirteen a lucky number or an unlucky one? I must ask the question, although in most circumstances I reject all superstition — and that would include astrology, the supernatural, necromancy and all forms of the occult.

My "bloody-minded closed-mindedness," as Aleister Crowley termed it on numerous occasions, was a source of many a fierce argument, especially during my younger years, when seances, planchette, reincarnation and other spiritualist claptrap were all the rage. Once in a moment of weakness, I allowed myself to be persuaded to attend one of Conan Doyle's lectures on spiritualism, only to reconfirm my opinion of him as a consummate storyteller who was appallingly credulous on matters nonliterary. I must also confess to having permitted Crowley to perform esoteric rituals at several of my salons. However seriously Crowley and some of his acolytes viewed them, I regarded them as little more than fatuous entertainments.

I put an end to Crowley's charades the time he claimed to be effecting his voodoo on Victor Neuberg. A camel, indeed! And Algiers? In a zoo? I knew Victor to have been in Swiss Cottage at the time, most likely in Runia Tharpe's bed. After I refused him further carryings-on of that nature, Crowley attempted to reclaim the painting he had given me, a portrait of his former mistress, Ninette Shumway. I retorted that if his powers were as formidable as he claimed, he was welcome to employ them to spirit the portrait back into his possession. He refused to speak to me after that.

Ninette no longer hangs above the mantel in my front room. My nephew's Primus is now the sole occupant of that honored place. Some years ago I relocated Ninette to the first-floor washroom, an admittedly petty act, but one that I have no intention of reversing. Should Ninette's daughter Louise outlive Jeremy, I shall have him bequeath it to her. Otherwise, it will go to Marc-Allan.

How easy it is to get sidetracked in these writings. I was speaking of the number thirteen. I was speaking of it because Jeremy and I were married *on the thirteenth and today is our thirteenth wedding anniversary. Ought that to mean something? Is it an augury of some sort? Does it portend good fortune? Is it an omen of a more diabolical variety? None of those, I'll warrant. Regardless, it is a droll piece of serendipity.*

I cannot say how many more of these anniversaries I shall be here to celebrate. At ninety-two, I imagine that only a few specks of sand remain at the top of my particular hourglass.

On our fifth and tenth anniversaries, in 1966 and 1971, we returned to Regent's Canal and the Cotton Blossom, *where Andrew piloted a leisurely champagne cruise for two that launched from behind The Palm Tree and meandered back there several hours later for an informal gathering, not unlike the one we enjoyed on our wedding day. If I am here and can still manage it in three years' time, Jeremy will no doubt arrange something similar for our fifteenth.*

Today, being less of a milestone, opened with breakfast in bed. I am an execrable cook, yet Jeremy is a master — not that it takes a master to produce a fry-up. Jeremy's version, however, would be unrecognizable in Mile End: poached duck eggs, Lincolnshire sausage, fried tomatoes fresh from our neighbor's garden, thinly sliced portobello mushrooms, home-baked bread with Dundee marmalade, a pot of Royal Blend tea, a glass of freshly juiced oranges and a flute of Bollinger. Dinner at Claridge's last night was not so heavy but equally delicious, even if not Jeremy's handiwork: Cornish lamb so tender it nearly melted in my mouth was accompanied by crushed new potatoes and tapenade. We ended with a poire Williams parfait.

When we returned and Jeremy unlatched the front door, Elvis Presley was waiting for us. No, I do not believe all the folderol about Elvis having falsified his death. Rather, Gwendolyn McHugh, she of this morning's garden tomatoes, had crept into the house at Jeremy's direction and switched the cassette player onto a continuous loop of "Surrender," a popular song the week of our wedding. We danced to it in The Palm Tree thirteen years ago, and we danced to it again this evening.

Won't you please surrender to me

Your lips, your arms, your heart, dear

Be mine forever

Be mine tonight

Jeremy treats me like a duchess, which is more than I deserve when you consider how often I treat him like a serf. It has been a fine thirteen years, unexpectedly fine. Exceptional, I would have to say. I may have been a reluctant bride at seventy-nine, yet not for an instant since have I regretted my decision to marry him. Whatever happens next, my time with Jeremy will surely prove itself to have been a remarkable finale to a most singular life, and I am grateful for every breath of it, as I am grateful to Jeremy for insinuating himself into this latter chapter.

43

Erik traced a frown-like arc into the dirt path with his shoe. "I'm dying, Mac," he said. He gazed down at the London skyline, picking out St. Paul's Cathedral, the Houses of Parliament and, a few blocks from 33 Fitzroy Street, the BT Tower. He walked on, until the panoramic city view offered by Parliament Hill could no longer be seen.

"I know," Mac said. "I'm sorry."

"Me, too." Erik stopped and forced a smile. "That was a dumb thing to say."

"No it wasn't," Mac said. "The only dumb thing would be if you didn't say anything. That wouldn't be dumb. Just not smart. Not when you're surrounded by people who love you so much."

"All these months later I still can't wrap my mind around it," Erik said. "Not really. Even though I've had the pneumonia and even though two doctors in two different countries have said it's definitely AIDS. And even though I know other people my age who have died. Even with all that, it doesn't seem like it's possible that it can be happening to me. Some mornings I wake up and for a split second I think it's all been a bad dream. The worst kind of dream. Then I remember."

He continued toward Parliament Hill Cafe and lunch. "I sometimes forget during the day. It's easy to forget things you want to forget." He looked at Mac. "That's not true. It isn't easy to forget. My body won't let me forget…not for long. Not anymore."

Mac said nothing. What was there to say? He couldn't take away Erik's AIDS. He couldn't take away Erik's intolerance to the drugs that could keep him alive, that might have spared him from PML, a brain infection for which there were no drugs…or cure. He couldn't reunite Erik with his mother or sister. Britta's immune system was now as compromised as was her son's and she needed KC to take care of her. All Mac could do was give Erik a home in a city that would never be his home…or Mac's. All Mac could do was get Erik to Sir Michael Bevan, an old RAF chum who was now one of Britain's top AIDS doctors. All Mac could do was listen.

"Thanks for coming out with me." Erik lowered himself onto a bench. "I'm getting scared to go out by myself, in case my legs give out. I'm not ready for a wheelchair. Not yet."

Mac sat next to him. A robin perched itself in the tree across from the bench, warbling loudly. It reminded Erik of the robin in *Mary Poppins*, the one that had trilled with Julie Andrews early on in the film. *It'll take more than a spoonful of sugar to help my medicine go down. There isn't enough sugar in the world for that.*

"I love Bernie," Erik said, "but I can't be with him sometimes. He cares so much and he hurts so much. It sounds cruel to say, but I just can't handle his stuff on top of mine."

"It can be hard to know you're going to lose someone you love," Mac said softly, "and to feel powerless to stop it from happening. I know."

"Bernie's mother?"

All these years later, Mac still experienced a bittersweet twinge when he thought about Esther Freed; sweet at the time they shared, bitter that it had been so brief. Each of the two times Esther had suddenly entered his life and just as suddenly left it, he had felt both grateful and bereft. Most of all, he had felt alone. The one person with whom he had longed to share his feelings was the one person who wasn't there. Instead of reaching out to friends, he had thrown himself into his work. He had cut himself off from the world.

"Promise me something," Mac said.

"If I can."

"Promise me you won't shut Bernie out. I'm not asking as Bernie's father. I'm not asking for Bernie. I'm asking as your friend." He draped his arm over Erik's shoulder. "Love matters, Erik. It doesn't matter whether you have six weeks, six months or sixty years left together. Your art matters, of course. But love matters more. Bernie doesn't want you to protect him. He wants you to let him love you."

Mac thought about Bernie, who he knew in that moment to be

sitting across from 33 Fitzroy Street in front of *View*. Alone. "Bernie's love won't make your AIDS go away," he said. "I wish it could. What it can do is help make it more bearable…maybe even beautiful. Let him love you, Erik. Not for him. For you."

44

"I've been an idiot," Erik said. He rested his head against Bernie's chest and shut his eyes. As sumptuously elegant as the Claridge's suite was, the only thing Erik wanted to be aware of was Bernie… of Bernie's arms around him…of Bernie's heart beating against his cheek. He would have been happy crammed into a tiny attic garret or a windowless cellar, as long as he could be there with Bernie. Forever.

"It'll be forever for me," he said to himself. "I just wish it could be a longer forever for us."

This was to be the first of Erik and Bernie's two honeymoon nights in the hotel's royal suite, a wedding gift from Mac. Mac had offered a longer stay, but Erik knew that he didn't have that luxury. He was running a losing race against his body's decline. If he was going to deliver the promised paintings, he needed to get back to work.

Once he had conspired with Sarah, Sylvie, Sadie, Mac and the Fitzroy Square Frontagers' and Garden Committee to arrange for an outdoor ceremony, Erik invited Bernie to join him on his favorite bench across from *View.* "I know we can't get married, not legally," he said, reaching for Bernie's hand. "I never thought I'd want to, even if we could. It felt like so much bullshit. Now, it seems like the most important thing in the world. I know it won't be legal and that it doesn't really mean anything—"

"You're wrong," Bernie interrupted. He squeezed Erik's hand. "It means a lot. It means everything."

"For me, too." Erik gestured toward the sculpture. "I wanted to ask you here in front of Naomi Blake because she's taught me so much about how to keep living in the face of…" He swallowed hard. "In the face of death."

Bernie pulled Erik toward him and kissed him gently but passionately.

"Is that a yes?" Erik asked into Bernie's neck.

"Do you have to ask?" Bernie kissed him again. "What did you have in mind? I'm guessing that it won't be a big church do like Princess Di's was. Should I check train schedules for Gretna Green? Isn't that where all the illicit marriages happen?"

"Hell, no." Erik jerked away, pretending to be offended. "It may not be at St. Paul's like Di's was. I still want the wedding every girl dreams of, with vows and rings, and a cake. And presents. And tuxes."

"I don't know how many girls dream of tuxes...unless they're lesbians."

"You mean I never told you I was a dyke?" Erik snickered. "Is that going to be a problem?"

"Nope. I'm, um, broad-minded."

Erik groaned.

"I'll make a deal with you." Bernie said.

"Another deal? Everyone wants to make deals with me. Is that some sort of Jewish thing? We Lutherans don't make deals."

Bernie leapt to his feet. "Erik Donnekin," he shouted. "Come on down!"

"That was *The Price Is Right*, silly, not *Let's Make a Deal*. You know bupkis about game shows."

"Bupkis? Forget being Lutheran. We'll turn you into a Jew yet."

Erik tugged on Bernie's arm, pulling him back down to the bench. "So what's the deal?"

"I'll give you your fancy schmancy wedding if you give me a honeymoon."

"I'm one step ahead of you, handsome." Erik giggled. "The wedding's next week, right here with Naomi Blake as witness, and Mac's booked us for two nights at Claridge's. The royal suite, if you please. Just like at the Ritz, and perfect for two queens. If that isn't tempting enough, we're all finally going to get to meet Sadie's elusive boyfriend."

"Pretty sure of yourself, aren't you, mister?"

"No," Erik replied, suddenly serious. "Not really."

#   #   #   #   #

"I've been an idiot," Erik repeated. He lifted his head so that he could look into Bernie's eyes.

"What do you mean?" Bernie mumbled, drowsy from hours of lovemaking.

"I've been pushing you away since we got to London. Probably since before. I don't know why." He let his head drop back onto Bernie's chest. "Yes I do," he whispered. "I was scared. Scared for me and scared for you."

Bernie stroked Erik's hair. "Me, too."

"It won't be pretty, you know. What's coming, I mean. You heard what the doctor said. The muscle stuff is only going to get worse. I could get paralyzed. I could go blind. I could end up in a coma." He hesitated. "You know what I'm most scared of?"

"Uh-uh."

"I'm terrified that I'll forget how much I love you." He began to spasm.

Bernie hugged him tightly.

"Promise me something," Erik murmured when the shaking subsided.

"Anything."

Erik took a deep breath to stop himself from weeping. "Promise me that if I forget how much I love you, that you won't forget. Promise me that no matter what I say or how I act, even if I'm bitchy or horrible to you, that you'll always remember…that you'll always remember that I've never loved anything or anyone as much as I love you right now…that I never will." He couldn't hold back the tears any longer. Neither of them could.

45

J oseph removed the platter from the fridge and set it on the counter. With a long, non-serrated knife, he meticulously sliced through the three layers of pâte feuilletée, two layers of crème pâtissière and white-and-chocolate fondant icing. Then, using a stainless steel spatula, he slid two of the mille-feuille pastries onto individual chilled plates. Finally, he steamed the milk for the cappuccinos and spooned the froth into the two doubles warming on top of the St. Gallen espresso maker.

"You're taking a long time, Joey," Sadie called from the dining room. "Can I help?"

"And ruin the surprise?" Joseph replied. "Two more minutes."

Sadie pushed away from the table, already cleared of its main course, and gazed out the window of Joseph's Morpeth Terrace flat toward the brick-and-concrete neo-Byzantine complex that was Westminster Cathedral, now bathed in the golden glow of dusk. Joseph had taken her on a quick tour of the cathedral on their way to his flat and she had been astounded by its soaring majesty and transcendent light. Although Sadie had lived all her life in Catholic Montreal, she had never set foot in a Catholic church. It wasn't something that good Jewish girls did, any more than they spent time alone with Catholic boys in their apartments. But Sadie was no longer a girl and Joseph was no boy. And as ridiculous as it was at her age, Sadie was in love. *Maybe not so ridiculous. Look at Emmeline.*

Not that Sadie was trying to follow Emmeline to the altar. "Who needs to get married anymore?" she had asked Sarah after Bernie and Erik's ceremony. "I just want to be with him, if he'll have me."

"*If* he'll have you?" Sarah exclaimed. "The way he ogles you, he would have you right now, right here on the grass."

"Sarah!" Sadie blushed a deep scarlet and turned away so that no one would notice, especially Joseph, who was a few yards away chatting with Erik.

"He'll have you," Sarah continued after Sadie had regained her color. "More than that, I bet he asks you to marry him. He's that kind of gentleman." She lowered her voice. Joseph was moving in their direction and she didn't want him to hear. "You done good with this man, Sadie. He's a real mensch." She kissed Sadie's cheek and whispered in her ear. "After all this time, you deserve some happiness. You may not believe it, but it's true."

Was it true? Some days, Sadie felt like two different people: the severe, censorious shrew she had been for much of her life and the not-quite naive, not-entirely gentle woman she had been for less than a year. "Can you really teach an old bitch new tricks?" she murmured while she waited for Joseph to emerge from the kitchen with dessert. "Have I really earned a few years of love and happiness?" It didn't seem possible.

Dinner had been more than a meal. It had been a banquet, with Joseph calling on everything he had learned through his months of Cordon Bleu workshops. They started in the living room with a marinated feta hors d'oeuvre and a bottle of Joseph Mellot Sancerre. From there they moved into the dining room for a starter of cucumber salad with yellow peaches, ginger and sesame dressing, followed by a rabbit ravioli with foie gras, mushroom emulsion and roasted hazelnut, both accompanied by a Château-Grillet Viognier. "I'm not sure the courses go together," Joseph apologized, "but we haven't taken a class in menu preparation yet. Same goes for the wine. I hope everything's okay."

"After what I was eating before London," Sadie said, "it's more than okay. More than that, it's batamt."

Joseph regarded her quizzically.

"That means it's delicious." She scraped the last of the ravioli onto her fork and let it rest on her tongue. "I love that you cooked for me," she said, "but let's do it together next time, like we've always done in class."

Joseph raised his glass. "Here's to many next times," he toasted.

\#   \#   \#   \#   \#

Joseph removed the engagement ring from its red-leather Cartier box and gently placed it atop one of the pastries. He would have asked Sadie to marry him weeks ago, but he had wanted to wait until after Bernie and Erik's ceremony and until after Sadie's Fitzroy Street family had met him. Now there was no longer any reason to put it off. He was seventy-nine. Of course he could live as long as Mac's Aunt Emmeline. Then again, he might not. However long he had, he wanted Sadie with him.

Sadie turned away from the window when she heard the dining room door open. She beamed at Joseph, dressed as usual in wrinkled pants, white shirt, crested Cambridge tie, elbow-patched corduroy jacket and worn carpet slippers, and down at the delicate mille-feuille he was carrying, her favorite dessert. Then the flickering light from the twin tapers on the table glinted on the heart-shaped diamond. She pressed her eyes shut and opened them, expecting the ring to be gone. It wasn't. "Are you sure?" she gasped.

Joseph set down the tray, lifted the ring from the icing and eased it onto Sadie's finger. "More sure than I have ever been about anything," he said softly, "in my life."

46

Erik dipped his paintbrush into the emerald-green daub on his pallet and held it up to the blank canvas. The tremor in his hand was barely noticeable today. But it would be back. Each day's respite, and there were fewer and fewer as the weeks passed, only made the inevitable return of his symptoms that much more severe. He could be on his feet today, but who knew what tomorrow would bring. If he was lucky, only his legs would give out and he would still be able to paint, if sitting down. If he wasn't so lucky, he would spend the day in bed, twitching and jerking uncontrollably while Bernie held him. On days like that, Bernie, Sarah and Mac took turns washing him, feeding him and taking him to the bathroom. On days like that, he almost wished that the pneumonia had killed him in Italy. Almost.

He steadied his right hand with his left and directed the brush to trace a broad spiral in the upper right-hand corner, filling the empty space with loop after loop after loop of vibrance. By the sixth turning, though, he lacked the strength to steer the brush. He gripped it as tightly as he could and let his spasms paint for him. They careered wildly, leaving a labyrinthine pattern of color in their wake. Erik willed his arm to still, if only long enough to switch brushes and colors. This time, he held two brushes — one loaded with vermilion, the other with ultramarine. Once again, he began with a measure of control, if less than previously, and when the tremors recurred, he surrendered to them. He repeated the ritual twice more. That was all he had the stamina for.

Erik let his brushes and pallet drop to the canvas tarp that now covered every inch of Emmeline's front room floor. Bernie would collect them later and clean them for him. All he could do now was collapse onto the nearest chair, itself covered in an acrylics-stained throw.

He would not be able to do art for much longer. Bernie tried to convince him otherwise, but he knew…just as he was now certain that he would not make it to his October show. There would be a show. He was determined to produce enough work, even if it killed him. AIDS was killing him anyhow, so he might as well give it a good run for its money.

Erik scanned the completed canvases leaning against the wall, barely recognizing them as his own work. The painstaking strokes that had marked his earliest painting had been replaced by something feverish…frenetic…chaotic. It's not that his pre-AIDS creations had been overly controlled. In their own way, each had been an act of surrender to paint, brush and canvas. At least that's how he had viewed them at the time. He smiled grimly at his naiveté. He hadn't known what real surrender was like until his body started to refuse his mind's commands. Only then, had paint, brush and canvas truly been in charge of his creative enterprise.

Was any of it any good? Jeffrey and Pierre at Galérie Cinq Arts thought so.

"This is the best work you've ever done," Jeffrey gushed over the phone when he received the latest photos. "Whatever you're able to do, we want it, even if it's just these few."

Erik doubted that he would make it to the dozen originally promised, but who knew? If the God he had prayed to in the Siena hospital was an art lover, he might keep him going just long enough to make it to twelve. *Only four more to go after this one.* He shut his eyes, leaned back into the chair and gave in to the palpitations that convulsed through his body. *Right now, it might as well be forty.*

47

"You've got to slow down, hon. Please." Bernie hugged Erik tightly then quickly released much of the pressure of his embrace. Erik had always been trim, his weight and height a near-perfect match. Being sick hadn't turned him into a fragile skeleton. Spending eighteen hours a day painting had…or at least as many of those hours when he could, when his body would let him. He barely slept now, stuffed only enough food into his mouth to keep going and spent the rest of his time willing his legs to support him and his hands to grip a paintbrush. Those were the good days. On the bad days, Erik lay in bed, his mind muddled and his body in seizure.

This had been one of the good days, and as the grandfather clock one floor down in the front hall struck midnight, Erik curled up against Bernie, the moonlight shining in through the open bedroom window casting a deathly pall on his already pale complexion.

"I'm not going to make it through this—"

"Erik—"

Erik covered Bernie's mouth with a bony, paint-spattered hand. "Let's not pretend anymore. We've run out of time for miracles." He pushed himself up to sitting and kissed Bernie. "All I have left, love, is you and my art, and time is running out for me on both of those." He rolled out of bed and pulled Bernie with him to the window. Now that it was June, *View* was veiled by the garden's lush greenery. But he knew it was there, still speaking to him as potently as it had that long-ago afternoon with Sadie.

Once he had recommitted to the show, Erik asked Mac to see if he could get Naomi Blake to come by the house. Unfortunately, she was out of the country; ironically, in Canada. He would have liked to talk to her again, but he knew he didn't need to. He had her sculpture to keep him on track.

"I wish it hadn't taken me so long to find this voice," he continued. "I wish I hadn't had to get sick to find it. It isn't fair." He laughed softly. "When I was a kid, Anders kept saying that life wasn't fair. I guess he was right after all."

He slipped on the jeans that he had draped over the chair before joining Bernie in bed. They had fit snugly once. Now they hung loosely on him as though they were two sizes too big; they would have fallen to his ankles without a tightly cinched belt. "I know it's late," he said, "but can we go across to the park for a bit?"

Bernie pulled on a pair of shorts and a t-shirt. Neither bothered putting on shoes and they padded across the road barefoot, dropping onto the bench across from *View*.

Even close to one in the morning, the air was warm, chilled only slightly by a damp breeze off the Thames a few miles away. The park's trees helped muffle the ever-present hum of traffic from Euston and Tottenham Court roads, and it sounded more like a distant tide than a steady stream of cars, trucks and buses.

"We both know that I'm not going to make it through this. We've known it pretty much all along." Erik felt Bernie tremble, and he knew that Bernie was trying to force back his tears. Erik wanted to cry, too. He had to get these words out first. If he let himself cry, the words might never come. They had to.

"I fucked things up at the beginning," he went on, "and I wasted a lot of time feeling sorry for myself. Too much time. At least it feels that way now that there's so little time left. It's coming, Bernie." His voice cracked. "I know it is." Too soon, he would be spending all his days in bed, barely able to function…if at all.

He somehow found the strength to go on. "Now that I've found this voice, I can't let it die with me. I have lots to say and I have to get it out before…before…while I can still paint." His eyes glistened. "I don't have time to slow down, Bernie. I can't afford to slow down. I know I can't win the race against death. I need to win the race against what this PML is doing to my body. Will you let me do this? Will you help me?"

"I hate this," Bernie wanted to shout. "I hate what this is doing to you, what this is doing to us. I hate that you're leaving me. I hate that everything is taking you away from me. Even your art. I hate it all." Yet he knew that had their places been reversed, he would be asking the same of Erik right now. He clenched his fists then released them. "You know I will," he said.

I thought a lot about dying when I was in my early sixties. Living through the Blitz will do that. Then the war ended and I found myself celebrating my first peacetime birthday in six years, at The Palm Tree. As the band broke into a syrupy Auld Lang Syne in the seconds before midnight, it struck me that through some feat of German incompetence, the pub and I had both managed to survive. Every structure around The Palm Tree had been destroyed, yet it still stood — alone amidst mountains of rubble. Swathes of my neighborhood were also gone, along with many dear friends; yet I still stood.

In that instant, in a building that had cheated the Luftwaffe, surrounded by so many who had cheated Death and with my glass raised to 1946 and the start of my sixty-fifth year, I thought, "Sod the war and sod dying; it's time to start thinking about living again."

So I did.

If it did not feel appropriate to reestablish my weekly literary salon — the concept felt too frivolous in the aftermath of so much death and destruction — I would find other ways to support the artists and writers I admired, including my nephew, Marc-Allan. As soon as it was possible to do so, for example, I flew to Canada to view his first-ever art exhibition, in that backwater he had insisted on emigrating to. His art was as outstanding as I knew it would be, which is why I defied his parents to encourage him. Halifax, alas, was a dull and dreary desert.

Once upon a time, I had labored for women's suffrage; now that the war was over, I would fight for women to be permitted to retain their wartime jobs, and I would work for other causes of import. A national health service, for example. By then, I had made my peace with the Labour Party, after years of resenting their brutal assimilation of the more progressive British Socialist Party, and I resolved to campaign aggressively on their behalf.

I had loved recklessly during the early years of the Blitz, never knowing whether I or "mon amant du jour" would survive until morning. By war's end, having lost so many of the men and women I had made love to, I withdrew into myself, fearing the loss of any further intimates. Now, I would compensate for those lost years by rekindling my passions. Even as the sexual openness of the war years congealed into the bland Spam of the 1950s, my appetites only increased. Thank heavens they did. Otherwise, there could never have been a Jeremy. Otherwise, I would certainly have died long before now.

It is passion that has kept me alive and healthy. Passion for causes. Passion for love. Passion for life. Yet passion can accomplish only so much. Today, more than halfway to my ninety-third birthday, I am more aware than ever of the ticking of a clock that before long will lose its capacity for rewinding. Perhaps Jeremy will not have to carry me out to the back garden with a pistol on the eve of my hundredth birthday after all. That would be good. He dislikes firearms so.

48

Bernie, Sarah, Mac, Sylvie and Sadie crowded together around a kitchen table that had never been large enough to accommodate all of them, their chairs turned to face Erik, who had propped himself up against the wall by the door. Joseph stood behind Sadie, his hands massaging her shoulders.

No one knew why Erik had called them together on this Summer Solstice morning. All eyes were fixed on him, and his, more piercing now that his cheeks were washed out and hollow, moved slowly around the table before coming to rest for a full minute on Bernie.

"This feels like one of those country house mystery stories," Erik said, "where the detective gathers all the suspects together to unmask the murderer. Like an Agatha Christie book. But there's no mystery here, is there."

No one said anything.

"The other cliché would be for me to say, 'You're probably wondering why I asked you here today.'"

His audience waited expectantly. They all had questions and concerns. None dared voice them. Erik's emotional state had improved since he started painting for the gallery show, but his physical condition had deteriorated. Whatever stamina he could muster, he now channeled into his art. He could no longer paint through the day. Some days he could not paint at all. Some days he could not get out of bed. Some days it seemed as though he would never get out of bed again, only to unearth some hidden reserve of energy that fueled him enough to get back to brush and canvas. If he had taken precious time away from painting to call them together, it must be important.

Erik inhaled deeply. "I've been rehearsing this little speech for days and it's still going to be hard to deliver, so please don't interrupt. If you make me stop, I don't know if I'll be able to get started again. Okay?"

As everyone else nodded their agreement, Joseph raised his hand. "I can wait upstairs if you want," he offered awkwardly. "I know I'm not really part of your family here."

"The hell you aren't," Erik declared forcefully. His voice softened. "I'd like you to stay. What I have to say also affects you."

Joseph edged closer to Sadie. She took his hand.

"I think the best way to start is by acknowledging the elephant in the room. So here goes: I'm dying, and it doesn't look like I have that much time left. We'd all like it to be different, me especially. But that's the way it is." His right hand started to twitch. He covered it with his left and ignored Bernie's attempt to give him his chair.

"You're as much my family, all of you, as KC and my mom. More in some ways cuz you're here with me and they can't be." His voice quavered and he paused to collect himself. "I couldn't have asked for a better second family. Sarah and Sadie, my twin Jewish mothers. Sylvie, my little sister. Mac, the father I wished I'd had. Joseph: You got seduced into this weird family without knowing what you were getting into and you stuck with us, with me. And Bernie, my husband in every way that matters: You've stood by me even when I tried to push you away. I—" He shook his head. "Even if I was gonna live as long as Emmeline did, there would never be enough time to tell you how I feel about you, how I've felt about you since the first moment I saw you." He shut his eyes, willing away the convulsions that he knew could soon prevent him from going on.

"I love you all and I'm grateful to each of you for putting your life on hold to help me through this," he resumed after a few minutes' focused breathing, "but it has to stop. How do you think it makes me feel, knowing that you're all waiting around for me to die before you can get on with your own lives?" He scanned the table. "Not good, that's how.

"In that spirit, I have a message for each of you." Supporting himself from chair back to chair back, he crossed the room to Sadie and Joseph. "Will you two just get married already? I may have less time left than you do, but you're hardly spring chickens. Besides, you have to do it while I can still walk Sadie down the aisle and give her away. So before you guys leave this room, I want you to promise to set a date." He leaned down and kissed Sadie. Joseph pulled him into hug.

Mac was next. "This queen has a message for you from *The* Queen: 'Start on my damn portrait or I *will* have your head chopped off.'" He winked at Sarah, who was sitting across the table, then returned his attention to Mac. "Promise me you'll call Her Majesty's minions in the morning and get that first sitting set up. Oh, and you don't really need Sylvie here, do you?"

"I—" Mac began.

"That was rhetorical." Erik covered Mac's mouth with one hand and mussed Sylvie's hair with the other. "First, Sylvie, you come out here to help get Sarah and Sadie settled. Then, you haul off to Italy to deliver me and Bernie to London. Meanwhile, all your research is back in Nova Scotia and your magnum opus isn't getting opused. Am I right? Don't answer. I know I'm right. So get your French-Irish Canadian ass back to Kings County and stop babysitting me. I won't be around to see your definitive hagiography of the big guy here. But if you don't get cracking, he won't be either." Sylvie squeezed his hand.

Erik shuffled over to Bernie and embraced him from behind. "It's time to get back to your painting, love. I've held you back long enough. If you're gonna be the supernova that eclipses your superstar pops here, you'd better not let this sick queen get in your way. Paint with me if you want. I've gotten over my shit about that. Or paint up in the attic. But paint, goddamn it. You're too good, way better than I could ever be, to let anything stop you. Capisci, signore?"

"Capisco, amore mio." He pulled Erik onto his lap and kissed him.

"You've all got your assignments," Erik said, "so...class dismissed." He leaned his head back into Bernie's chest.

No one moved.

"Sir, sir. Teacher, sir!" Sarah waved her arm wildly in the air, breaking the tension. "You forgot about me."

Erik grinned. His face was so gaunt that his smile now filled most of it. "Forget you? Narishkeit!" He giggled. "I haven't completely lost it, you know. It's just that you're the only one in this motley gang who's doing what she needs to be doing. You came here to write a book, and you're writing book. And what a book! Wait till you guys read it. If you thought *Sara's Year* was a page-turner, you ain't seen nothin' yet." He scratched his chin. "You want an assignment, Sara Schumacher, author? Here it is: Finish the book. I want to know how it ends." He continued, barely audibly. "While I'm still alive to enjoy it."

49

Sadie and Joseph were married the following week, by the same minister who had presided over Bernie and Erik's ceremony and, again, in front of Naomi Blake's *View*. It was one of Erik's more challenging days, so Bernie supported him as he walked Sadie up Fitzroy Square Garden's abbreviated aisle and handed her over to Joseph, but not before hugging her as tightly as his strength would allow.

There would be no honeymoon, at least not until October when Sadie and Joseph planned to fly to Montreal for Erik's show. That had been one of Sadie's conditions for agreeing to an immediate wedding. The other was that she and Joseph would spend half of each week on Fitzroy Street and the other half in the Morpeth Terrace flat.

Joseph had readily agreed to Sadie's conditions. Not Erik.

"Tough luck, mister," Sadie said to him. "That's the way it's going to be."

And it was.

50

"I think I can. I think I can. I think I can." Erik gritted his teeth and braced himself against the front room wall. His legs wanted to give way. He could feel it. "I think I can, I think I can, I think I can," he repeated. It wasn't working. "Damn it," he grunted. "It worked for *The Little Engine That Could*. Why can't I get it to work for me?"

He gripped the magenta-tipped paintbrush more tightly and willed his arm toward the canvas. "I'm not asking for a cure, for God's sake. Just a few more days. Just long enough to finish this painting."

Self-Portrait 1989 was the last of the twelve paintings that Erik had promised Galérie Cinq Arts. The other eleven rested against the walls of the front room, now Erik's bedroom as well as his studio. Mac had initially considered a stair lift for Erik. However, his legs could no longer be relied upon to get him over to it and his fingers could no longer be counted on to operate its controls.

The paintings followed a peculiar progression. Each of the first six was more disturbing than the one before it, the imagery growing increasingly menacing, even gruesome. *Number 7* — only the self-portrait was identified by anything but its number in the sequence — was a pastel bouquet, as light and airy as its predecessors had been bleak and cynical. Each succeeding painting was brighter and more vivid, and *Self-Portrait 1989* was a vibrant explosion of color, an unbridled expression of optimism.

Erik touched his brush to the canvas as Vera Lynn's voice filled the room from Emmeline's cassette deck.

Dream, when you're feeling blue
Dream, that's the thing to do

His hand shuddered and the drop of magenta expanded into a rough blob. He took a deep breath and started to guide the brush shakily upward. His hand jerked. His arm spasmed. All sensation fled from the right side of his body. He collapsed, still somehow gripping the brush, which sliced a magenta gash down the side of the canvas.

"Shit," he tried to say, but couldn't. Then he blacked out as the music played on...

Dream when the day is through
Dream, and they might come true
Things never are as bad as they seem
So dream, dream, dream

51

Bernie clutched Erik's hand, mercifully stilled from weeks of escalating jerks and tremors. It was ten days since Erik had fallen into a coma, five weeks since his collapse in mid-painting had badly weakened the right side of his body, and Bernie had barely been out of the room. He slept in a cot next to Erik's bed and ate all his meals from the trays that Sadie, Sarah or Mac brought up for him. Sylvie had returned to Nova Scotia after Sadie and Joseph's wedding. As he had done in Siena, Bernie left only when absolutely necessary — to shower and change his clothes, for example. But not often and never for long. When he wasn't holding Erik's hand, he was sketching him — not as he had been when they first met; as he was now.

As for Erik's art materials, they had been pushed into a corner of the front room to accommodate the apparatus that now monitored his vital signs. However, all his paintings, including the unfinished self-portrait, sat on easels that formed a semicircle around his bed. "When he opens his eyes," Bernie declared, knowing that "when" was more likely to be "if" and "if," according to Sir Michael Bevan, was unlikely, "the first things I want him to see are me and his art."

While Erik was still conscious, Sir Michael had urged him to move into a hospice. But Erik had begged Mac to allow him to remain in the house. If he could not see his mother again; or, in all likelihood, his sister — Britta was as sick as he was, and KC was with her in Halifax — 33 Fitzroy Street was where he wanted to live out whatever time remained to him. It was his only home now, its residents his only family.

Even with Erik in a coma, Sarah continued to read to him from *The Emmeline Papers*. She had nearly finished her first draft and she was determined that, coma or no coma, he would get to hear the ending. Sadie and Joseph had moved into Fitzroy Street full-time and they read to him as well, from Emmeline's library. Mac had asked Buckingham Palace to reschedule his sessions with the Queen and instead sat with Erik, sharing the latest news from the art world or from back home in Canada, or simply sitting with him in companionable silence.

One morning in late August, Erik's eyelids fluttered, then blinked open for a few seconds. A single tear formed at the corner of his left eye. His mouth moved, too, as though he was trying to say something. Before Bernie could pick up the phone to call Sir Michael, Erik had lapsed back into unconsciousness. Ten minutes later, KC called from Halifax: Britta had just died.

Bernie said nothing to Erik about Britta. Why bother when it was clear that at some level Erik already knew? Instead, he told Erik to expect a visit from KC, "really soon," all the while praying that Erik would still be alive when she got there.

He was, and KC immediately joined the daily vigil in the front room, recounting quirky stories about herself, about their childhood and about Britta, in the hopes of drawing out the faintest of smiles. But Erik's lips, like the rest of his body, never budged.

52

"You have to let him go," Sarah murmured to Bernie late one Friday evening toward the end of August. She had noticed a light burning in the front room as she and KC came in from seeing a movie and she assumed that Bernie had fallen asleep in his chair. She would just slip in, she told KC, and switch off the light.

Bernie wasn't asleep. He was hovering over Erik, willing him to open his eyes. "Wake up, damn it," he cried, tears streaming down his face. "Don't leave me like this. Please!"

Sarah moved silently into the room. She stood next to Bernie, not saying anything. Then she pulled a handkerchief from her purse and pressed into his hand. He clenched it in his fist but refused to look away from Erik. "He can't die," he moaned. "I won't let him."

Erik's chest rose and fell, the only movement in his body. Such a beautiful young man, Sarah thought. Such a waste. Would Naomi Blake, who had seen so much death, call it a waste? Or would she dig deep inside her artistic soul to find the hope, the meaning, the grace? *I'm also supposed to be some sort of artist. Bernie, too. Why is it so hard for us to see what Naomi Blake would see?*

Sarah turned her gaze to the son of her oldest friend, a young man who had experienced more loss than was right for a boy his age. He lost a father. He lost a mother. Then he lost that father again when he found out that someone else was really his father. If that wasn't enough, he lost years of his life trying to be someone he wasn't. And now, having found the someone he could be that real self with, that someone was also being taken from him. "God has a plan," Sarah's mother had always reminded her whenever she complained about how unfair life was. "Some plan," the teenage Sarah had inevitably retorted. Fifty years later, it was hard to argue with that assessment.

"He's not going to get any better, boychik," Sarah said softly. "You know that, right? In here, you know that." She tapped his chest.

Bernie didn't move.

"He's just going to lie there like that until you let him know that it's okay. You have to let him know that it's okay. You have to let him go."

"I can't," Bernie whispered. "How can I?"

"You can. You have to. For him, you have to. For you, too." She maneuvered him toward the door. "Come," she said. "Let's go for a little walk."

"I can't leave him."

"Erik's not going anywhere. I promise. Not without you saying so." Sarah propelled him out to the street and steered him up Fitzroy to Warren, then the few blocks east to the traffic and commercial bustle of Tottenham Court Road. When they got to Caffè Nero, she pushed him into a wicker seat at one of the outdoor tables and disappeared inside. She returned balancing a foamy decaf cappuccino for him, a mug of tea for herself and a giant slab of Sachertorte and two forks.

"I brought you here," she said, "to remind you that life doesn't stand still, even at this hour. Look around you. People are walking up and down the street. People are going into hotels and restaurants. People are sitting in cafes, like us. That's just on the sidewalk. On the road, cars are driving back and forth. So are those strange two-story buses. I'll shush for a minute so you can listen to the noise." She waited a few breaths, until an ambulance screamed by. "It isn't all good noise, I know. But it's life noise. It's living noise." She cut off a piece of Sachertorte with her fork and pushed it into Bernie's mouth. "I brought you here, Bernele, to remind you that you're also alive."

Bernie chewed mindlessly, barely aware of the moist, chocolatey richness of his favorite kind of cake. Erik's too. Erik… Erik was lying in his bed back at the house, alone. Did he know he was alone? Had he retained some awareness of what was going on around him? Bernie had to believe that he did, or… He couldn't think about the alternative. There was no "or."

Sarah was talking. He tried to focus on what she was saying but couldn't. He forced down a gulp of scalding coffee to jolt him back to the present moment.

"Do you think Erik is happy in that stuffy room day after day after day?" Sarah was asking. "Do you think he's happy that you're sitting in that stuffy room with him? You aren't painting. You aren't sketching anymore, unless it's pictures of Erik. You're hardly eating. You aren't sleeping. You aren't taking care of yourself. You think that makes him happy?"

Bernie shrugged.

"He's a good boy, your Erik, and I love him like I love you." She reached across the table for Bernie's hand. "You don't want him to die. Of course you don't. But your Erik has one foot there already, Bernele, and he's not coming back. He's just not. He can't. As bad as he wants to, as bad as you want him to, it isn't going to happen. I know you don't want to know that. But I know you know it. And I know you know that the longer you hold on, the harder you make it — for him and you both."

Bernie studied the traffic on Tottenham Court Road. People coming from places. People going places. People living their lives. He said nothing for ten minutes. Then he wiped his eyes with the handkerchief he was still clutching. "I need to go back," he said. "Alone."

I am about to die. I ought to have seen it coming, at least in more than the theoretical terms in which I have frequently addressed it in these pages. I did not. Perhaps we never do. Perhaps we always expect to live forever, even as we pay lip service to the Angel of Death's inevitable call.

Is it the nearness of a final breath that has provoked from me another absurd reference to an Angel of Death? More than absurd. Incontrovertibly absurd because devils — angels, too — fall into the realm of the religious and the supernatural, all of which is superstitious codswallop. At their witless best, these fictions are harmless distractions. At their worst, they are virulently malignant, as destructive as nationalism, elitism and most other "isms."

Perhaps I ought to believe in devils. Anyone who lived through the genuine horrors of two world wars and the engineered terror of a Cold War could well be tempted. What else would you call the genocidal slaughters of a Hitler or a Stalin? What else would you call the heartless indifference in the face of such barbarisms that polluted the halls of power in so many nations, including our own?

Yet it is too easy to dismiss all the malefactors as devils. It is decidedly more difficult to acknowledge them as men...and women. When we so name them, they are no longer "those others." They are us. And we are them.

Jeremy calls me an ill-tempered old misanthrope when I blather on like this. He is correct, of course. I can be a right misery, so much so that he has taken to hiding the newspapers from me to spare him from another of my intemperate rants. He is also wrong. Although I sometimes act as if I have no use for the human race and see little hope for the future of humanity, it is a pretense...a pretense borne of my inability to mold the world into my image of what it ought to be.

Why should I expect to have been able to shape the larger world in a particular way when I have not managed to do so with my smaller, less *significant slice of it? Clearly, I am as delusional in my own way as those I rail against.*

No, my life is not what I imagined it would be. I was raised to expect a suitable marriage, a gaggle of offspring, a social position and a respectful subservience to the father of my children. Even after I rejected that presumption as the most nauseating bilge, I carried other expectations, prime among them was that I would be the instrument of radical change — in this country, at the very least. I would join Nancy Astor in the House of Commons or I would read law and join Ivy Williams at the bar. Instead, I catered to the inflated egos of Fitzrovia's cultural set.

I have no regrets. I possessed none of the diplomacy or spirit of compromise necessary for an effective career in politics. And I lacked the requisite conviction in the supremacy of laws and precepts to have been any kind of jurist. As for the arts, my gift was as a catalyst, never as a creator in my own right.

No, my life is not what I expected it to be. Is yours? Is anyone's? Yet there is not a single minute of it that I would do over in the hopes of a different journey or an alternative outcome. Not many can claim that they have lived life wholly on their own terms, with little concern for how others might regard their words or actions. I have been privileged to have been one of those few.

I cannot know how old you are, you who read these pages. (I know someone is reading them because I know that Jeremy will ignore my instruction to destroy them.) However old you are, it is not too old. It is never too old. Not for anything. Take it from an old woman who knows.

If I learned anything from the wars I have lived through, it is that anyone can die at any moment, can die far younger than any God who claims to be omnipotent, omniscient and all-loving should permit. And if I have learned anything through my ninety-two years, eleven months and thirty days, it is this: It is not when we die that matters; it is how we have lived through whatever number of years of life we have — be they too few or, as in my case, too many. However many are left to you, Reader, live them.

As for me, if I make it through this day and to the eve of my ninety-third birthday, I intend to eat as good a dinner as this body is still able to digest, I intend to wash it down with a fine Bordeaux and I intend to complete it with a night of passionate lovemaking with the most accomplished lover I have ever taken to my bed: my young husband.

As for you, whoever you are, I urge you to do something similar. I guarantee that you will not regret it.

One concluding thought as I contemplate my final hours: It was never my intention that these words serve as any form of legacy. Their overriding purpose was to serve me, and they have performed that task with surprising efficacy. I do not need any words to outlive me, for nothing can outlive me.

If you knew me, whoever you are, I remain alive in your heart. If you did not, I live on in the memories and stories of others who did. I live on in the walls and floors of this old house. I live on in the streets of this city and in the river that runs through it. I live on in spring rains, the summer sun and the air you breathe. As long as these exist, so do I.

That is not spiritual claptrap. That is fact. I have lived. I have touched. I have been touched. In the end, and that end is so close now that I can feel it reaching out toward me...in the end that is all that matters.

1989

Montreal

53

The late afternoon sun gilded the fiery reds, yellows and oranges of Westmount's oaks, elms and maples as Bernie stepped out of Sarah's Kensington Avenue apartment building and turned south toward Sherbrooke Street. Sarah had suggested a taxi and Mac had offered a limo. Bernie had thanked them but said he would rather walk. By himself.

No one was offended. It was natural that Bernie would want some alone time before facing the expected throng at Galérie Cinq Arts. It was Friday, October 13, 1989, the opening of *Expressions,* Erik's show.

It seemed like lifetimes ago that Erik had joked about the date: "It's either gonna bring me really good luck or really bad luck." In the end, it had brought him both: Bad luck that he wasn't alive for the show; good luck that the influential art critics who had been granted a sneak preview were already raving about the depth and originality of Erik's vision and were predicting a rapid sellout.

Bernie smiled. Erik would have appreciated the irony. As for the quality of Erik's work, especially those final paintings, Bernie had never doubted it. "I shouldn't say I told you so," he murmured, "but I told you so."

This eight-block stretch of Sherbrooke held so many priceless memories for him, more now than did any other part of Montreal. Here is where he escaped after his mother's funeral. Here is where he discovered that Mac was his biological father. Here is where he uncovered a passion for making art he had never known he possessed, along with the gift to make a success of it. Here is where he met Erik Donnekin for the first time. And it all took place in a brief but life-altering thirty-six hours.

The gallery was jammed when Bernie pushed open the door and elbowed his way through the crowd. A few people recognized him and pumped his hand or patted him on the back. Someone thrust a catalogue at him. Another pushed an overflowing champagne flute into his hand. Most were too hypnotized by Erik's art to bother with him. He tried to pick out Sarah, Mac, Sylvie, Sadie and Joseph. However, if they had emerged from the back office, they had been swallowed up by the throng.

Bernie wove his way a to cordoned-off alcove, where Erik's unfinished *Self-Portrait 1989*, already bearing a red "sold" sticker, hung in front of a backless stainless steel bench, its seat pocked with swiss cheese-like holes.

Just outside the cordon stood Pierre, dressed in black jeans, a tuxedo t-shirt and crimson Vans. When he saw Bernie approaching, he jabbed Jeffrey, who was dressed in a real tux, the jacket the color of Pierre's shoes. Jeffrey clapped his hands loudly to get everyone's attention. Everyone ignored him. Pierre then ducked under the cordon, leapt onto the bench, pushed two index fingers into his mouth and let out a shrill, ear-piercing whistle.

"Mesdames et messieurs," Pierre shouted. "Bienvenue. Welcome to *Erik Donnekin's Expressions.*"

The crowd stilled.

"There is so much I could say about Erik Donnekin and this show, but Jeffrey made me promise to say nothing at all. Anyone who knows me knows how hard it is to get me to shut up." He smirked. "About anything."

Everyone roared with laughter, no one harder than Jeffrey.

"Without Erik Donnekin," Pierre said, "the man I am about to introduce might never have grown into the great artist he has become. And without this man's love and support, there could have been no *Expressions.*" He pronounced it the French way. "Mes chers amis et collègues, puis-je présenter Bernard Marc Freed!"

All attention focused on Bernie as Jeffrey pushed a stanchion aside for him to enter the alcove. Bernie said nothing at first. He scanned the gallery, acknowledging the handful of familiar faces and smiling at Sarah, Sylvie, Sadie and Joseph, who now stood a few feet away. He knew Mac was around somewhere but he couldn't see him.

"It was just over five years ago," Bernie began, "that I met this brilliant, talented, handsome, funny, gentle and kind — oh, so kind — man in this very spot. On this bench." He touched the bench, gazed at *Self-Portrait 1989* and let his mind travel back to that August afternoon. "It had been one of the darkest days of my life, and Erik Donnekin was a big part of what turned it into one of the brightest. *The* brightest." Bernie paused. He didn't want to cry because he wasn't sure he would be able to stop. He shut his eyes and saw Erik in front of him, encouraging him as he always had. He took a deep breath.

"Looking back, I— No, Erik wouldn't have wanted today to be about looking back. He would have wanted it to be about looking around, at paintings he himself never believed he could be capable of, at these expressions of fear, pain and darkness and of joy and wonder and light and color and love and courage that surround us here. Even in the midst of his most challenging days, even when I could see that he knew he was going to die and that he was sparing me by saying nothing about it, those expressions never left him. They still haven't left him…or us. They hang here, thanks to Jeffrey and Pierre, a constant reminder of the beautiful soul and gifted artist that was — that is — Erik Franklin Donnekin." Bernie started to tremble. He wasn't sure he could continue. Then Sarah caught his eye. He braced himself and went on.

"I once told Erik that he was a better artist than I could ever hope to be. Wherever you are Erik, these paintings prove that I'm right. For once, you can't argue back."

"Don't count on it!" a voice called out from deep within the crowd.

Bernie grinned. "That was Erik's sister, KC, another great artist, and she's right. Whatever bundle of disembodied light and love that Erik is right now and wherever it is he's hanging out, I just know he's working on ways to argue with me about that one.

"I know I've gone on longer than I should," he said, "but I have to add one final note before I free you back into this incomparable experience of *Erik Donnekin's Expressions*. I'm not sure if you knew this: All proceeds from the show go to fund the Erik Donnekin AIDS Hospice. *All* proceeds; Jeffery and Pierre are kicking in their gallery commission. This will be no ordinary hospice." His voice rose. "While open to all, its special mission will be to serve creative artists like Erik. It will be filled with art, literature and music, including the creations of those who come there to live out their final weeks and days.

"But don't buy Erik's work just to support the hospice, as terrific a cause as it is. Buy it to bring one of Canada's greatest artists and the best person you could ever have had the privilege of knowing into your home or office. Buy it to sell out this show and to prove me right and him wrong: He *is* the better artist of the two of us. For sure, he was the better person." Bernie's voice cracked and he forced himself to go on. "I can't begin to tell you how much I'll miss him. How much I already do."

Bernie touched the self-portrait, following Erik's final magenta brushstroke with his finger, then fled through the applauding crowd.

1990
Nova Scotia

54

Bernie held the silver-and-teal urn against his chest and gazed out toward the gray waters of Minas Basin, waiting for the sun to rise pink and orange over central Nova Scotia and throw its fiery glow into the bay. It was chilly in late January, but Bernie had rolled up his jeans and slipped off his Nikes. He wanted to feel the red sand squishing under his feet and between his toes, just as he had that long-ago winter dawn when Erik dragged him out of bed at Mac's to experience this, his favorite place at his favorite time of day. They had returned often over the next four years, sometimes with sketch-pads or paint and canvas, sometimes simply to stroll. The last time had been a few weeks before they left for Italy.

Today, Bernie had come back to the tidal flats for one final walk with Erik, to bring him home.

It was barely light enough to read, but Bernie eased himself onto the damp sand, crossed his legs, set the urn next to him and retrieved a padded envelope from his knapsack. Sarah had handed it to him at Dorval airport with strict instructions not to open it until this moment.

Bernie turned it over and over in his hand, as reluctant to know its contents as he was curious. Finally, he sliced it open and pulled out Erik's Walkman and headphones, an unmarked cassette tape and four folded sheets of computer paper. For an instant he was confused. Why had Sarah sent him to Blomidon Provincial Park with Erik's Walkman? Why did she have Erik's Walkman? He had been searching for it since before Erik died and had asked Sarah if she had seen it. He remembered now that she had been strangely evasive at the time. It hardly mattered anymore.

He looked from cassette to letter and back again. Which should he deal with first? Then he noticed the note taped to the back of the Walkman. It was in Sarah's nearly indecipherable handwriting: "Read the letter first, boychik. Play the tape after."

Okay. Bernie stuffed the Walkman and cassette back into the envelope to protect them from the sand and unfolded the letter. Even then, he refused to focus his eyes on the dot-matrix type in front of him. Instead, he projected a series of memories onto it: of the first time he set foot in Galérie Cinq Arts and saw the guy who would change his life; of the first time they made love in Erik's tiny Greene Avenue apartment; of the last time they made love, the night before Erik's collapse.

How he had loved this man.

He dried his eyes on his sleeve, let them refocus and began to read, hearing Erik's voice in the words...

Dear Bernie,

It's been hard finding the space to write this letter, with you hovering over me every hour of every day like a lovesick puppy that's scared of being left behind. Every time I'm able to open my eyes, there you are, waiting for me to die and afraid I'm going to die, all at the same time. Well, let's get it over with: I am going to die. I don't want to leave you, but it's time. And if you're reading this, I already died, and we're wandering together, you and me, along the beach at Blomidon, like we did our first day together in Nova Scotia all those happy memories ago. The only difference today is that you can't feel me holding your hand. You may think you're alone at dawn with an urn-full of ashes, but I'm with you. I promise. Where else would I be?

Sarah helped me write this. I couldn't do it myself because it's so hard for me to hold onto anything anymore, like a pen. It isn't easy to speak either, a lot of the time. But Sarah was so incredibly patient with me, especially cuz I don't have a lot of strength and we could only do this in bits and pieces, when you weren't in the room.

By the way, please don't be mad at Sarah for not telling you about this. I made her promise to keep this letter a secret and to only give it to you when it was time for you to take me home.

Even if I had been stronger, I think I would have had to put all this into a letter. I don't think I could have spoken it to you out loud.

I don't think I was ever that strong, or that brave. So I'm grateful to Sarah for helping me with this in all the ways she's helped. I'm more grateful still to her for bringing you into my life, even if she didn't know she was doing it at the time.

I know you're angry, Bernie. You're angry at this disease for taking me away from you. You're angry at whoever gave it to me for causing both of us so much pain. And although you would never say it to my face, I know you're angry at me, too. For leaving. Don't be. None of this is anyone's fault. No one did anything wrong. Life happens, and a lot of the time it doesn't seem fair or make any sense.

Here's what does make sense: you and me, together, for the time we had.

I love you, Bernie Freed. I love you more than anything or anyone I have loved. I love you as I sob through these words that Sarah is writing down for me. And I love you, whatever and wherever I am now, as you're reading them. You are the best thing that ever happened to me. Ever, ever, ever. And if I could trade these five years with you for a lifetime of perfect health, I wouldn't.

I said before that I'm having a hard time holding onto things. I didn't only mean things like pens and spoons and hands. I meant life. I won't be asking anyone to pull any plugs, but I am telling you that as I write these words, I'm ready to go. Not in sadness. In joy. In a joy that I don't have the words to express. Even if I was a writer like Sarah or Emmeline, I still don't think I'd be able to find the right words.

It isn't that I want my life to be cut short, especially my life with you. But like with my paintings, especially these new ones, it isn't about what I want. It's about what life wants from me. And it looks like life has spoken.

I thought I might be afraid to die. I'm not. Sure, I want an escape from all this AIDS crap. But that's not it. I feel strangely complete. I've painted the best work of my life and experienced the best love of my life. And while it might have been fun to stick around for more of the same, it almost feels unnecessary. It's trite and even cruel to say that I'm at peace, but I am. As long as I get to finish this letter, that is.

This will sound odd, but one of the things that has helped me as I've been cooped up in this house and trapped in this increasingly uncooperative body has been Emmeline. Sarah's Emmeline. She may have lived a completely different kind of life than mine, not to mention one that's three times as long as mine, yet lying here and listening to her story, it's like she's here with me, guiding me through these final months.

If this letter is already sounding like some over-the-top "As the Stomach Turns" sketch from *The Carol Burnett Show*, hang on to your hat. It's only gonna get worse. So take a deep breath.

You have to promise me something, Bernie. Look up from this letter. Look out past the bay. Look east toward the ocean. Look east toward the sunrise. Look east and make this promise *before* you keep reading. Make it now, cuz you won't like what I'm going to ask you to do.

Have you promised? Here goes…

With any luck, you've got a lot of years left before you come looking for me in the Great Beyond. Promise me now that you won't spend them doing what Mac did with your mother. Promise me that you won't mope through the next fifty years mourning what might have been instead of living what is.

I'm never going to leave your side, Bernie Freed. Not ever. But you're alive and I'm not. And if I've learned anything through these months of dying, it's the value of living.

Promise me that you'll live your life. Promise me that you'll keep growing as the great artist you are (the great artist that I could never have been, even with a hundred and fifty more years) until your art outshines Mac's. I know you can do it, and I know he knows you can do it. And I want to be able to watch you do it, from whatever watching place I'm sent to.

Promise me, too, that I won't be your last love, just your first. Be like Emmeline or my Mum and take on lovers by the troop-load (just do it safely) or be like Sarah or Sadie and find another soulmate. Just remember that the best way for you to honor our love is to keep on loving, and the best way for you to honor my life is to keep on living. So do it, love, and do it well. Cuz I'll be watching!

Yours, always and forever, and with more love than any one body can contain,

Erik

55

Bernie didn't move for what felt like hours yet couldn't have been more than a few minutes. He had expected to cry, especially after listening to the tape. It was one of Erik's favorite songs, Dolly Parton's "I Will Always Love You."

If I should stay
I would only be in your way
So I'll go, but I know
I'll think of you each step of the way
And I will always love you

To his amazement, he didn't cry. Perhaps he had no tears left. Or perhaps he was ready to move on, into the joy and happiness that Erik was wishing for him through Dolly Parton. Almost.

He stuffed the letter and Walkman back into his knapsack, picked up the urn and ambled out toward the water. As cold as he knew the ocean would be, he waded in, popped open the urn and began scattering the ashes, Johnny Appleseed-style.

"I'm not making any promises about the lover thing," he said. "That's not entirely up to me. But if you promise to hold onto one of my hands, I promise to keep the other outstretched and open to... I don't know what. To whatever.

"About the art? I won't let you down. I swear to you right now that I am going to be the best damn artist this country has ever seen." He grinned. "Now that the competition is out of the way." A rogue wave crashed toward him, soaking his pants. He chuckled. "So that's the way it's going be, is it?" He flipped over the urn and dumped out the final dusting of ashes. "You win, Erik. The best damn artist in the world."

The tide was rising now, the water launching its stealthy but inexorable push toward the crimson Blomidon cliffs. "You're wrong about one thing, Erik. You were, *are*, a great artist. I don't care what you say. I won't to let anyone forget that. Not ever."

Bernie turned away from the bay and followed the tide back the way he had come. "Mac wants me to go to London while he works on the Queen's portrait. He'll deed Emmeline's house over to me, he said, to give me a new home. I don't know. It'd be hard to be at Emmeline's after...well, you know. Maybe I should, though, just to bring some life and art back into the place. It might be fun to be in London again, to be with Mac but on my own." He considered his options. "Or maybe I should go somewhere that isn't London, that isn't Montreal, that isn't Nova Scotia. Somewhere I haven't been before. Somewhere that isn't so filled with memories. Somewhere new." He shook his head. "Like I said, I don't know..."

Then he did. As Bernie watched the pink light of dawn illuminate the red sand at his feet and the pine-crowned red-earth outcroppings around him, the idea for a new series of paintings came to him. They would be abstract, pulling in the ochers, blues and greens of Blomidon and bathed in this transcendent light, the light that births a new day. He would stay here, maybe at Mac's or maybe in a place of his own — in Wolfville or nearby in Canning, or closer to the park in Scots Bay — and he would paint it. He would paint it for Erik. He would paint if for himself. He would paint it for love. After that? After that he would know what to do.

Sara & Sadie's Yiddish Glossary

A hiltsener tsung zol zi bakumn (ah *HILL*-tsehn-er *TSOONG* zohl zee bah-*KOOM*-en) — She should grow a wooden tongue
Aleha hasholem (ah-*LAY*-ha ha-*SHOW*-lem) — May she rest in peace
Alteh machashaifeh (*AL*-teh makha-*SHAY*-feh) — Old witch
Balabusta (bah-lah-*BOOS*-tah) — Exemplary mistress of the household, good cook and housekeeper
Barimt biblyotek (bah-*RIMT* bib-lee-oh-*TEK*) — Famous library
Batamt (ba-*TAMT*) — Delicious
Bupkis (*BUP*-kiss) — Nothing, something worthless
Boychik (*BOY*-chick) — Term of endearment. Literally, young boy
Chaloshes (khah-*LOH*-shess) — Disgusting
Chaleria (kha-*LAIR*-eeyah) — Nasty, shrewish woman
Chazerai (khazer-*EYE*) — Junk, garbage
Chutzpah (*KHOOTZ*-pah) — Nerve, gall
Dershrokn (dare-*SHROHK*-en) — Afraid, terrified
Drek (*DRECK*) — Garbage, dirt, manure
Eingeshpahrt (*AYN*-geh-shpart) — Stubborn
Farblondzhet (fahr-*BLOHND*-jet) — Mixed up, lost
Farkakte (far-*KAK*-teh) — Lousy
Farshnickert (far-*SHNICK*-ert) — Drunk
Fartumelt (far-*TOOM*-elt) — Dizzy
Faygele (*FAY*-geh-leh) — Gay, often derogatory. Literally, little bird
Freylekh (*FRAY*-lekh) — Cheerful, happy
Gott in himmel (gohtt een *HIMM*-el) — Exclamation of shock. Literally, God in heaven
Gut yontif (goot *YOHN*-tiff) — Happy holiday
Hekdish (*HECK*-dish) — A decrepit place, a dump

Heymishe (*HAY*-mish-eh) — Homelike, homemade

Keyver (*KAY*-ver) — Tomb, grave

Kibbitz, kibbitzer (*KIH*-bitz, *KIH*-bitz-er) — Joke around or meddle; jokester, meddler

Kishke (*KISH*-keh) — Belly, stomach

Klafte (*KLAHF*-teh) — Bitch; literally, vagina

Kvell (*KVELL*) — Burst with pride

L'chaim (le *KHA*-yim) — Traditional toast. Literally, "to life"

Lekherlekh (*LEKH*-urr-lekh) — Ridiculous

Machashaifeh (makha-*SHAY*-feh) — Witch

Mamzer (*MUM*-zer) — Bastard

Mazel tov (*MAH*-zel tov) — Literally, good luck. Used most often to convey congratulations

Mensch (*MENCH*) — A good person

Meshugena, Mishigas (mi-*SHOO*-ghe-nah, mih-shih-*GUSS*) — Crazy, craziness

Mit fil respekt (mitt *FEEL* res-*PECT*) — With much respect

Modne (*MOHD*-neh) — Strange, peculiar

Narish, Narishkeit (*NAHR*-ish, *NAHR*-ish-kite) — Foolish, foolishness

Narish ligner (*NAHR*-ish *LIG*-ner) — Foolish liar

Nishtik mamzer (*NISH*-tick *MUM*-zer) — Worthless bastard

Ongepatshket (*OHN*-geh-pahtch-ket) — Overdone, bordering on tacky

Prost (*PROHST*) — Common, ordinary, not classy

Schmatta (*SHMAH*-tah) — Literally, rag, but refers to the clothing trade

Sheyner man (*SHAY*-ner mun) — Handsome man

Shlep (*SHLEPP*) — Haul/carry something heavy or awkward; take a tedious or difficult journey

Shmegeggie (shmeh-*GEGH*-ee) — Buffoon, idiot, fool

Shreklekh (*SHREK*-leckh) — Horrible

Shvitzing (*SHVIH*-tsing) — Hot enough to make you sweat

Tsufil (tsoo-*FEEL*) — Too much

Vos a talant (vohss ah tah-*LAHNT*) — What a talent

*** Yiddish pronunciations can vary widely and there is no universal standard for transliteration.*

How Emmeline Got Herself a Book

It's July 2015 and I'm tidying up the final draft of *After Sara's Year*, the book that completes, or so I believe, my *Sara Stories* novels. Suddenly, a flash of intuitive insight races through me: It's the idea for a third book in the series that was never meant to be a series. (It was only when *Sara's Year* readers kept demanding that I reveal more about their favorite characters that *After Sara's Year* was born.)

This new book would be called *The Emmeline Papers* and it would weave two interrelated threads: the story of Emmeline Mandeville, Mac's quirky, eccentric, single-minded aunt, and the story of how copies of her memoir happen to fall, independently, into several *Sara Stories* characters' hands.

That wasn't the book I wrote.

I began my first draft of *Emmeline* the same way I began my first novel: in a writing workshop that I was leading. This time, I was teaching at Unity Santa Fe, not in my long-ago Toronto living room. And unlike the first time, I assumed that I knew what I was doing. (Lesson: Never assume anything!)

Twenty-three years ago at that Toronto workshop, I chose to participate in a writing exercise that I was facilitating. The result eventually became *The MoonQuest*, and that evening's writing would become an integral part of the novel.

In Santa Fe I set out to do something similar. Once my workshop participants had begun writing, I pulled out a notepad and penned an opening prologue based on my *Emmeline* idea.

The morning after my *MoonQuest* experience, I picked up where I had left off the previous evening and continued writing. Something radically different happened the morning after my *Emmeline* experience: When I reread the prologue I had written, it felt all wrong. The writing was fine; the premise was not.

I had no idea how to proceed.

Then a few weeks later, author Karen Helene Walker sent me the first essays in an anthology on aging she was compiling and had asked me to edit. The more essays I read, the more I began to view *Emmeline* and her "papers" in a whole new way. It didn't take long before I realized that the book I thought I was writing was to be something else altogether — something more engaging for its readers and, for better or worse, more emotionally and creatively challenging for its author.

Unlike Karen's *Still Me…After All These Years, The Emmeline Papers* was not to be a book about aging. Aging would be a component of *Emmeline,* but the story would be more about what all of us face regardless of age. It would be about hopes and dreams. It would be about mortality and death. It would be about fear and courage. It would be about loss. It would be about love and relationship. It would be about compassion and perseverance. It would be about life.

"Okay," I said to my Muse, that mischievous entity that runs my writing life. "What about the title?" If *The Emmeline Papers* was ideal for my original concept, I couldn't see how it fit this new one.

"Remember *Sara's Year,*" my Muse replied somewhat acidly.

When I sat down in a Santa Monica Starbucks in 2014 to begin *Sara's Year,* I also had a concept and a title. Before I finished that day's writing, the concept had vanished, and over the next months I never stopped second-guessing a title that seemed to bear little relation to the story I was telling.

"It's perfect," my Muse kept insisting.

It's rare that I know the ending of a novel I'm writing before I reach the closing scenes. You see, I never outline. So it wasn't until the final chapter of the first draft that I understood why the *Sara's Year* title was, in fact, so perfect.

With *The Emmeline Papers* I was being asked to take that same leap of faith. Even if the story had changed radically, I needed to trust that the original title would still fit. It does. And as with *Sara's Year,* the finished story is far more evocative and compelling than anything I could ever have dreamed up with my conscious mind.

I'm certain the same will be true with what I expect to be the fourth and final book in these *Sara Stories.* This time, I have neither title nor concept. This time, all I have is a character and a time frame. Who knows whether either will prove to be accurate!

But that's a story for another day. Today's story is *The Emmeline Papers*. I hope it has engaged, inspired and moved you as much in the reading of it as it did me in the writing of it.

Mark David Gerson
July 9, 2017

Author's Note

Most works of fiction grounded in an actual time and place tend to be more fictional than factual. *The Emmeline Papers* is no exception. As with its *Sara's Year* and *After Sara's Year* predecessors, I have not hesitated to manipulate known facts to serve my story, even as I have done my best to reflect as accurately as possible the real-life places and situations portrayed in these pages.

Perhaps the best example is the London house where much of the story's action takes place. Thirty-three Fitzroy Street exists, if not precisely where I have placed it, nor is it identical to this book's cover image, which was photographed a half a block away on Fitzroy Square. Fitzroy Square Garden, however, exists as described, complete with Naomi Blake's *View*, commissioned for the Queen's Silver Jubilee through a process that I'm certain bears no resemblance to the one into which Emmeline inserts herself.

Although present at this writing with a menu similar to the one from which Sarah makes her lunch choice, the Fitzroy Street residents' favorite getaway, Caffè Nero on Tottenham Court Road, was not there in 1989; the chain wasn't established until 1997. That was the same year that the British Library left the British Museum, where Bernie was awestruck by the striking gold-ribbed dome of its famous Reading Room. It was also the final year that Montreal's Mirabel International Airport was used for overseas flights. Dorval (renamed Pierre Elliot Trudeau International in 2004), the same facility from which Bernie flies to Nova Scotia in one of the book's final scenes, now handles all passenger traffic in and out of Montreal. Time has shifted another of the story's landmarks: London's Le Cordon Bleu culinary school is no longer located at 31 Marylebone Lane. It moved to 15 Bloomsbury Square in 2012.

The Royal Family has owned a succession of Daimler DS420s over the years, the most notable being the one used for the funeral of Diana, Princess of Wales; I could never verify whether one might have been used in 1989 for royal guests.

Although all *Emmeline*'s characters are products of my imagination, several of the peripheral ones have flesh-and-blood counterparts, the most prominent, of course, being Queen Elizabeth II. Others include Sir William Heseltine, the Queen's onetime principal private secretary, former Canadian Prime Minister Pierre Elliott Trudeau, former Canadian cabinet minister and High Commissioner to London Donald MacDonald, McClelland & Stewart publisher Doug Gibson and artists Keith Haring, Anne Savage and Naomi Blake. Yet here, too, all resemblances are either coincidental or convenient, not intentional.

The Savage and Haring mural projects mentioned in the story are real. The one that Bernie's mother participates in at Montreal's Baron Byng High School no longer exists, nor does the school; Jeunesse au Soleil/Sun Youth now occupies building. *Tuttomondo,* the Pisa mural that Bernie and Erik contribute to, still stands. And although Anne Savage painted *Quebec Farm*, it has never hung in the Westmount Public Library.

All the artists and writers who attended Emmeline's literary salons were real Fitzrovia residents or regulars, including Betty May, who was an artist's model. However, there is no evidence that she ever stripped off her clothes and demanded that Augustus John paint her on the spot. The story about Aleister Crowley claiming to have transformed Victor Neuberg into a camel and deposited him in the Algiers zoo is true...at least according to Crowley.

It was not easy for me to turn the clock back to the late 1980s and chronicle the AIDS/HIV situation as it was back then — for both factual and emotional reasons. I hope I have honored the memory of the many friends I lost in those years by capturing the essence, if not necessarily the detailed specifics, of what was known and experienced at the time.

Gratitude

It may not take a village to write a book, yet it takes one to support each book's author. I am grateful to my many friends, online and off, who believe in me even when I have a hard time believing in myself and who consistently encourage, sustain and inspire me not only to keep writing but to do my best work. At the top of the list are Kathleen Messmer, Sander Friedman, Adam Bereki and Joan Cerio. However, there are many, many others, too numerous to list here. I must also thank the loyal readers of my first two *Sara Stories* books, without whose urgings there would never have been an *Emmeline Papers*.

As with *Sara's Year* and *After Sara's Year*, this book required the kind of research I never had to undertake with my *Q'ntana* fantasy novels. *Fitzrovia: London's Bohemia*, one of the titles in the National Portrait Gallery's *Character Sketches* series, was an invaluable aid in learning about many of the habitués of the Fitzroy Square area and in chronicling some of their more outrageous antics. I'm also grateful to Jeffrey Robinson's *The Hotel: Backstairs at the World's Most Exclusive Hotel* and the three-part 2012 BBC documentary *Inside Claridge's* for taking me behind the scenes at Mac's favorite London hotel. I was able to capture the essence of Mac's favorite Montreal hotel with the assistance of Adrian Waller's *No Ordinary Hotel: The Ritz-Carlton's First Seventy-Five Years*. Artist/art educator Anne Savage may have played a larger role in *Sara's Year*, the first installment in this series, yet I found myself turning back to Anne McDougall's *Anne Savage: The Story of a Canadian Painter* for this book as well.

Although I lived through the early AIDS years of the 1980s, I relied on two physicians for their more detailed information and insight into that period: Dr. Orin Rosengren of Montreal and Dr. Chris Mathews of UC San Diego Health. Despite their indispensable assistance, I take full responsibility for any medical or historical inaccuracies related to HIV/AIDS that you may encounter.

If you have ever wandered into one of the many cafes that double as my writing studio, you will no doubt find me huddled over my laptop mumbling like a madman. Unlike Sarah, I'm not chatting with my long deceased friends. Rather, I'm reading aloud as I write — to the annoyance, no doubt, of those at adjacent tables. To the patrons and baristas who indulged my idiosyncrasies at various Satellite coffee shops in Albuquerque and at Starbucks outlets in both Albuquerque and Los Angeles, thank you for your patience.

There are two places in the United States that have stirred my creative juices more than any other through my twenty years in this country: New Mexico and Southern California. If I crafted most of *The Emmeline Papers* in Albuquerque, I also worked on bits of it in LA. I am grateful to both cities for their inspiration, as well as to the city that forms the spine of these *Sara Stories*, my hometown of Montreal, and to Blomidon Provincial Park, a favorite spot of mine when I lived in the Kings County house that inspired Mac's and which has now played a role in two of my books. It also inspired a scene in *The MoonQuest*. As for Halifax, I feel sure that had Emmeline given it a second chance some decades later, she might have revised her negative postwar impression and might even have come to share my affection for the city.

When Aunt Emmeline made her first appearance in *After Sara's Year*, little did I know that she would return in a book whose title would not only bear her name but would be set largely in her house. I had a similar experience with Sadie, who spent most of *Sara's Year* in the background only to demand a top-of-the-bill return engagement in *After Sara's Year*. My characters are not merely squiggles on a page. They are as real to me as any flesh-and-blood personage, and I am grateful to them for continuing to live out such fascinating lives and for continuing to compel me to tell their stories.

I am grateful, too, to that incorporeal entity that I call my Muse. From its first tricksterish manifestation in my life nearly half a century ago, it has continued to push and prod me to open my heart and mind to the stories that teach me as much about myself as, I hope, they inspire and entertain you. May those promptings continue for many more years to come...or at least as long as it takes to write the fourth and, I believe, final book in these *Sara Stories*.

Final Words

I came out as a gay man in 1975 and so was very aware of early reports of the "gay cancer" that later came to be known as AIDS/HIV. I considered dedicating this book to the memory of the friends I lost through the 1980s and 1990s. Then I asked myself what Erik would have wanted. I don't think it would have been a "memoriam."

Instead, I offer *The Emmeline Papers* as a celebration of the many lives that touched mine so profoundly through those years only to have been extinguished tragically and prematurely by AIDS. In particular, I single out Roy Salonin, who was so integral to my own coming out journey, a story I share in *Acts of Surrender: A Writer's Memoir.*

I also offer this book as a tribute to the living, to those in my life who live with HIV: Thank you for your courage, your determination and your open-spiritedness. You are an inspiration.

You loved them in *Sara's Year.*
You laughed and cried with them in
After Sara's Year and
The Emmeline Papers.

Now, get ready to join your favorite
characters on one final journey!

The Sara Stories, Book 4

Coming Soon!

www.thesarastories.com

www.ingramcontent.com/pod-product-compliance
Lightning Source LLC
Chambersburg PA
CBHW050349190726
48284CB00007BB/2207